TRAITOR'S STORM

TRAITOR'S STORM

M. J. Trow

CRÈME de la CRIME

This first world edition published 2014
in Great Britain and in the USA by
Crème de la Crime, an imprint of
SEVERN HOUSE PUBLISHERS LTD of
19 Cedar Road, Sutton, Surrey, England, SM2 5DA.

British Library Cataloguing in Publication Data

Trow, M. J. author.
  Traitor's storm. – (A Tudor mystery)
  1. Marlowe, Christopher, 1564-1593–Fiction.
  2. Walsingham, Francis, Sir, 1530?-1590–Fiction. 3. Isle
  of Wight (England)–Fiction. 4. Armada, 1588–Fiction.
  5. Great Britain–History–Elizabeth, 1558-1603–
  Fiction. 6. Detective and mystery stories.
  I. Title II. Series
  823.9'2-dc23

ISBN-13: 978-1-78029-062-1 (cased)

All Severn House titles are printed on acid-free paper.

Severn House Publishers support the Forest Stewardship Council™ [FSC™],
the leading international forest certification organisation. All our titles that
are printed on FSC certified paper carry the FSC logo.

Typeset by Palimpsest Book Production Ltd.,
Falkirk, Stirlingshire, Scotland.
Printed and bound in Great Britain by
TJ International, Padstow, Cornwall.

ONE

L ittle Gonzalillo hated the Escorial. He was the King's
jester, for God's sake, born to a life of laughter, with
music and merriment – and a little mayhem from time
to time. When the Court moved to Madrid or Valladolid he
came into his own, tumbling and eating fire and teasing
the children. After all, he was their height, and while they
were kicking the shins of their elders and betters, he could do
the same to them. In fact, little Gonzalillo hated children almost
as much as he hated the Escorial.

The place was a palace in name only. It was also a
mausoleum and a reliquary. Its evil little windows reminded
the dwarf of the gun emplacements along the hulls of His
Imperial Majesty's ships of the line. They were dark and mean
and held nothing but death. Gonzalillo pattered along the
labyrinth of corridors, through the library with its shelves of
polished oak and richly embossed leather. There were 40,000
books here – he'd get round to reading one of them one of
these days. Then he was bounding up the stone steps to the
reliquary, wondering if anyone had yet spotted the fake prepuce
of St Basil he had slipped in there a few months ago.
The goat it came from wasn't likely to tell anyone of the ruse
and, even if no one ever detected it, it brought a smile to little
Gonzalillo's lips every day.

He paused at the black velvet arras, pulled himself up to
his full four feet two inches and straightened his doublet.
Mother of God, it was cold up here. It was supposed to be
May but the wind from the Sierra de Guadarrama whistled
and whirred along the passageways and rattled the shutters.
Hail had bounced off the roofs for much of the night and the
Courtyard of the Evangelists was white when Gonzalillo had
padded across it. It was not dawn yet and the whole place felt
like a tomb.

The dwarf twisted the ornate key and the little door in the

high wall creaked open. The hinges were never oiled; not because the room's occupant was afraid of the shadow of the assassin that waited at every king's elbow, but because he so valued his privacy and wanted to know immediately that it had been violated.

King Philip sat in his closet, his long, pale face lit by a solitary candle. It looked as if he hadn't slept for a long, long time. Gonzalillo took the briefest of looks, then bowed low and held that position, as only an acrobat could, staring at his shoes. Behind him, the velvet hissed back into position with the sibilance of sin and he waited.

'The English ships, Gonzalillo,' the King said at last, without looking up from the papers on his desk. 'They are faster than ours.'

'Indeed, Felipe.' The dwarf knew the signs, had rehearsed the moment so often. When the King spoke, that was the time to drop the bow and start the day's work. Gonzalillo smiled. No one in the Escorial; no one in the whole wide world called His Majesty 'Felipe'. His children called him Papa and his wife My Darling. His Pope and his God called him My Son. Only his half-brother, Don Juan of Austria, called him Felipe – and Don Juan of Austria was dead these ten years. Gonzalillo crossed to a barrel of water and cracked the thin film of ice on its surface. He filled a jug from it, wiping the bottom on his doublet with a grimace, and carried it to his master. Then he placed it on the table, well away from the clutter of charts and maps he saw there, and dabbed the King's temples with a damp cloth. Philip of Spain leaned back and sighed. The first fingers of light were lending an eerie creeping glow to the closet. He closed his eyes.

'How much this time?' Gonzalillo asked him, fussing around the King.

'Hmm?' Philip's mind was elsewhere, his mind racing through the surf of the Channel, bringing his ships' guns to bear on the man his sailors called El Draque, the dragon: the English pirate Francis Drake.

'How much sleep have you had?'

'I don't know,' the King said in that hoarse whisper of his. 'Enough, I expect. And their gunnery is good.'

'Hmm?' It was Gonzalillo's turn to be elsewhere.

'The English fleet,' Philip explained. 'Their gunners are good.'

'Let's take this thing off.' The dwarf gently lifted the golden chain of the Fleece from his master's shoulders and let it clatter on the sideboard. 'Gives you a headache, that, doesn't it? Ready for breakfast?'

Philip looked up sharply, his pale blue eyes wide and urgent, his brooding jaw thrust forward. 'The enterprise,' he said softly. 'The enterprise of England.'

Gonzalillo stopped fussing. He put his hands on his hips and looked up at the most powerful man in the world. 'Yes,' he said, with all the gravitas of a Santa-Cruz, 'the English ships are faster than ours. And yes,' he suddenly became the Duke of Parma, 'their gunners are good. But we, Felipe el Prudente, have God on our side. The English can never claim that. Now,' he quietly took the quill out of the King's hand, 'will you *please* have some breakfast?'

'It all depends,' said Philip as the dwarf took his hand and led him away, 'on our friends in England.'

'Disappeared?' Nicholas Faunt was not sure he had heard all of what Francis Walsingham had just said. They were moving upstream from Placentia, following the curve of the river and the wind was roaring in his ears as they took the centre of the waterway to round the Isle of Dogs.

'Has not been heard from.' Walsingham thought that perhaps his chief projectioner had lost the plot somewhere.

'Since when?'

'Last month,' Walsingham told him, pulling his cloak tighter round him against the weather. He grimaced up at the leaden sky where thunder clouds loomed to the east. 'It is May, isn't it? I've lost all track of time, with this weather. It feels like November.'

'Where did you say he was again?'

'The Wight.' Walsingham leaned forward, lowering his voice lest the boatmen, bending their backs against the wind, should have ears.

'We are talking about Hasler, aren't we?'

Walsingham leaned back. He had known Nicholas Faunt

since he was a boy. Few men in England had so sharp a brain or so loyal a heart. But Walsingham was not a well man. Back in January he had taken to his bed, all but blind in one eye, and that had frightened him. For more years than he cared to remember, he had been the Queen's Spymaster, the dagger ever-vigilant at her back. One day, and it might be soon, he would have to pass the chains of office to a younger man. Was Nicholas Faunt *really* that man?

'You know we are,' the Spymaster said.

It was Faunt's turn to lean forward, into the biting wind. 'What I mean, Sir Francis,' he said, 'is that you know Harry Hasler as well as I do. He'll have found a doxy somewhere or a tavern or probably both. It's his way.'

'Yes, it is his way,' Walsingham agreed, 'but we both know that underneath that loutish exterior is a projectioner of rare talent. His last report talked of danger and he couldn't, he said, be more specific. That was on the sixteenth ult.'

'From where?'

'Newport. He was working for George Carey at Carisbrooke Castle.'

'What do you propose?' Faunt asked.

'We send somebody else. Track Hasler down. Find out what's going on.'

Faunt nodded. 'Me?' he said.

'No.' Walsingham shook his head, his face greyer and deader looking than ever in the early morning light. 'I need you here.' He patted his doublet. 'You haven't seen the latest report from Lisbon. I have. And believe me, it makes for grim reading. When I've seen the Queen and the Privy Council, we'll have a better understanding of what's going on.'

'The enterprise of England.' Faunt nodded, as though he dreaded the sound of the phrase, even from his own lips. 'So who will we send, then? To the Wight, I mean?'

Walsingham narrowed his eyes, taking in the roofs of the houses that loomed out of the mist to right and left, the wharfs of the Queen's quays. 'Marlowe,' he said. 'We'll send Kit Marlowe.'

'Kit.' Tom Sledd was feeling his way along the gallery of the Rose, with a lot of care. The cleaner hadn't been in yet and

Tom was theatre born and bred so knew what might be underfoot. There had been a lot of vegetables thrown last night and who knew but a rotten orange might still lurk in the shadows. Or worse. Tom Sledd had known a lot worse.

'Tom?' The voice came out of the darkest corner. 'Over here.'

Sledd sidled along the edge of the gallery, kicking aside anything firm enough to move. Something ran ahead of his kick, but rats were the least of his troubles.

'What is it, Tom?' Marlowe's voice was indistinct, his face being buried in his arms, which were folded on the rail. He raised his head and his eyes gleamed in the dim, rain-washed light that came from the roof. 'Let me guess,' he said, before the stage manager could get a word out. 'Are we going to be able to go on with this drivel very much longer before the crowd burns the theatre down? Would we all be better off setting up as grocers, because after all, we have the vegetables for it?' A hand came up and tossed an apple in the air, catching it and then throwing it at the stage.

An actor looked up, affronted, as the wormy fruit whistled past his ear. 'Oy!' he roared, looking into the darkness. 'You could have had my eye out! I get enough of that every afternoon; I don't need it in the morning as well.'

'Sorry!' Marlowe sang out, then sagged back into his folded arms again.

Tom squatted on the bench and looked at Marlowe. He tried a few platitudes in his head, but none of them sounded right, so he let them go. He knew Marlowe would fill the gap very soon and he wasn't disappointed.

'I will admit that I suggested this play to Henslowe,' Marlowe said. 'I also admit that I felt sorry for Thomas, always going on about his play. I thought, what with one thing and another these days, that a play called the Spanish Tragedy couldn't help but pull the crowds.'

'It has pulled the crowds,' Sledd said. If you couldn't say something nice, just tell a tiny bit of the truth, that was what the great Ned Sledd had taught his protégé and sticking to that had got him through some sticky times.

Marlowe sat up straight now and leaned back, looking Sledd

in the face. 'The crowds. The jeering. The rotten fruit. I won't tell you what is lurking at the back of this gallery, but let's just say that when they get to cleaning this bit of the place they will need a big bucket and a sturdy shovel.' He sighed again.

'Well, never mind, Kit,' Sledd said, risking a matey punch on the playwright's shoulder. 'You'll have something for us soon, I have no doubt.'

Silence.

'Kit?'

'I was writing, yes.'

'And?'

'It promises to be my best yet.'

'Not the play with Dr Dee in it?'

'No. No, that one will have to wait. It must be . . . special. No, this one is set on an island. A strange man is the main character, foreign, enigmatic. But I can't quite see him, I just don't seem to be able to get it right. And meanwhile, we have . . . this.' He waved his arm to the stage where the rehearsal was stumbling along.

'I meant to ask you about that,' Sledd said. 'Why are we rehearsing still?'

'Henslowe asked me to make some cuts. He made a list last night of when the vegetables started to fly and asked me to rewrite the scenes.' He gave a shrug. 'Tom Kyd should be doing that, but nobody knows where he is just now.'

'Travelling's all I heard.'

'Yes, well, that's not very helpful when there are rotten apples flying through the air. Anyway, what did you want me for?'

Sledd put a hand to his mouth, stricken. 'Sorry, Kit. I was looking for you for . . .'

'Don't fret yourself.' A cold voice came from the back of the gallery. 'I'm here now.'

Marlowe didn't turn his head. 'Nicholas.'

'Kit.'

Sledd spoke low and fast. 'Master Faunt is here,' he muttered.

'Thank you,' Faunt said drily. 'Now, if Master Marlowe and

I could have some privacy.' Tom Sledd started to sidle back the way he had come.

'Before you go,' Faunt said, in the special tone he had which could stop a glacier in its tracks. 'You might want to bring a bucket and a shovel when you are back here next. There is . . .'

'I know,' Sledd said, shaking his head as he reached the steps down into the groundlings' pit. 'I know. How they even get the pig up the stairs, I will never understand.'

TWO

The two men walked out of the Rose and strolled down Maiden Lane. They leaned over the wall of the Bear Pit and watched for a few moments as Master Sackerson rolled this way and that in a shallow puddle. The bear eventually got up enough momentum to regain his feet, shook himself in a shower of muddy drops and ambled off to the shelter of an overhanging canvas, green with slime and half off its supporting poles.

Faunt flicked a finger at the animal. 'I'm surprised he's still here,' he remarked.

Marlowe shrugged. 'No reason he shouldn't be, is there?' he asked. 'He's Master Henslowe's favourite person, anyway, so I think anyone wanting to remove him would have a fight on their hands.'

'Hmm.' Faunt wiped an invisible speck of dirt from the front of his doublet and resumed his walk down to the main thoroughfare at the end of the lane. He needed somewhere warmer and drier; would this rain never end?

Marlowe caught him up with a hop and a skip. 'Nicholas,' he said, 'you didn't come all this way to discuss bears.'

'No. But I won't talk in this drizzle. Let's get in the dry somewhere. A tavern would be best; a tavern with a fire burning better still.'

At the crossroads, Marlowe turned left and then sharp left again through a low doorway. It was like entering another world. A dark, fusty world perhaps, that smelled of old ale and older tobacco, but one that was warm, dry and, most importantly from Faunt's point of view, apparently empty; the sign of the Angel, at Southwark. Looking into the gloom, a figure was just discernible standing behind a rough trestle table. The figure didn't speak but took a step forward and resolved into a man of no particular age, with a dirty apron wrapped around his middle. He was polishing a beaker with a cloth even dirtier than the apron and yet much cleaner than the beaker. Marlowe held up two fingers and the man replied with a guttural, wordless sound.

Faunt looked around and nodded. 'Quiet,' he remarked.

'And no wonder,' Marlowe said, taking a seat with his back to the fire. Faunt looked at him with a wry smile. Marlowe knew full well that the projectioner never sat with his back to a door or a window. Faunt took the chair and turned it through ninety degrees, sitting slantways to the table, his long, elegantly stockinged legs stretched out to the fire. 'The ale is awful. The wine is worse. It's filthy. But the fire is warm and the innkeeper stupid, so we can talk as privately here as anywhere and in reasonable comfort.'

The innkeeper, stupid or not, was fast enough and was at the table with two brimming beakers. He also slammed down a plate of gingerbread, cut into cubes and dusted with powdered sugar. Faunt looked dubiously at the drink and the food but good breeding precluded him from commenting until the man had gone. He then pushed the beaker and the plate away. Marlowe took a swig from his drink and a bite of the gingerbread.

'I thought you said the ale and wine were bad,' Faunt said.

'They are. The cider is excellent, though, and the gingerbread some of the best in London.' Marlowe smiled at Faunt. 'You forget that Ned Alleyn is of the company up the lane and where Ned Alleyn drinks there are always perks to be had. Especially from innkeepers' daughters who like to keep Ned Alleyn's friends sweet.' Marlowe raised his beaker to a trembling curtain at the back of the inn and was rewarded with a distant giggle, followed by a grunted curse from the innkeeper. The playwright pushed the plate back towards Faunt. 'Try some. It's just right.'

Faunt took a tiny nibble from just one corner and nodded. 'Are you tired of London yet, Kit?' he asked, suddenly getting down to business.

Marlowe, mouth full of gingerbread, shook his head. 'No,' he said, swallowing. 'Why should I be? I admit this play is heavy going at the moment, but I am writing one of my own which . . . well, why lie to you, Master Faunt? I am going to be writing one soon, but things keep getting in the way of my beginning.'

'What kind of thing?' Faunt asked, interested to know what this man of fire and air might be doing that had passed his intelligencers by.

Marlowe looked up at him over the rim of his beaker. 'You, for one,' he said.

Faunt spread his hands and tried to look innocent, something that he found increasingly difficult to do convincingly. 'I?'

Marlowe leaned forward. 'You didn't come to the theatre looking for me just to say hello and join me in a drink, Master Faunt. I have felt the hot breath of too many of your intelligencers following me around to think you had forgotten me. What is it you want me to do? I want to warn you that I will not be going abroad for you in a hurry. News from Spain does not make me anxious to get any nearer to that spider's web – and anyway, in this weather, I don't want to do a Channel crossing.'

Faunt looked injured. 'A Channel crossing? Heaven forfend, Kit. No, no, although . . . a boat may be needed.' He leaned back and patted the table rhythmically with his fingers for a moment, thinking. This man was too tricky for his own good, sometimes. He had almost let the cat out of the bag and there was no way of knowing which way the animal might jump.

'Ireland?' Marlowe broke the silence. That Godforsaken place was the graveyard of many a good man.

'No, no, not Ireland. Governor Parrott is keeping the lid on things there, at least for the time being. No, it's much nearer than that.'

'Is this a guessing game?' Marlowe said, a little testily. 'Well, how about . . . the Isle of Dogs.'

Faunt narrowed his eyes. 'Let's not be frivolous, Kit.' He motioned him nearer and leaned in himself. He dropped his voice so that the distant innkeeper would have no chance of hearing, even if he wanted to. 'I'm talking about the Isle of Wight. One of our men is . . . missing. Perhaps not missing, but certainly unaccounted for, as we speak. He was investigating . . . well, you don't need to know that now. If you can't find him, that will be the time to tell you more.'

'Rubbish!' Marlowe leaned back and spoke at a normal level. 'How can I possibly find him if . . .' He stopped, as any man would who suddenly felt the point of a dagger pricking the inside of his thigh.

Faunt raised a sardonic eyebrow.

'. . . if I don't know what he was doing there,' Marlowe continued, in a whisper.

'He was working for Sir Francis,' Faunt said, 'and that really is all you need to know. He was working for George Carey at the castle at Carisbrooke. His story was that he was a garden designer but we may have blundered there. As far as I know he didn't know a dogrose from an actual dog, so it may be that his cover has been blown.'

'I don't know anything about gardens either,' Marlowe protested, 'so I can't be his replacement.'

'No, no,' Faunt said. 'Because he might be just absent, rather than missing, we won't draw attention to it by replacing him. I thought you could pretend to be a writer . . .' He saw the look on Marlowe's face and quickly redirected the rest of the sentence: 'Which of course you really are, so the cover is perfect in that respect. No, I thought – that is, Sir Francis thought – you could go down as a writer looking for inspiration on an island.'

That was so near to the truth that Marlowe was open-mouthed. Perhaps he had not spotted all of the intelligencers after all.

'It's a peculiar place, the Wight,' Faunt went on. 'Odd people at every turn and so you might even find inspiration. The supernatural, all that rubbish is a bit up your street as I recall.'

'History,' Marlowe corrected him. 'History, not magick.'

'Well, make your own cover story,' Faunt said dismissively, taking a final swig of cider and a bite of gingerbread. He glanced over to the window and peered out. 'I do believe the rain is easing off. I have had your man pack you a bag. He'll be at the theatre with your horse about now, I should think.'

Marlowe smiled. That was pure Faunt. The man always assumed and it never made an ass out of him.

Walsingham's right-hand man stood up and wrapped his cloak over his arm. 'Keep in touch, of course. There will be a boat waiting at the Hamble this time tomorrow.' He waved at the twitching curtain and was rewarded by another gale of giggling. 'The cider *is* good,' he remarked. 'Not something I would usually drink but very . . . appley. Good day.' And he was gone.

Marlowe swilled back the last of his drink and smiled. It was a good batch. The last one had had rather more rat in it than he really enjoyed, but that was the thing about cider. It was always a surprise.

Marlowe's horse was indeed waiting at the Rose but of his servant there was no sign. He always had other fish to fry and clearly didn't want to risk being inveigled into accompanying Marlowe in his trip south. Tom Sledd held the animal's head and he was looking far from happy. Apart from anything else, the man was a stage manager, for God's sake. He held horses for no man.

Marlowe took the reins and lifted the flap of the bag thrown across the cantle. It didn't seem very big for an extended stay, but he would doubtless manage. He nodded to the stage manager, who had transferred his grip to a stirrup leather. He still hadn't spoken. 'Tom,' he said, with a smile, and tried to walk the horse a few steps, but Sledd was like an ox in the furrow. Marlowe had seen him in this mood before. He wasn't often moved to anger, but a twitching nerve in his cheek was giving it away.

'Kit,' he replied, through clenched teeth. Then, as if the words had built up so that they overflowed the dam of his tongue, 'I thought you were finished with all this. I thought you were a playwright now, that you would stay here, help . . . help with . . .' He looked down angrily at the ground and kicked a muddy stone viciously. He let go of the stirrup and stepped back.

Marlowe needed to get away, but not before he had put his friend's mind at rest. 'Tom, I'll just be away a day or so. I need to go . . . to somewhere and do . . . something. Oh, God's teeth, Tom, you know I can't tell you anything. I'll be back soon, that will have to be good enough.'

'But, the play!'

Marlowe smiled. 'Ah, the play. I thought it wasn't me you were worried about. Get Master Shaxsper to give you a hand.'

'He won't work with Ned,' Sledd said with a sigh.

'Tell Ned he has to behave. Apologize to Will over whatever it is he has done. Tell him otherwise you'll replace him with Burbage.'

'Burbage won't work with Shaxsper.'

Marlowe leaned his forehead on the saddle. He could stay and sort out the shambles at the Rose or he could go off for a few days on a nice, quiet island, staying in a castle, which sounded a cut above his normal lodging. He could have a brief look round for the missing ladies' man, Hasler, and then come home. By then, any number of situations may have resolved themselves. If his prayers were answered – should anyone be listening to answer them – then the whole boiling would have fallen down a hole in the ground and they would have to start all over again. Perhaps Tom Kyd would have come back from his travels with a new play that somebody actually liked. He drew a deep breath, stepped back half a pace and sprang into the saddle. He looked down at the stage manager. 'Goodbye, Tom. Expect me when you see me.' And he walked his horse down Maiden Lane and trotted through the half-timbered suburbs that hugged the road to the south.

It seemed a long time since Christopher Marlowe, Bachelor of Arts, Cantabriensis, had started out on a road like this. And when was that, exactly? When was the first step of this long journey? When he had splashed through the puddles of the Dark Entry on his way to school in the shadow of the great cathedral? When he had jumped on the back of a passing cart out of Cambridge and taken an apple offered to him by Francis Walsingham? For three long years he had been on that road to London and every time something had got in his way. And here he was, leaving it again. Just how insane was he? Nor' by nor-west.

The inn had not been of the best, but the bed had been reasonably soft and at least Marlowe had had it to himself. Walsingham's purse strings were not loose, but they did allow enough money out to ensure a reasonable degree of comfort.

Marlowe had never been to this part of the south coast before and he couldn't help feeling that he had gone rather out of his way. For a harbour, the Hamble kept itself very much to itself and Marlowe suddenly found himself at the head of a little street of houses, all leaning on each other in what looked like a slowly failing attempt to keep themselves out of the river. Moss was growing over the steps and up the wall and some of the buildings seemed more part of the river bank than the land. He would not have been at all surprised to see a giant water vole drinking smoke from a pipe at the doorway of the most decrepit. But it was a man, dressed all in drab and with a low cap pulled down over his eyes. His beard seemed to join the cap and his chest. As the only living thing in sight other than himself and his horse, Marlowe had little option but to speak.

'Hey, there,' he called. 'Is this the Hamble?'

The man didn't stir, but his little eyes glinted, swivelling from side to side in the shadow of his cap. 'Ar.'

Marlowe dismounted and went a step closer, slipping only once on the slimy green pavement. 'I was to be met here,' he ventured. He was usually rather more circumspect, but he didn't see how this creature would be likely to be a danger. He looked as though he might be actually growing into the low stool he sat on.

'Oh ar?' Again there was no movement, except from the piggy eyes.

'I need to get over to the Wight.'

The man finally took his pipe from his mouth and looked out to sea in a vague fashion. 'Ver the Woight, I wunt start from yere at'all. I'd start from Portsea, I shud. Oh, yes, Portsea, that's where you wants to be, Master.'

'I was told I could get a ship here.' Marlowe was beginning to think that he should have listened to Tom Sledd and stayed in London.

One bright eye closed and the other one surveyed the few little rackety boats pulled up on the river mud. 'Ship? No ships yere, Master. Just our little boats, poor things as they be. Just a bit o' fishin' we do yere. Oh, yes. Just a bit of fishin'.'

Marlowe wound the reins round his hand to stop him winding

his hands around the idiot's throat. He had been brought up within salt smell of the sea, but his had mainly been an inland life. He hated sailors and all who sailed with them, for all his mother hailed from Dover. 'A boat, then. I was told I could get a boat to the Wight.'

Again the eye roamed up the river and back again. 'Not at this tide, Master. Perhaps this evening there'll be somebody'll take you.'

'In the dark?' Marlowe asked. He had had enough of boats and the dark. He preferred to know where he was going, even if it was to the bottom.

'I shud say, s'arternoon. It's low tide now, see. High tide in about six hours.' The eye now looked at him. 'That's how it works, see. Tides. Low tides, high tides, twelve hours apart or near as makes n'difference. I would have thought you would have known that, Master Marlowe. Canterbury isn't so far from the sea and you've lived on a tidal river this eighteen months since.'

Marlowe looked sharply at the man, who looked scarcely any different from before. But both eyes were looking at him now and an intelligent look was in them. 'I didn't know . . .'

'Well, no, you obviously didn't. I have spent years building my reputation here, Master Marlowe. Looking the other way as the villagers smuggle all night and sleep all day. I am, in a manner of speaking, the village idiot. Daft Harry is my name, but you can call me Daft.'

'Daft Harry what?' Marlowe had been caught on the back foot and wanted to be able to sound intelligent when he saw Faunt next.

'Just Daft Harry, I think, Master Marlowe. You seem a little too lax to receive too much information. I was told to expect one of Sir Francis' best men.' The brown mound shook with a chuckle. 'I wonder when he will get here?'

Marlowe sighed and sat down on the low wall opposite the cottage door. It felt a little slimy and something skittered out from under his thigh, but he didn't really care. He had a feeling that he was going to undergo far worse at the hands of this self-trained salty sea dog. 'Are you going to take me across?' he said.

'Ooh, tha's a rum un,' came a voice from behind him. 'Daft Harry take you out on a boat? You'd need to be as mad as him to do that, I'm reckoning.'

Marlowe twisted round and looked over a wall. The beach was about six feet below and sitting on an upturned lobster pot there was a man wearing a stocking cap and an oiled jerkin. He was mending a net, but not very well as far as Marlowe could tell. There seemed to be a lot more mend than hole. 'And you are?' he asked, wondering how much he had heard.

'Gabriell,' the man said, 'Gabriell's the name.'

'Gabriell what?' Marlowe asked, feeling as though he had arrived in the middle of a game to which he didn't know all of the rules.

'Gabriell. Gabriel Gabriell.' The man gave a throaty laugh, coughed and spat on the weedy stones. 'My old mum, she'd just straight run out o' names when I come along.'

'You have a lot of brothers, Master Gabriell?' Marlowe asked politely. As far as he could see, high tide was at least five hours off and he may as well be civil while he killed time.

'No,' said the sailor, closing his mouth with a snap. 'Just me. Poor old mum. Ar.' He lapsed into a nostalgic silence and Marlowe straightened up, assuming the conversation was over.

'But if you'm be wanting to go over t't'Wight, I can take you. I got a fair little boat down on the shore.'

Marlowe looked at Daft Harry, who lifted a shoulder and gave a small nod.

'Don't ask him,' came the voice from below. 'If that's Daft Harry you'm talking to, he don't know his arse from a hole in the ground.'

'Aaaarrr,' Daft Harry shouted, shrugging again at Marlowe and winking.

'Is your boat far?' Marlowe asked, trying to get the conversation back on an even keel.

'Just down to the shore. A matter of ten minutes' walk if you can shake your stumps.'

'Is there anywhere I can leave my horse?' Marlowe asked. In his head, he added *where you won't eat it*.

'Up at t'big house,' Gabriell said. 'You can't miss it. Go up t'road where you came in. Turn t'other way from where you came and about half a mile along, there she'll be. The groom there will take your mare in for ye. She'll be safe enough along there 'til you come back. Old Lady Dunton, she lives there. Soft for horses, she is.'

'And when I come back, we can go down to your boat? Get across to the Wight?' Marlowe was beginning to feel as though he may have wandered into one of John Dee's secret worlds of faerie. Everyone was as mad here as a March hare and that month had gone.

'For sure, Master. That we shall.'

Marlowe got up from the wall, trailing green slime for just a second before it gave up its grip on his breeches. He glanced again at Daft Harry, who nodded and winked again, sprang up on to his horse and was gone up the lane.

The Hamble returned to its silence, the grey sea mist lying at the mouth of the river like a curse, the quiet lapping of the turning tide making the boats boom as they rocked and tapped against each other. Daft Harry sat there in his doorway, sucking his pipe and occasionally giving vent to a random whoop. He liked to stay in character, even with no one to see. Gabriel Gabriell carried on mending his net, biding his time.

Marlowe had made his turn and was almost at the big house before something struck him like a thunderbolt.

THREE

How did Gabriel Gabriell know which way he had come? The question racketed around in Marlowe's head half the way to the big house and all the way back. He left his mare in the care of a groom no worse than many he had known and a good deal better than some insofar as he seemed to know which end of a horse was which. As he walked the short distance back to the riverbank, the question started to shout in his ear and so by the time he got back within earshot of Harry's mad oscillating screams and Gabriel Gabriell's idiot grin, he was in no mood to discuss matters.

He had his hand on the hilt of his dagger as he stepped over the slippery cobbles of the last few paces. Gabriell was sitting on the wall, a bag thrown carelessly over his shoulder. Daft Harry was peering into his pipe, a mournful expression on his face. He looked up at Marlowe's approach.

'Pipe's out,' he said. 'No smoke.'

'There is indeed no smoke without fire,' Marlowe said shortly. He looked at Gabriell. 'Are we away, Master Gabriell?'

The sailor got up and flexed his knees. 'As ready as we'll ever be,' he said and turned to face downstream.

'Have you got a light for my pipe?' Daft Harry said, beckoning to Marlowe. The playwright looked at him for a long minute. The idiot was winking and grimacing wildly, tossing his head and one shoulder towards Gabriell's back. Marlowe decided not to help him.

'No.' He turned his back on him and followed the sailor's rolling gait.

'But . . .' Daft Harry dropped out of character momentarily and Gabriell spun round. 'Oh, sir, master,' he whined, quickly reverting. 'Surely, for a poor . . .'

Marlowe waved a hand. 'Sorry,' he called, using his best projection, learned at the knee of the great Ned Sledd himself, 'I don't drink smoke. I have no tinder.'

'Suit yourself,' the intelligencer muttered. 'When you're drowned, don't come whining to me.' Aloud, he added, 'Take care, then, masters all,' and slumped back on to his stool. It might be years before another of Sir Francis' men came by but while he waited, it wasn't such a bad life. He got three hot meals a day from the ladies of the parish and as many hot ladies of the parish a night as he could manage. Lady Dunton looked kindly on him too. With the men away all night fishing, an idiot who had the brains and other attributes of a donkey could do quite well. He gave a little chuckle and watched the retreating playwright almost fondly.

Down at the beach, Gabriell gestured to his boat, pulled up on the sand. It looked very small, but then the journey wasn't long.

'How far is it to the Wight?' he asked Gabriell.

The sailor narrowed his eyes and looked out into the widening of the River Itchen, which in turn led out to the Solent. He licked a finger and held it up and then kicked a clump of brownish, leathery seaweed. Finally he turned to Marlowe and said, 'I have absolutely no idea. I rather hoped you might know.'

Marlowe's dagger was at the man's throat before another wave lapped the shore. 'Who in hell are you?' he said. 'As if it's not bad enough having to deal with an idiot far too convincing for his own good, now I have a sailor who doesn't know his rowlocks from his arse.'

Gabriell eased his head back a fraction but the blade went with him. 'Idiot? What idiot?'

'Daft Harry. Do you have more than one idiot in your village?'

Gabriell held Marlowe's wrist steady while he swallowed. 'Daft Harry? No, he's just the village idiot. We only have the one.'

Marlowe gathered up a handful of Gabriell's jerkin and lifted him a little off his feet so he had to balance on tiptoe to stop the blade pricking under his chin. 'Daft Harry is an agent of Sir Francis. As, I assume, are you, although I find it hard to credit.'

'I am, as a matter of fact, but just as well, old chap, eh, or we would all be a bit in the soup. Are you usually this indiscreet?' Gabriell was chancing his arm to speak like this to someone with a knife at his throat, but he had been told a lot about Marlowe and thought he could tell whether a man was a homicidal maniac or not. And this man seemed not.

Marlowe let him go suddenly and he fell into the fine sand at his feet. He felt a warm trickle on his neck and wiped it. He looked in horror at the back of his hand – he had cut him. The man had actually cut him. He felt quite ill suddenly and put his head between his knees.

'I don't mind being indiscreet with men I am about to skewer,' Marlowe said, 'but I fancy you might know more about this business than I do, so I am prepared to let you live long enough to tell me what's going on.'

'I don't know that much,' Gabriell whined. 'I didn't know about Daft Harry, to name just one part of my ignorance.' He looked up, shielding his eyes from the weak sun which was struggling out through the clouds. 'Are you certain about him?'

Marlowe inclined his head and wiped the tip of his blade on Gabriell's shoulder before slipping it back into the sheath at his back.

'I get a letter once a week from Nicholas Faunt. I don't know who brings it. It is here, in my boat, every Monday at dawn. The Wight has always been somewhere they keep their eyes on. With the Back of the Wight facing France, if there aren't spies landing, then there's brandy. You can't afford to take your eyes off them for a minute.'

'And yet, here you are,' Marlowe said sardonically, 'up the Itchen without, it seems, a paddle.'

'My boat is ready to take to the water,' Gabriell said huffily. 'I could be landing on the Wight in, ooh . . .'

Marlowe kicked the boat dismissively. 'Can you sail this?' he asked.

Gabriell looked him up and down. 'I hope you don't think that I lied to Master Faunt,' he said. 'He placed me here as a sailor, and sailor I am.'

Marlowe narrowed his eyes and felt again for the dagger in the small of his back.

Gabriell shook his head. 'No, no, I am afraid I don't know how to sail this boat,' he said, scrabbling backwards in the sand. 'But,' he rolled over on to his hands and knees and got up, 'I *do* know about what is going on in the Wight. I commit every letter to memory each week and then burn it. I remember them all. What would you like to know?'

Marlowe had a finely developed sense of his own well-being and had no intention of getting into a boat with this man, but on the other hand he did need to know as much as could be gleaned about the situation over the water. He took a step forward, matched by one of Gabriell's going back.

'Stand still, Master Gabriell. I won't prick you again, you can be sure. But we must find someone here to sail us across to the Wight. Surely, not *everyone* in your village works for Sir Francis. Think, man.'

'There are any number of sailors,' Gabriell said, 'but they go out at night. They *say* to fish, and their boats do come back laden down. But whether it is with fish or more valuable cargo, I couldn't say.'

'I know I have asked this before,' he said patiently, 'but is it true that you are an agent of the Crown?'

'Why do you ask, Master Marlowe?'

'Because you don't seem to be able to see further than the end of your nose.'

'If I were to capture every smuggler,' the man said reasonably, 'there wouldn't be a man left out of gaol on the whole of the southern coast and I would get nothing else done. As it is, I talk to some of the men, about what they do on the Island. They think I have a rich lover somewhere nearby to keep me clothed and fed. Otherwise, how would I live?'

'Do you?'

'Live?' Gabriell was confused.

'Have a rich lover?'

The man blushed to the roots of his hair and opened his mouth, though he had no reply that would pass muster.

'There is no need to explain to me,' Marlowe said. 'Needs must when the Devil drives and I know Sir Francis can be tardy when it comes to sending your dues.' He stepped forward quickly and put his arm around the man's shoulder before he could back away. 'Master Gabriell, we are on the same side. Shall we just find a quiet rock or two, out of the drizzle and we can sit and take our ease. Do you have some food in that sack?'

Gabriell nodded.

'Well, that's splendid. We can sit over here and you can tell me all about the Wight. And then, I will go back into the village, say you have fooled me over my fare across to the other side and someone will pity me for an idiot and will think the more of you for your cunning. How does that sound?'

'You're a good man, Master Marlowe,' the intelligencer said. 'A good man and a kind one.'

'If you say so,' Marlowe said. 'But for now, tell me what you know.'

Gabriel Gabriell did not know much more than could be found in the average Almanac. The Captain of the Wight, who was Governor too, was George Carey, kinsman to the Queen. The best ale was to be found in the King's Town of Brading, but Newport, the chief town, was awash with rabid Puritans who had banned Sunday trading, cards, dice and skittles. The locals spoke a peculiar dialect and Gabriel had heard, though he was not sure he believed it, that in the west of the Island there were Anthropophagi, headless men with their faces on their chests. Oh, and the place was haunted.

Marlowe had settled himself at the man's feet, ready to be enlightened, but now rose with a sigh, brushed the sand from his Venetians, removed a crab from a crease in his boot and walked across to the mouth of the river to await a boat to the Wight.

Richard Turvey was captain at Cowes Castle and he did not suffer fools gladly – least of all that idiot Norris whose estate lay across the broad estuary of the Medina from his. He trained his shiny new telescope on the little skiff that was bobbing its way below the cannon on his walls and could make out a single passenger. He believed he was possibly the only man in England to own one of these marvels of modern science. Certainly, he was the only man in the Wight who did.

'What do you make of that, Stanley?' he asked, passing the glass to his lieutenant.

'What am I looking at, sir?'

'The skiff, man.' Turvey was not known for his patience and he was already beginning to wonder what Stanley was actually for.

'Gentleman,' Stanley murmured, twisting the brass this way and that. 'Roisterer, I shouldn't wonder. He must have more money than sense to pay old Ben's price for a crossing. He wouldn't be one to give him any money off the fare for him being a light load.'

Turvey chuckled and nodded. 'No sword, though,' he said ruminatively.

Stanley waited until the boat had rocked past. 'Can't see one. Flash cloak, though. Londoner, I'd say.'

'Would you?' Turvey snatched back the telescope. He knew perfectly well the man had never been north of Salisbury in his life. 'Would you really? Well, one thing's for certain – Jimmy Norris won't have seen him.'

Captain James Norris was furious. He had told old Winchcliffe to take that oak down more often than Dick Turvey had made a fool of himself at the old Leet Court. The boughs were not coming into leaf yet in this wet, late spring, but the trunk was *exactly* blocking Norris's view of the skiff bobbing down the river. He took his job seriously. He was lord of East Cowes, the guardian of the river mouth and he watched *everybody* who sailed in – especially now, in these dark days. There were beacons on the high land of the Wight along the ridge that snaked like a coiling serpent from Yarmouth to the Bembridge Ledge. The parish guns had been hauled out of storage and the cobwebs brushed off them. Militiamen marched and counter-marched on St George's Down. There were rumours . . . and James Norris was drowning in rumours. The man in the skiff, what was he? Mid-twenties, perhaps. Flash dress. Soldier? Too well dressed for a scholar. Anyway, the Wight was crawling with apothecaries and comptrollers. There simply was not room for any more.

He called down from the battlements. 'Cransford!'

'Sir?' The sergeant-at-arms popped his head up from the jakes.

'Skiff coming past. Get yourself to the quay and find out who that is.'

'Now, who the hell is that?' John Vaughan was sitting on the quarter deck of the *Bowe* that afternoon, an open ledger on the table in front of him. Ahead of him, trimming sail as it took the last bend in the river, a little skiff was wending its way towards the quay. Vaughan blotted the page and closed the ledger. The passenger in the skiff did not look like a member of the Privy Council, but it paid to be careful.

'Benjie!' Vaughan called down into the hold. 'Probably not a Comptroller of Wines and Spices, but let's pretend he is, shall we? Call it a drill.' He flicked out the expensive timepiece that had reached his hands from the Scheldt. 'I'm timing you.'

There was a thunderous roll as Benjie set to work below decks, hauling barrels, spreading canvas and tying intricate knots. He had done this so often, he could almost do it in his sleep. Up on the deck, John Vaughan watched the skiff slide under his stern, vanish for a moment, then reappear. The helmsman was throwing his rope and the quaymen caught it, turning the rough hemp around the iron stanchions and holding it fast. The single passenger clambered out, his legs wobbling a bit at first, and he strode away up the hill, past the huge house of John Vaughan, the one that was so large it counted in the town's tax records as two.

Kit Marlowe was glad to be on dry land again. Ahead of him stretched a smoky little town with gabled houses that jostled each other along Quay Street. There was a huge house to his right, new and opulent, clearly the home of a well-appointed gentleman. Beyond that and to the left, the Bridewell loomed grey and grim. Gnarled old hands groped out between the bars at street level and myriad voices called out to him: 'Alms, master. Help us. For the love of God.' There was only so much help Kit Marlowe had to give, for the love of God or anyone else. Even if he had thrown a coin or two through the bars, the inmates would have torn each other apart trying to get to

them and keep them. He could see a church ahead, its spire
tall above the rickety rooftops. This must be St Thomas's, if
Gabriell had told him true, where the former Lord of the Island
lay in his alabaster armour with his rapier at his side.

The man had gone of the plague not six years before and
Kit Marlowe had a dread of the plague. As a boy he had seen
it, the grey bodies piled on carts clattering over the cobbles
of Canterbury on their way to a pit, which, in his child's eye,
had been Hell, the Abyss itself. Marlowe turned into the High
Street with its workshops and awnings, its inns and its stables.
If it was Spain's plan to land here, as some men said, there
would be rich pickings indeed.

A drunk stumbled out of the Castle Inn and collided with
Marlowe. The playwright projectioner steadied himself and let
him fall gently to the mud of the street. He was a militiaman by
the look of his clothing, with the rose of Hampshire sewn to his
sleeve. Marlowe smiled grimly to himself. Yes, if the Spaniards
came, people like this man would soon see off the Duke of
Parma's veterans.

Clear of the town, he took the hill towards the castle. He
could see the river sparkling to his left and men drilling on
the high, bare ground beyond that. He stood and watched them
for a while, pikemen going through their drills and archers
aiming at the butts on the lower slopes. But there was not a
caliverman in sight and, without guns, the men of the Wight
might just as well wave at the Spaniards and throw a welcome
party for them.

It was the drum towers he saw first, new, smooth-surfaced
turrets below their flagged roofs, above the rough Medieval stone.
Briefly they reminded him of the Westgate at home in Canterbury,
where his old dad had done time for crossing the powers that
be. Guards wearing the Queen's livery stood carelessly at the
gates. The huge oak doors were open and women with laundry
baskets strapped to donkeys were wandering in and out. For a
while, Marlowe thought he might be able to walk straight in,
but then two halberds clashed across his face.

'Name?' one of the guards asked him.

'Christopher Marlowe.'

'What's your business?' the other guard wanted to know.

'That's *my* business,' Marlowe said.

'Oh, a comedian,' the first guard smirked.

'Comedian, tragedian, poet.' Marlowe smiled. 'What you will.'

'What you talking about?' the second guard asked him.

'That rose on your tunic,' Marlowe said, flicking a parchment scroll from his purse. 'Look.' He pointed to it. 'There's a similar one. Can you read, thick knarre?'

'Of course,' said the guard, somewhat affronted.

'Then read the signature.'

The guard did. His eyes widened and his halberd slid over his other half's, back to upright. 'Elizabeth R' he had read through the scrolls and curls. 'What is your pleasure, sir?' he asked.

The other guard stood to attention too, careful not to make any more eye contact with the newcomer.

'I have business with the Governor,' Marlowe said. 'Don't worry.' He swept past them under the shadow of the murder holes. 'I can find my own way.'

FOUR

From the shadow of the gatehouse, Marlowe turned left and found himself almost on the step of a house, so new he almost expected the plaster still to be wet. The timbers were full of sap and were swelling and moving in the damp air and there were signs that ongoing repairs were constantly in progress. Despite this, the house was magnificent and he stepped back to admire it while he waited for his rap on the knocker to be answered. He was looking up at the roof gables and smiling at the faces carved there by a craftsman with a ready wit and time on his hands. A slight cough attracted his attention and he jumped slightly and looked at the doorway.

A woman stood there, looking at him from under a heavy brow. Her clothes were magnificent, but the front of her gown was covered by a sacking apron and her face was coarse and looked unwashed. Her hair was pulled severely back from her face under a cap and she carried a single white lily in one hand. When he didn't speak at once, she leaned forward, her free hand on the door and snapped, 'Yes?'

Marlowe was adept at charming women – and men too, for that matter, if they could help him in a quest. But he could tell from the outset that this woman was not put on earth to be charmed by him or any other man. Even so, he could scarcely help going through the motions, so he put down his bag and swept a low bow. 'Mistress,' he said, 'I have come to stay in the house of Governor Carey as his Writer in Residence.'

She made as though to shut the door. 'Thank you,' she said sharply, her voice deeper than Marlowe's own. 'My brother can write. And should he need more writing than he can manage, he has a secretary. Good day, sir.' And with that, she shut the door.

Marlowe felt that it had not gone well. He looked to his right and saw some old buildings, sagging on their foundations, but topped with newer structures in wood, with steps running up against the old stone walls. There seemed to be no one about but he must at least look. The woman had looked as though she would stop at nothing to prevent writers taking up residence. He listened carefully and could hear distant shouts from the training ground beyond the castle wall and the snick of a spade on a flint from what he took to be the kitchen gardens, over in a sheltered corner, beyond what appeared to be a chapel. He was not usually indecisive, but he had been thrown from his purpose and had to rethink.

Suddenly, a head popped out of a casement in the upper storey of the old building. 'Master Marlowe?' the head's owner called.

'Yes!' At last, someone who seemed to be expecting him.

The head withdrew and then reappeared, along with the rest of the person, at the top of the stairs. The man waved and then gave his attention to the steps, which were steep and narrow with no outer rail. When he got to the ground, he strode across the gap between them, hand outstretched.

'I do apologize, Master Marlowe, for not being here to meet you,' he said. 'Sir George is in town on business, but he asked me to keep watch for you. I'm afraid I got a little wrapped up with what I was doing. Accounts, you know.' The man's eye sparkled. 'I do love balancing columns of figures. Do you?'

Marlowe smiled with the memory that this man conjured up of Philip Henslowe, his box on the table in front of him, counting on his fingers, toes, nostrils and any handy body parts of others in the room, flicking the coins into piles quicker than a wink and then coming up for air with a deep sigh and a lugubrious murmur of, 'A loss again, lads. A sad loss.' Sometimes he could control the twitch at the corner of his mouth, sometimes he couldn't. Marlowe answered the comptroller. 'I don't love it myself, but I know many who do – I understand what you mean although I don't understand it, if you follow. Words are more my thing.'

Taking the penultimate sentence into account, the man would wait to have confirmation of that, but meanwhile, these were troubling times. 'I hate to have to ask for this,' he said, 'but may I see your . . .' He glanced from left to right and dropped his voice so low Marlowe had to read his lips. 'Your letter from the Queen.'

Marlowe delved into his bag, but allowed his hand to come up empty. 'And you are?' he said, a tiny tight smile on his lips.

'Did I not say?' The man struck his forehead with an inky palm, leaving just the slightest imprint there, like a fledgling bruise. 'Martin is my name.'

Marlowe clenched his teeth and held his breath. Please, he prayed to all his Muses and even God, for good measure, please don't let his name be Martin Martin. He couldn't bear it.

'Martin Carey. I am Sir George's nephew, I suppose, but so many times removed that it makes no matter. Only the name remains to say there is any relationship at all. We're all cousins under the skin, aren't we? To prevent confusion, everyone calls me Master Martin and I do very well like that. They usually keep me up there.' He pointed behind him. 'I have my own office in the keep, so it's aptly named. Gives me peace and quiet for the world of numbers.'

Marlowe handed over his letter and then shook the man's hand. He was a pleasant enough looking fellow, with corn-coloured hair that flopped limply over his eye and was constantly being tucked behind his ear. His inky fingers had dyed it a very faint blue. His eyes were hooded and were constantly moving up and down, searching for an invisible row of figures to add or subtract. He was around Marlowe's height, but had no substance to him. A gust of wind would blow him away.

'I met a woman at the house . . .' Marlowe began.

'A woman?' Martin said, looking at him with one eye cocked, like a sparrow after a worm. 'Big. Wearing some kind of apron?' He sketched the garment across his front.

'That's her. Speaks like so!' Marlowe dropped his voice almost an octave and the comptroller laughed and nodded.

'You have met the Lady Avis Carey. You have lived to tell the tale, which I believe is not something that can be promised to everyone. She doesn't let many past her door.'

'Avis? That is Latin for bird,' Marlowe mused. 'I wonder which one.'

'Not a peacock, that's for sure,' Martin said. 'But she can't guard her brother's door against the Queen's seal, so let us go and see if we can find someone more congenial in the house. There are plenty more to choose from; you were just very unfortunate.'

'If she is Sir George's sister, why is she opening the door? Surely, she has people to do that for her?'

'Any number, but she is like Cerberus; she guards her gate well. She doesn't think that anyone can do it quite as well as she.'

'And the apron?'

Martin laughed and ushered Marlowe ahead of him towards the door. 'No one can sweep like Avis, cook like Avis, mend, make beds or for all I know dip tallow like Avis. She is a whirlwind, but like the whirlwind nothing is done well, just thrown into the air. We have to have twice the staff we could otherwise do with if we didn't have Avis. One lot to be shouted at by her for their idleness, and one lot to go around behind her setting things right.'

Marlowe leaned nearer. 'Is she quite . . . normal?' He was thinking of Daft Harry and how he could come here for lessons.

Again, the comptroller laughed. 'Of course not. No one is normal here. I thought that was why you had come, to get ideas for a play!'

Marlowe shrugged. 'I need people in the audience to recognize my characters, if only a little,' he said. 'I may need to look elsewhere.' Martin reached around him and pushed open the door and he looked in, taking in the luxurious interior. 'But here will do nicely for now,' he said, stepping in and putting down his bag.

He looked round to see Martin watching him, a proud smile on his face. 'It is lovely, isn't it? I always enjoy seeing people's first reaction.' A huge ancient fireplace stood to one side of the room, no logs in the grate for all it was a bleak, cold spring and elegant tapestries from the Gobelin works hung between the long windows opposite. Marlowe smiled to see Dido,

Queen of Carthage, rolling in the woven embrace of Aeneas, arrayed in martial splendour under a canopy of roses.

'This was the Great Hall,' Martin explained, 'built by Isabella de Fortibus herself.'

Marlowe realized he was supposed to be impressed and whistled through his teeth.

'She was the last independent ruler of the Wight,' Martin told him proudly, clearly as much of a history bore as he was with figures. He glanced over his shoulder and reached out an arm to Marlowe, shepherding him on. 'But don't let's linger here. I can hear Avis in the distance and she's getting closer.'

Sure enough, there was a distant hooting, like a bullock lost in the fog and calling for its fellows. The deep mooing was definitely getting louder and without further ado, the two men ran for the stairs and by the time Lady Avis reached the hall all that was left of them was some dust settling out of the weak sunbeam that lit the second landing.

Although Marlowe's room was tucked away in one of the furthest gable ends, it was still luxurious by anyone's standards. The bed was goose down and the drapes were heavy and clean. A small table had been placed under the window, with a pile of fresh paper, some uncut quills and a bottle of ink, with the wax still on the stopper. Clearly, someone could housekeep in this place, even if it wasn't Avis. Unpacking was the work of moments and the playwright lifted out shirts and a spare doublet in one pile and arranged them in the press. He picked up his bag and looked around for somewhere to put it out of the way, and as he folded it across, he heard it crackle. He walked over to the window, opening the mouth of the bag as he did so, looking inside. Tucked half into the lining was a piece of paper. He reached in and pulled it out. He recognized Faunt's spidery hand as soon as he saw it and wasn't sure whether to be glad or sorry. He had felt all along that there might be some reason even more clandestine than usual for his being here and this letter hopefully would hold the key. He was tired of waiting for the other shoe to drop. Unfolding the paper, he leaned closer to the casement to read. 'Kit,' he read. 'In haste, I must tell you more of what you may find in the mansion of Sir George Carey. Hasler is your quarry, not only because I do not like to lose a man in the field but also because we fear there may be a cuckoo in the nest. A cuckoo that works for Spain.'

A hullabaloo outside broke into Marlowe's reading. He threw open the window and looked out to see, squat and foreshortened in the courtyard below, three men. The guards were hurrying up from the gate and everyone seemed to be shouting at once. One of the guards gave one of the men a shove that sent him sprawling. It looked as though there might be real trouble when some gardeners came running up, forks and sickles in hand. Marlowe had seen enough brawls to know that angry and excited men and sharp implements rarely ended well. He tucked the paper under his pillow and raced for the stairs.

Down in the hall there was a twitter of maids and the distant boom of Avis in the corridor. Marlowe squeezed past and opened the door a crack. There were by now yet more gardeners and another couple of guards had materialized from the gate house, one rubbing his eyes and the other lacing his breeches; the night shift and one with a rather better social life than the other, Marlowe guessed, seeing the girl slipping out through the far archway, keeping her face to the wall. Opening the door as little as possible, he slipped through and pulled it closed behind him, keeping well back until he could see who was shouting what at whom and who was most likely to swing something deadly first.

The three men who had begun it all were standing at bay on the first step, shouting at the guards who seemed intent on arresting them or at least laying them out one by one. The youngest of the intruders was holding a grubby rag to his forehead, staunching a rivulet of blood which nonetheless was making its way to his chin, where it mingled with a scrubby beard. The other men were older, of an age and looking alike. They had weaselly faces, eyes close together under narrow brows and their mouths seemed very short on teeth, but they were dressed in decent clothes, clean and mended where their work had made it necessary. Looking with his intelligencer's eye, Marlowe had them down for smallholders, not rich certainly, but not poor. He couldn't think why they had run so precipitately through the archway and he decided to find out.

He took one step down and edged round the crowd. He plucked the sleeve of a gardener who was clearly feeling underarmed as he was only carrying a hoe. Whilst a sharp hoe could be a weapon in the right hands, these were not the right hands, as the lad was clearly very low in the pecking order of Sir George Carey's gardeners. The lad turned, spinning on the ball of one foot, hoe at the tilt and ready for anything. Before he could strike, Marlowe reached out one hand and removed the hoe from his grasp, pulling him at the same time away from the crowd.

'What's going on here, boy?' he asked.

'Who're you?' the lad replied, voice going up and down the scale in an adolescent discordance.

Marlowe cocked an ironic eyebrow at the crowd, who seemed to be doing a lot more threatening and brandishing than they had before and everyone had taken another step forward. 'Is this the time? But since you ask, I am Christopher Marlowe, playwright and poet. So, again, what's going on here?'

If the boy thought that it was an odd question for a poet to be asking, he didn't show it. 'I don't know, not rightly. George Urry, that's him over yonder, poking that bastard guard in the chest, he reckons he do have found a body down in one of his drains, down there.' The boy gestured out to the meadows that lay to the south-west of the castle.

Marlowe pulled the boy's arm back down to his side. 'No wild gestures, lad,' he muttered. 'You don't want to lose a hand, I don't suppose.'

The boy rolled his eyes and folded his arms tightly to his chest. He was by nature a gesturer, finding that a pointing finger could cover more than a thousand words sometimes. He certainly didn't want to lose any odd extremities to a sickle at his tender years. He nodded with his head to the south-west instead. 'He says there is a body, dead as a nit, it be, down in one of the drains. He had noticed that his cattle were all drinking from the same trough and that's not normal, not when there's another one over the other side o'field. So he went down with his brother.' He nodded at the almost identical man in the middle. 'And his boy.'

'Do we know who the body is?'

'No. He be stuck head-first in the drain. He's stinking up the water, that's why the cattle wouldn't drink there.'

In London, news like this wouldn't cause anyone to turn a hair, let alone cause a riot, but he had met the guards himself and he could see how it had happened. Three overexcited and shouting men had barged past them and really the rest was inevitable. He took a deep breath and stepped back into the crowd, raising his voice to make himself heard. Ned Alleyn would have been proud – such projection, such breath control!

He positioned himself between the Urry brothers. 'Gentlemen!' he thundered. 'Can we all calm down for one moment?' It was a question but it sounded like an order.

Hearing coherent speech from a stranger caught the attention of the crowd and slowly, by ones and twos, fists, forks and sickles began to be lowered. Several people were bleeding now and they were grateful for an excuse to get out of the situation with some kind of dignity and the right number of ears intact.

Marlowe nodded to the guards, who were still in somewhat martial poses, halberds threatening and fists clenched around studded staves. 'Gentlemen,' he said to them. 'If we find there has been a crime committed here, I am sure these estimable gentlemen, the Masters Urry, I believe –' the smallholders straightened and tried to look important – 'meant no harm when they ran past you. They have some important news for Sir George.' He looked from man to man with a raised eyebrow and they nodded. 'Which they were anxious to share. So, if you would all like to disperse . . .'

The crowd didn't move.

'. . . or alternatively, wait there quietly, while we find someone in the house who can hear their story, I am sure we can get to the bottom of this in a moment.'

'You bugger off,' someone shouted from the crowd. 'Coming down here with your Lunnon ways, telling honest men what to do.'

There were cries of agreement and a few sickles came back
to chest level.

'There's some poor bugger dead down in Harry Urry's drain
in Bottom Field. We'll *disperse* . . .' The speaker paused for
the chuckles he knew would come. Whoever he was, he knew
his crowd. 'We'll *disperse* when we know who he be, and
who did put him down that there drain.'

There was scattered applause and Marlowe was almost
tempted to give the man a job as warm-up at the Rose. The
crowd hung by a thread and Marlowe thought fast.

'I am a stranger here, it's true,' he said. 'I didn't mean to
interfere, but I didn't want any of you hard-working gentlemen
to do something you might live for a short while to regret.
Murder is easy when sickles are flying through the air and I
know no one wants to hang for the sake of a dead body, now,
do you?'

This time the mutters were more muted and everyone took
a couple of steps back, making the crowd bigger, but much
more thinly spread. Everyone suddenly wanted an arm's length
between him and his neighbour.

'Sir George is not at home,' Marlowe said. 'Is there a
Constable here?'

Every head turned to left and right. Then each one shook.

'Then how would it be if *I*, who cannot have been responsible
for any of this, having only landed at the quay this afternoon,
went with these gentlemen down to the drain to see who this
dead man is? I would need a hand or two and perhaps some
spades. Is that a good idea?'

The crowd was silent and looked rather confused. They
were not used to having their opinions sought by men dressed
like Marlowe and sounding as though they had swallowed a
primer. Eventually, a few men nodded and others followed
suit.

'That's splendid.' Marlowe clapped each Urry brother on
the shoulder. He pointed into the crowd and picked out two
who had seemed less demonstrative than the rest when it came
to shaking sharp things over their head. 'You and you,' he
said. 'Come with us.' Then he turned to George Urry. 'Will
you show the way?' he said.

Urry looked up from under sparse brows. 'I dunno,' he said. 'I come up to see Sir George.'

'He ain't here, though,' his brother said reasonably. 'The Constable's off at Mistress Sanford's; she's having words with her old man again. Young Joseph came and got him, noontime. He'll be locking him up by now, it is to be hoped. Let's go with this gentleman, our George, and get that corpse out of our stream. T'ain't healthy nor lucky, leaving him there.'

Marlowe and the two younger Urrys looked at Harry, standing like an ox in the furrow. The crowd had melted away, including one of the diggers chosen by Marlowe. The guards stood back, at attention and waiting for what the playwright would do next. After all, he did have a letter from the Queen.

George Urry suddenly stamped both feet, and turned for the tunnel to the outside world. 'Let's go, then,' he said. 'Sooner we're gone, sooner it's done.'

Feeling that you could certainly not say fairer than that, Marlowe shepherded the men into line and fell into step at the rear. He was practically certain that the man in the drain would turn out to be the elusive Hasler and if so, he could get out of this asylum before too many more tides had turned. Unearthing any number of corpses would be worth it for that alone.

FIVE

D on Alonso Perez de Guzman, the Duke of Medina
Sidonia, looked in the mirror that evening in May.
Beyond the mirror's foxing he saw what he had
become. He was in full armour, blued and gilded by the best
craftsmen in Toledo. The chains of the Fleece and of Santiago,
the Moor Slayer, hung around his neck and his chin was held
high by the elaborately starched ruff made lovingly for him by
the nuns of the convent of Alcalar. He blinked, looking into
his own watery grey eyes. He was the Captain-General of the
Ocean Sea and 125 ships and 30,000 battle-hardened troops
skipped to his every word. Yet he knew in his heart he was
essentially a secretary, a carrier of inkwells and a sharpener of
quills. He was the commander of the greatest Armada in the
history of the world and he had never heard a shot fired in
anger on the water before.

Men who had heard that sound now trooped on to his quarterdeck; he could hear their boots on the planking of the timbers
overhead. He adjusted his sword, cleared his throat and clattered
up the narrow wooden ladder. In the light of the huge poop
lantern, they saluted him, their pinnaces bobbing in the dark
water below the bulk of the *San Martin de Portugal* as it rode
at anchor. Under their dark cloaks, Medina Sidonia's captains
had come to pay their respects in readiness for the great enterprise that was about to begin.

Alongside the commander, his right-hand men bowed to
each man as he approached. Diego de Valdez was High Admiral
of Spain, as arrogant a bastard as ever sailed a ship. He also
had a temper shorter than a Protestant's rosary and it did not
help that the man he hated most in the world was his cousin,
Don Pedro, bowing curtly to him now, as commander of the
Andalusian squadron. Francisco de Bombadilla was the army
man. If Valdez knew how to fight at sea, Bombadilla could
fight on land; he had proved it a dozen times. It was

unfortunate that the man spent most of his time fighting with officers under his command. But Medina Sidonia was under no illusions. He had lost count of the times he had written to the King, begging to be released from this command. Felipe el Prudente did not know whether to be hurt or outraged and he had returned eloquent letters in his own spidery hand, with all kinds of reasons why Medina Sidonia it had to be. In the end, out of patience at last, he had written: 'Medina Sidonia. Be there. P.'

So that was the true purpose of Valdez and Bombadilla and everybody knew it. They were King Philip's bloodhounds, making sure that the Captain-General of the Ocean Sea did not try to slip *his* leash.

Old Juan de Recaldé could be heard wheezing and struggling up the *San Martin*'s rope ladder. He was sixty-two and a martyr to sciatica, but he was also Medina Sidonia's second-in-command and as brave as a lion. He would lead the Biscayan squadron to hell if he had to and come out laughing the other side. He resolutely refused the chair offered to him on the quarterdeck and leaned on the ship's rail to ease the pain in his joints.

Alonso de Leiva had no such difficulty because he was forty years younger than the old man. His carrack *La Rata Santa Maria Encoronada* was the pride of the Genoese squadron in Philip's fleet and it bobbed on the water across the sweep of Lisbon's harbour. He was tall with long, golden hair, a poet of sorts and loved by his men. He bowed low before Medina Sidonia, the cross of Santiago shining against the severe black of his doublet.

The Captain-General clapped his hands once they were all assembled, like a schoolmaster trying to control an unruly class, and they came to order. Servants mingled with them serving goblets of the finest Spanish wine from Recaldé's own vineyards and Medina Sidonia raised his in a toast. He was about to hold forth when a last head appeared above the quarter rail, the lion mane of Hugo de Moncada, captain of the galliasses. He hated Medina Sidonia, knew him for the over-promoted idiot he was, and could not understand why *he* was not in command.

'Sorry I'm late, Captain-General,' he said, not meaning a word of it and helping himself to a goblet, passing by him on a tray at that moment.

Medina Sidonia smiled at him indulgently. Keep them all sweet now, he thought to himself. They had not set sail yet and there was a long way to go. He raised his goblet. 'Gentlemen,' he said. 'The enterprise of England.'

'The enterprise of England!' they all thundered and sipped their wine. Then, as they all fell to what they did best, bickering and sniping, a messenger arrived from His Majesty at the Escorial, addressed to the Captain-General. Medina Sidonia tore the seal quickly and read it briefly by the guttering flame of the poop lantern. He could not make it all out in that bad light, but it had something to do with the place the English called the Isle of Wight.

Marlowe and the Urrys trudged down the hill from the barbican. The going was steep here and the hawthorn hedges that lined the sunken lane closed in dark and deep. This had been the old way up to the castle in the days of Isabella de Fortibus and few people used it now. It emerged on to flat fields, enclosed for two generations. The River Medina twisted through them as a little stream, full after the constant rain.

'Over here.' Harry Urry led the way, striding along the path that led to the hedge. The three men were standing at the entrance to a culvert in a ditch, the grass growing over its curved brick roof. But it was not the ingeniousness of the water supply that Marlowe was looking at – it was the pair of legs sticking out of the low tunnel. The boots were good, of stout Spanish leather, and they were caked in mud.

'Gentlemen,' the playwright said, 'would you do the honours?'

The Urry brothers had handled dead bodies before. Their old man had gone of the plague six years ago and while others kept well away from even the most beloved victim of the pestilence or sent for the plague doctor, remote behind his beaked mask, the Urrys had just stayed with the old man, wiping his fevered brow and patting his hand in comfort. Then they had carried him to the new graveyard at Church Litten and buried him themselves. As for them, marked for death by their proximity, they developed not a pustule, not a bubo, not so much as a sneeze and a shiver.

What had scared these two was the sheer surprise of what they had found. Men died at their work – a carelessly swung crane at the quay; a mean bull suddenly gone rogue – but they did not crawl into a culvert to do it. They screwed their courage to the sticking place and each of them grabbed a boot. The owner of those boots slid out with a strange sucking noise and then stopped. Marlowe peered up into the culvert and saw the problem. The dead man's elbows had caught on the brickwork on both sides and his arms were stiff and rigid. He made a twirling motion behind him with his hand and the brothers turned the legs clockwise. The elbows came free and the body came loose, rushing into the ditch with an afterbirth of mud, water and loosened grass.

When the head appeared, grey eyes staring through a film of mud up at the sky, the Urrys crossed themselves. Marlowe noticed it – the old faith still had its followers this far south.

'Do you know who this is?' he asked.

'Walter Hunnybun,' Harry Urry said. 'He owns the land yonder.'

Marlowe followed the man's pointing finger. The Hunnybun lands stretched away over the slope of the fields where the squat tower of a church nestled in a valley.

'His lands end here?' Marlowe checked.

'That's right,' Will Urry told him. 'We're standing on our land now, his'n is over the hedge.'

Marlowe paced backwards and forwards, frowning. The Urrys were still staring at the body, caps clasped to their chests. 'So,' the poet said. 'He died on your side of the hedge.'

'Did he?' Harry Urry asked.

'It's easier, I would think,' Marlowe said, 'to push a body in head first than feet first, wouldn't you say?'

'I dunno,' the farmer conceded with a shrug. 'Sheep. That's what I know. What are you, then, some sort of constable?'

Marlowe laughed. 'No,' he said, 'I'm some sort of play-wright. But I have seen murder before.' He crouched in the mud under the hedge and looked at the corpse of Walter

Hunnybun. The man was, he guessed, forty, solidly built and well dressed. His Venetians and doublet were soaking wet from their time in the culvert and his hat, if he had been wearing one, was gone. Marlowe hauled the body over on to its face, to the sound of a swallowed gasp from Will Urry. It seemed so wrong to the man that his neighbour should have his face pressed into the mud, even though it could make no difference to him now, wherever he had gone. There was no dagger at the man's back, no sword at his side. He had come out to meet a friend, that much was obvious, or at least someone who posed no threat. But there he had been wrong. Marlowe rolled him back.

'Where's his house?' he asked.

'Yonder.' Harry Urry pointed, but there was no building in sight.

'He has family?'

The Urrys shook their heads. 'Widower,' Will said. 'No nippers.'

'Keeps to 'isself,' Harry chipped in.

'Is he . . . was he a farmer, like you?'

'Not like us,' Harry grunted. 'I don't like to speak ill of the dead, but . . .'

'But you're going to,' Marlowe suggested.

'Had airs and graces, did Walter,' Will said, not looking down at the man's staring face as he spoke. 'Always hobnobbing with gentry, even when he weren't welcome.'

Harry gave him a sharp nudge. 'You don't know that,' he said in an undertone.

Will was affronted. 'Well,' he said stubbornly. ''E were.'

Harry turned to Marlowe. 'He were stuck up, Walter were,' he said, already consigning the man to history. 'Lickin' the arse of Sir George.'

'Always up at the castle,' Will chimed in, not to be outdone.

'That's where we'll take him, then,' Marlowe said. 'Can you lift him, gentlemen?' He looked up the hill. 'It's a steep climb.'

It was. But these two were used to it, having carried more dead sheep than Marlowe had rhymed couplets, and they tossed a coin as to who would take the heavy end. Will lost and lowered himself to take the shoulders. The limbs were loosening now, the head lolling back.

And all the way up the slope, Marlowe couldn't help noticing the biceps on both men. Either of them could have demolished Walter Hunnybun's skull. They were First Finders; they had come across the body in the first place. But was that because they knew just where to look?

Marlowe had timed his arrival well. On the second Friday of each month, Sir George Carey, Captain of the Wight, held a lavish banquet for the great and good of his Island and the wine flowed freely and the playing of pipes and lutes was exquisite. The orchestra had come gratis, lent by the Earl of Southampton, who owed George Carey a favour. Marlowe found himself as guest of honour on the high table, the candles flooding the room with light. George Carey was an alert-looking man with large dark eyes and tightly curled hair. He was the heir to the Hunsdon estate and his father was first cousin to Her Majesty. His fingers glittered with rings as he dabbled them in the bowl between courses and an emerald sparkled in the trinket hanging from his left ear.

'Well, we're delighted to have you, Master Marlowe,' he said, raising his goblet to the man. 'As you can see, I'm trying to bring a little civilization to this arse-end of the universe, but such things take time. I've been trying to get young Master Nashe down here for a while, but he's never available.'

'Nashe?' Marlowe raised an eyebrow.

'The satirist and university wit.'

'Is that what he is?'

'Do you know him?' Carey asked, sensing a raw nerve.

'Intimately. He's a skinny little fellow, gag-teeth. Got a fuse shorter than any of your calivermen, I'll wager.'

'You don't like him?'

'On the contrary, Sir George, I am very fond. All right, he is a mere lad and made the mistake of attending St John's College in Cambridge, but we have a mutual hatred which keeps us friends. Young Tom and I both hate with a passion Dr Gabriel Harvey, also late of Cambridge. Do you know him?'

Carey shook his head.

'That's as it should be.' Marlowe smiled and sipped his wine. If a courtier like George Carey had never heard of the obnoxious Harvey, then Marlowe's work was done. He looked down the table, changing the subject. 'Are all these gentlemen of the Wight?'

'After a fashion,' Carey said, flicking his fingers for a lackey to fill his goblet. 'Over there, for example.' The governor casually jerked his head to his right where a large man was holding forth on the current state of Carey's Militia. 'Henry Oglander. That man could bore a cannon. Papist, of course.'

'Really?'

'And it's not a good time to be of the old faith, Marlowe, you'll agree?'

'Oh, indeed,' the poet said, he who had no faith at all, unless it was in his own quill and his own dagger.

'Over there.' Carey nodded to his left. 'John Vaughan, merchant.'

'In what goods?' Marlowe remembered having seen the man on the quarter deck of a ship in the quay when he came ashore.

'Somebody else's,' Carey said.

'Oh.'

'Don't look so amazed, Master Marlowe.' The governor chuckled. 'You're from London. There are more pirates along stretches of your river than in the whole of Barbary. I can't complain; the man goes to church on a Sunday, gives freely to charity and his wife turns a pretty ankle . . .' Carey caught sight of his own wife sitting on Marlowe's left and quickly changed the subject. 'See those two, at each end of the far table?'

Marlowe did.

'The one on the left is Richard Turvey, captain of Cowes. On the right, James Norris, captain of East Cowes.'

'The forts I passed as I came in?'

'Would be, yes,' Carey said. 'Well, I couldn't ask for stouter hearts in these trying times, what with the war and so on, but they haven't spoken in six years.'

'What happened six years ago?' Marlowe asked.

'I took over the governorship. For all I know the feud between those two has been going on since the Flood.'

'George.' The governor's wife leaned closer to Marlowe, rubbing his forearm as though it were a favourite pet. 'You're boring our guest. He's not interested in our local politics. Master Marlowe –' she clicked her fingers to have their goblets refilled – 'tell me all about yourself.'

Elizabeth Carey was a striking-looking woman, with long, almost black hair wound up in coils held in place with pearls. Her teeth were even when she smiled, which was often, and her lips were red and full. Her breasts heaved at the margin of her stomacher but as this was the Isle of Wight she had not adopted the London style of revealing her nipples, rouged, to the world.

'There's little enough to tell, madam,' he said.

'Oh, come now,' she trilled. 'We have all heard of the great Christopher Marlowe, he of the mighty line. George saw your *Tamburlaine* at the Rose last year. He was full of it, quoting all the best bits.'

Marlowe laughed. 'That couldn't have taken long,' he said.

'Christopher Marlowe,' she said, looking into the eyes as dark as hers, the finely chiselled mouth, the hair hanging in fashionable ringlets on to his collar. 'Before you became the Muse's darling, what were you then?'

Marlowe raised an eyebrow at her and lifted his chin. 'You're teasing me, madam,' he said.

'No, I'm not,' she said earnestly. 'I really want to know. And please call me Bet.'

'Very well . . . Bet. I was a Cambridge scholar – Corpus Christi College.'

'Eughh!' She gave a weak shudder. 'So I could have been sitting by a churchman tonight?'

'A fate worse than death, Bet?' he asked with a wry grin. He could certainly think of a long list of churchmen who he would rather never break bread with again.

She was suddenly serious and he felt her hand brush his thigh under the tablecloth. 'There are many more fates worse than death, Christopher,' she said. 'Or may I call you Kit?'

'Yes, Bet,' he said, smiling. 'Of course you may.'

'George.' Bet Carey was suddenly on her feet. 'It's time for the dancing.'

'Oh, lord,' the governor sighed. Beyond him, at the far end of the table, Avis Carey snorted and banged out of the room, already ripping pins out of her coiffure and hauling off her ruff.

'Was it something anyone said?' Marlowe asked Bet, seeing the woman go.

'I'm sorry about Avis,' Bet murmured. 'Have you been introduced yet?'

'Not exactly,' Marlowe told her.

'Lucky you.' Bet smiled. 'Avis doesn't like dancing. Doesn't approve. Bit of a puritan, I'm afraid. But then, there's rather a long list of what Avis doesn't like. Firstly, there's—'

'Come, come, now, Bet.' George Carey was on his feet. 'Now *you're* boring Master Marlowe. Ladies and gentlemen, before the dancing begins, I'd like to propose a toast.' All the men were on their feet, goblets in hand. 'To the galleons of Spain,' he said. 'May they sink to the bottom!' There was a roar of laughter and the pounding of tables and healths were drunk to all and sundry.

Bet Carey was known throughout the south as a dancer of rare talent. The Satyr's dance was her favourite, although she had been known to join the Shipman's and the barefoot dances along the quay when one of John Vaughan's ships came in. She took Marlowe's arm and led him across the long gallery and down the great staircase to the old Medieval Hall where her husband's dogs lay in the open, cold grate.

The servants had lit the candles here in the roof lights and the tables had been carried to the walls to leave ample space. The governor's players had abandoned their places in the dining hall and took up positions at the bottom of the far stair.

'Candle dance,' Lady Carey commanded and everybody took their positions. Each lady and each gentleman was given a wax taper to hold and servants bobbed between them, touching their lit tapers to each one, along the hall, pair by pair. The lute struck up and Marlowe and his lady walked towards each other, nodding their candles in time. The little flames fluttered and flew, their reflections a myriad pricks of light in the dancers' eyes. He bowed to Bet; she curtsied to him, then the fortunes of the dance swept them apart and the couples whirled around the floor, each man with his candle in the air and his free hand behind his back, each lady with her free hand holding her gown out to the side.

Carey's dogs got up and ambled away. Whatever this nonsense was all about, it had no place in the canine world. They would wait for the morning, running and leaping through the tall grass after the hares in their master's warren. Marlowe found himself, in the new pass, facing a red-headed beauty with grey eyes that flashed in the candles' flames.

'Cicely Meux,' she said as she curtsied, allowing as much of her cleavage to show as she dared. 'You must be Christopher Marlowe,' she purred.

'If you say so, madam.' He bowed and the dance carried them apart. Those wallflowers around the wall and the grumpy old men who were too Puritan or too old to dance, kept time, heads nodding, shoulders swaying. Carey's borrowed musicians were excellent.

'Master Marlowe.' The playwright's next partner nudged candles with his. 'Ann Oglander. Welcome to Carisbrooke.' The girl had glorious blonde hair piled high with Spanish combs, and rubies glittered at her throat.

'Madam,' Marlowe bowed and swayed on.

'You must come to Ningwood,' the next partner insisted as she dipped in front of him. 'I am Ferdinanda Hobson. Wonderful to meet you at last, Master Marlowe.'

'Er . . . likewise,' the poet said and was almost glad when the music came to an end and he could bow to his last partner, a snaggle-toothed old merchant who had got so hopelessly confused in the sets that he had been dancing largely by himself for the last five minutes. And his candle had gone out. There was a flutter of applause.

'La Volta,' Bet Carey commanded and there was an inrush of breath around the room. The Master of the Musick looked at George Carey, who merely shrugged and spread his arms. He was glad to be able to sit this one out and wandered off to natter to John Vaughan. The music struck up and four ladies made a beeline for Marlowe. It was all done seamlessly except for the odd stepping on toes and Bet Carey seemed to have won the race.

'This is a little fast for me, my lady,' Marlowe said.

'Nonsense,' she laughed. 'We'll get to the full galliard later and then we'll put you through your paces.'

The music struck up and Bet slid forward, her feet tapping on the rush-strewn floor. Marlowe did too, slapping his hand against hers as they twirled. Other couples took to the floor, most of them noticeably younger than those who had danced the Candle Dance. As the rhythm beat faster and the couples swayed more suggestively, Marlowe's left hand slid across Bet's right hip; his left caught her between her legs and he lifted her high across his body, to the whoops and delight of the watchers.

Each time, she came down to earth with a sigh that only he could hear and a light in her eyes that only he could see. He felt himself smiling. No doubt the Lady Avis was alone somewhere in the bowels of George Carey's house, tutting and frothing about the filthy gropings and the fire of lust going on under her brother's roof. Dancing! Did no one read their Bibles any more?

The dancing went on into the early hours when various carriages rattled and clattered in under the arch of the barbican and people took their leave and said goodnight. Farewells were loud and hearty, steps vague and unsteady. It was always the same after one of George Carey's parties; no one wanted to go home.

The last wavering light disappeared down the hill and the castle settled into silence, broken only by the occasional bark of a fox over in the forest of Parkhurst. A shadow detached itself from the darkness of the chapel wall and waited; a light appeared at the door of the mansion and a slim figure slipped out, covering the lantern with a shutter. Without a stumble, the man carrying the light made his way to the chapel door and slid the key into the lock. Without looking round, he spoke.

'Shall we?'

The waiting figure grunted softly and they both disappeared

into the cool of the chapel, smelling of old stone, decay and also the muddy wetness of Walter Hunnybun's slowly drying clothes.

Martin Carey put the lantern down on a tomb lid, turned up the wick and turned to Marlowe. 'Do you think anyone saw us?' he asked.

Marlowe shook his head. 'It's going to rain soon but even if it was the best night of the year, no one in the house is in any state to be up watching. There may be lots of people padding along landings tonight, but no one looking out at the chapel. No one will see.'

Master Martin moistened his lips. 'Why are we being so secret? Everyone knows that Hunnybun is lying here.'

'Yes, that's true enough, but not everyone knows he was murdered and I want to keep it that way if at all possible.'

'Odd reasoning from a playwright, if you don't mind my pointing it out.'

Marlowe smiled. 'Everything is grist to my mill, Master Martin. Who knows when perhaps I might write a play about a murder and then this will all come in handy. Let's get on. Bring the light nearer and hold it up.'

Martin held the lantern at shoulder height and adjusted it so that it threw no shadow. The corpse of Walter Hunnybun was laid out flat on a hurdle across two chairs. Nothing had been done to make him more respectable than the act of laying him on his back. One hand was clawed up to his throat, the other was splayed out across his private parts. Marlowe took hold of a finger and moved it gently to and fro.

'The rigor has passed,' he said to Martin. 'I will move his hands down to his sides, but remember where they are now. This was how he died, one hand to his throat, the other to his pocky. What does that tell us?' As he spoke, he bent the arms so that they were alongside the body, out of the way. Before he let go, he looked at each hand.

'He was pushed into a drain,' Martin pointed out. 'Couldn't that explain it?'

'It might,' Marlowe said, leaning closer to the body. 'But it doesn't explain this.' He pointed to the front of Hunnybun's breeches. The laces were undone and a flag of white shirt was pulled through.

Master Martin looked closer and then looked at Marlowe, raising one shoulder. 'He may have been taking a piss.'

'He may have been,' Marlowe agreed. 'But why do that in a field when his house was just over the next hedgerow? No, I think that Master Hunnybun here was out walking to meet a lady.' He pulled open the man's jerkin. The shirt beneath was grey from the drain water, but was clearly made of good linen and freshly laundered. There were no creases from wearing, no marks at all except from the damp. 'He's dressed in his best, look. Even his boots are not everyday. I think that our farmer here was not expecting to meet death on his walk last night. I think he was in the mood for love.'

Again, Martin shrugged. 'But, surely . . .'

'Yes?'

'He is a widower. He could have who he wanted up to the house. Indeed, I have heard stories of him and his maidservant . . . but we shouldn't gossip, perhaps.'

Marlowe clapped him on the shoulder, making the lantern light waver over the dead face and giving it a momentary semblance of life. 'You are very kind, Master Martin. Perhaps Master Hunnybun liked a change now and again. Although –' and he looked dispassionately at the coarse features – 'I would not have imagined that he had to beat the ladies off with a stick. Not with a nose like that.'

Martin stifled a laugh and crossed himself piously. 'Poor man,' he said. 'He certainly does suffer from the Hunnybun nose. I can't think of any ladies from around here who would think it worth meeting him on a damp and cold night such as we have been having lately. Unless . . .' He gestured to the unlaced breeches.

Marlowe shook his head. 'Even allowing for the usual ravages, I don't believe that Master Hunnybun had any secrets to share in that department.'

'So . . .' Martin looked at Hunnybun for a moment, then made up his mind. 'So, I'm sorry, Master Marlowe. My money is still on his taking a piss. He isn't young. Men sometimes get urges when they are his age that won't wait.'

Marlowe looked down at the dead man too. He nodded. 'They do, Master Martin. Indeed they do. I think we will have to agree to disagree because although I have seen many an old man take a piss in the street and other public places, I have never seen one,' and he leaned over to pull the collar away from the livid throat, 'be strangled for it.'

It rained during the night; the windows of heaven shut up. Lovers lay entwined under their canopies while those of clean heart snored unaware. On the battlements of Carisbrooke, the drops bounced hard and fat off the morions of the night watchmen and the guards peered out into the darkness. They trudged the wall walk under the arms of the oaks, glancing down into the deserted, silent knot garden behind the chapel where the dead man lay and out across the impenetrable blackness of the Downs. That was the way they would come, if they were coming at all, the galleons of Spain. And the beacons would flare into light across the Island's backbone to tell the Wight that the Devil was on his way.

But perhaps the Devil was here already.

SIX

That was the day the sun shone. That solitary day, in an otherwise blustery, wet May. It warmed the stone of George Carey's castle and sent shadows dappling the curtain walls. The lord of the Island led his visitor up the steps behind his mansion and out on to the narrow wall walk. His militiamen, in heavy morions, breast and back plates, trudged and cursed along the crenellations. Yesterday, they had cursed because it was wet and cold. Today, they cursed because it was dry and warm. The pads of moss which had flourished in the damp were now treacherous underfoot as the slimy layer beneath made them as slippery as glass. As they stumbled, slipped and complained their way around their beat, it was a worry to Sir George that these were the men who would have to stand against the veterans of the Duke of Parma, the finest soldier in the world.

'Do you think they'll come, Christopher?' the governor asked, locking his hands behind his back and half turning to the playwright.

'Who, Sir George?'

'Why, the dons, man. The Spaniards. The whole island's bristling with more mercenaries than the King of Spain has confessors. Look, here.' He pointed suddenly to an arrow slit in the wall. 'That's Heynoe's Loop. The story goes that when the French invaded in 1377, Philip de Heynoe put a crossbow bolt through their commander's brain, fired from that very spot.'

Marlowe squatted to check the trajectory. 'Impressive,' he said.

'Oh, I don't know,' Carey muttered. 'Anyone can shoot a crossbow. My own dear sister damned near killed me with one once.'

'Did she?' Remembering the biceps on Mistress Carey, Marlowe was not too surprised.

'Oh, she was distraught, of course. In fact, between you and me, she never quite got over it. It was only a scratch and you know how tense everyone gets during a hunt.'

Marlowe knew.

'She has never touched a crossbow since and she hasn't come hunting with us either. Which is no bad thing, I suppose. She used to put the men off their stroke. A stunning looking girl she was, in her day.' Sir George looked to a far horizon that only he could see. 'Hmm, yes.' Then he stood upright, squaring his shoulders. 'But that was then.' He looked out grimly to where the labourers toiled in the meadows that fell away to the south. 'Now it's all calivers and culverins and sakers. Do you know how thick these walls are?'

'No, sir.' Marlowe was no fortifications engineer. He was also too polite to guess; there was nothing more embarrassing for guest or host than a guess that got the answer bang on the nose. He waited to be enlightened.

'Only two feet in places and the centre filled with rubble. That's where they'll come.' He pointed out over the ground rising below the walls. 'They won't try the north, the town side. It's too steep. They'll never get their cannon up the hill. But over there . . .' Carey shook his head and clicked his teeth. 'Man, it's a gunner's dream.'

He walked on, fingering the rough stones as he went. They climbed a long stairway, the stones uneven and worn with the years, to the ancient keep. George Carey, used to the climb as he was, was wheezing by the time he reached the gate. 'We don't use this part of the castle any more. Oh, except for Martin, of course; he has a little mathematician's eyrie. Says it helps him count. But if we *are* attacked, we can take refuge here. There are ovens and a well – one hundred and sixty feet deep, they say.' Then he stopped. 'It's my fault, of course. If I hadn't frittered the money away on the hall and the mansion, I might have been able to put up some modern earthworks.' Carey became confidential. 'They say Giambelli's in London.'

'Giambelli?'

'Federigo Giambelli, the engineer. Apparently the Italian bastard offered his services to Spain but the King turned him down. So, naturally, he came over to us. You heard about the hellburners last year, Drake's fire ships at Cadiz?'

'I heard.' Marlowe nodded.

'Giambelli.' Carey tapped the side of his nose. 'The man's a genius . . . Still, there it is. I can't afford him now.'

'Er . . . the garden's lovely.' Marlowe looked down at the tangle of verdure behind the chapel.

'Oh, my dear fellow, here I am, burbling on about fortifications and impending doom. And you have come with your poetry and wit to lighten our lives for a while. Oh, God.' Carey was frowning down. 'Johnson, where's Hasler?'

The governor clattered down the steps, wobbling here and there but making it safely to the bottom.

'My Lord?' An ancient gardener was leaning on his hoe in the middle of a green mess, but the Hall obscured his view now and for a moment he could not see Carey at all. He gazed vaguely into the sky.

'Hasler.' The governor trotted around the corner of the chapel, Marlowe in tow. 'The man to whom I paid a fortune to create a knot garden down there. He's created nothing at all.'

'I haven't seen him, sir. Not this three weeks or more.'

'Three weeks?'

'Hasler?' Marlowe saw his chance. 'Not Harry Hasler?'

'I believe so. Do you know him?'

'Tall fellow, blond . . . well, auburn, really.'

'That's right. What a small world.'

'Isn't it?' Marlowe smiled. 'Is he staying here at the castle?'

'Well, it looks as though he isn't staying anywhere at the moment.' Sir George looked again at the gardener, now tickling the ground with his hoe. 'Why wasn't I informed, Johnson?' The old man ignored him, lost in thought as he tended what looked like a rather untidy cabbage patch. Carey gave him another moment to reply, then turned to Marlowe again. 'No, he wasn't staying here. He was only a gardener, you know. He has lodgings in the town; Quay Street, I believe. Has he gardened for you, then?'

Marlowe laughed. 'The last time there was any greenery in Hog Lane, Sir George,' he said, 'Brutus was founding London. No, I know him as a poet of sorts. The odd play . . .'

The governor looked again at his knot garden. Given a lot of imagination and a good nature, he decided that you could just about make out some kind of pattern, but it seemed to peter out about halfway across and the knot unravelled into chaos. He sighed again. Another purseful he would never get back. He turned to Marlowe, still standing there on the path. A pleasant sort of chap. A thought occurred to him and his face brightened.

'That's it!' he shouted, clapping a heavy hand on Marlowe's shoulder. 'That's what we need. A play. To brighten the moment. Everyone's so keyed up with this wretched Spanish business. Look, I hate to ask it of you, Christopher, when I know you are here to write something more serious, but a masque, perhaps . . . something with music. A comedy. Nothing heavy. No death or anything like that.'

Marlowe raised both hands. 'That's not the sort of thing I write, Sir George.'

'No, no, my dear fellow, of course not. What was I thinking? No, Dido, Tamburlaine . . . pure fire and air. No, I just thought . . . well, a little light relief, you know.'

Marlowe looked at the man. George Carey was a governor on the edge. His little island was the most southerly along the south coast. He was standing in the path of a Spanish juggernaut and everybody knew it. If he wanted to whistle in the dark, it wouldn't ruin Marlowe's reputation if he helped him, just this once. 'Well,' he said. 'I do have a man in London who might be able to help. We'll need timber for a stage and flats, a few costumes. Would your people be prepared to perform?'

'Well,' Carey said, lowering his eyelids modestly. 'I myself have trod the boards. At Trinity, I was Queen of the May. Who had you in mind – in London, I mean?'

'His name is Sledd. Actor-Manager at the Rose in Southwark. He's up to his Venetians in something that's not going too well at the moment. Er . . . his expenses?'

'Consider them paid.' Carey beamed. 'This is marvellous, Christopher, marvellous. I'll go and tell the ladies.' He looked at the knot garden and frowned. 'I suppose that explains why he made such a hash of my garden.'

'I beg your pardon, Sir George?'

'Hasler. If he is a poet and a playwright, that explains why he didn't turn out to be much of a gardener. I wonder why he even applied for the job?'

Marlowe smiled. 'A man must live, Sir George. The theatre is a precarious profession.'

Carey nodded, still frowning. 'It would be for him if his poetry is as bad as his gardening, I should think, wouldn't you, Christopher? Hmm. Yes.' But Marlowe had no need to reply. Sir George Carey was climbing the steps to his ramparts again, worrying about the way the Spaniards would come.

That night, having sent his letter to Tom Sledd via Sir George Carey's man, Kit Marlowe went out on the town. He did not take one of the horses in the governor's stable, though they were at his disposal, but he did take his dagger, just in case. The warmth of the day had long gone and a chill breeze shook the darling buds that were only now peeping out of their hoods. He followed the little brook that babbled over the stones of the ford and watched the cowherds bringing their lowing animals home. Dim lights burned in the church of St Thomas and drunken soldiery were rolling around the square outside it, laughing and farting to their hearts' content. If Kit Marlowe had been an Old Testament man, he would have read Gomorrah into Newport and seen the destruction of the Lord. As it was he did not believe in fairy stories and he had places to be.

The house in Quay Street was just like all the others that ran down to the docks where the black ships rode at anchor. It leaned at a precarious angle and ivy clung to the walls. It was hard to tell whether the building was holding up the plant or the plant the building. He tapped at the low oak door with the pommel of his dagger and slipped it away again behind his back.

A young girl dragged the warped timber back. She was perhaps fifteen, with clear blue eyes and light, fair hair underneath a white cap. 'I was looking for Harry Hasler,' Marlowe said.

'Not here, sir,' the girl said and tried to close the door. But

Marlowe had done this before. His boot was in the way; so was his hand.

'When are you expecting him back?' he asked the girl.

'Who is it, Mary?' a rough voice called from the darkness of the kitchen.

'No one, father,' Mary said and again tried to close the door.

'No one, child?' Marlowe smiled. 'Less than kind, lady.'

The man was at the girl's elbow. 'Who are you and what do you want?' he asked.

'I want Harry Hasler,' Marlowe told him. 'And my name is my business.'

'Never heard of him.' The man shrugged.

'I was told he lodged here.'

'You was told wrong.' And this time the door did slam. Marlowe took stock of his situation. Master Martin *might* have misremembered the number in Quay Street, but his description of the house seemed to fit. He was about to knock again when the girl Mary appeared from a side door and beckoned him into the shadows.

'Sir,' she whispered, 'I'm sorry about all this, but Father . . . well, he don't like Harry . . . er . . . Master Hasler.'

'So he *is* here?' Marlowe dropped his voice to match hers, in deference to the obvious panic written over the girl's face, even in the half light.

'*Was*, sir,' she corrected him. 'I haven't seen him these three weeks.'

'Did he say where he was going?'

'No, sir.' Mary looked downcast. 'He didn't say he *was* going, even.'

Marlowe smiled and lifted up the girl's chin. 'Forgive me, Mary,' he said, 'but what was Harry Hasler to you?'

'Nothing, sir.' She sniffed defiantly. 'He lodged at our house, that's all. While he worked on the governor's gardens up at the castle.'

Marlowe glanced down. He was not familiar with these things, but it did seem as though Miss Mary's gown was a little stretched across the stomacher. 'How long has Harry been with you?' he asked. 'Staying here, I mean.'

'Ooh, about three months,' she said. 'Forgive me, sir, I have to go. Don't think the worse of father. These are strange times for us all.'

'Strange?' Marlowe asked.

'The Island, sir,' Mary whispered, wide-eyed. 'There are strange goings-on. Ghostly things, if you get my meaning.'

'I don't believe I do, Mary,' he said. 'Has your father let Master Hasler's room yet?'

'No, sir. In case he comes back.' She suddenly beamed. 'I hope he comes back.'

'Yes.' Marlowe nodded. 'We all do, Mary.' He flicked a silver coin from his purse. 'Is there a time when your father goes out? When I can take a peek at Master Hasler's room?'

Mary looked horrified. 'Oh, I don't know, sir.' But the reflected light from the coin was dappling her face and she found it hard to look away. 'Well, maybe tomorrow. He do go to market at cock crow.'

Marlowe flipped the coin and the girl caught it, hiding it quickly in her apron. 'Cock crow it is, then,' he said.

By the time Marlowe reached the castle, all was in darkness. The guard at the gate grunted something incomprehensible to him and let him through the wicket. If there were supposed to be guards on the walls after dark, they were not there now; nor was there one on George Carey's front door.

Marlowe passed the little chapel where the body of Walter Hunnybun still lay and went on up to his rooms in the east wing. In the hallway the expensive clock obtained from Jobst Bürgi, the one that George Carey was pleased to announce to all visitors kept accurate time to the minute, read half an hour past eleven. One of the governor's wolfhounds had been dozing on the old straw in the corner. He lifted his head briefly, whined once and went back to sleep.

It was at his own door that Marlowe felt a prickle of appre-hension at the back of his neck. It was unlatched and he had not left it that way. A careless maidservant, perhaps? Perhaps, but he was taking no chances. Dark corners and shadows in Gloriana's England were places to avoid; men died in them. He slid the blade out of its sheath and prodded the solid oak door with the tip. It opened noiselessly and he was inside, watching, waiting. There was no one there. The only conceivable hiding place was the Arras in the corner. He made no sound as he crossed the floor, the light through the lattice window illuminating his way. He felt the rough tapestry under his hand and wrenched it aside, dagger ready. Nothing.

He relaxed and lit his candle. The bed was made and turned down for him. There was a platter of bread and cheese under a cover on the sideboard, a pitcher of water and a jug of wine. And then, there were the books. Sir George Carey's library was one of the finest in England and Marlowe had borrowed half a dozen for his bedtime reading. He had left Sir Thomas More on top of the pile and Ralph Holinshed on the bottom. Now they were the other way around, *Utopia* relegated and the *Chronicles* in pride of place. Marlowe might have put this down to an illiterate maid or manservant who, in dusting, could not tell one from the other, were it not for the papers slotted inside Holinshed's corners.

Marlowe peered at these with the help of his candle, but he closed the door first. The papers were set out like the pages of a book but they were handwritten in a scholarly style. He read them, then read a page or two of Holinshed. They were very similar, except that the handwritten version was scurrilous: *And Lord Thomas delighted in the girl's body and would chase her through the knot garden and slap her backside bare. She would howl withal but seemed to enjoy it and never more than when the Lady Catherine held her down.*

Marlowe leaned back, trying to make sense of this, but it got more lurid. *The doctors found an oddity under her clothes, of the hermaphrodite kind, which meant that she would be barren all her days. It was God's judgement.* The most cryptic comment of all however was on the last page in the form of a rhyme: *Three steps from door to floor, Three steps for the taking, Three steps back and three steps fore, And the whole world's shaking.*

There was nothing else, merely these random jottings, and yet they seemed to tell a story. One thing was certain; the papers had not been there when Marlowe left and now they were, teasing the projectioner's brain, making the hairs on the back of his neck crawl. Three steps. Three steps. The words whispered in his head like the first rush of flames that were still burning people across Europe, like a dagger hissing from a sheath. He looked out of the window and saw faint points of light far away beyond the south wall of the castle. Will o' the wisps dancing on the night air, out in the fields where the Spaniards would come.

The cocks were crowing as Kit Marlowe went back to Quay Street. A grey dawn was breaking over the sleeping town and drovers were herding their cattle to the makeshift pens around the Cross. The poet had never known a town quite like this one. Canterbury, where he had been born in the shadow of St George the Martyr, was full of bells and books and candles. The King's School with its Dark Entry had filled his life there, along with the sound of his father's awl and the smell of the tanneries. Cambridge had been cloistered, invaded by children for most of the year as the scholars scurried to their lectures, noses blue and red from the cold wind straight from Muscovy. And London . . . well, London was London. There was no city in the world like it. From the Standard in Cheap to the Smock Alleys, the Dagger, the Woolsack . . . Marlowe knew them all. The stench of Billingsgate and the rush and tumble of the Bridge.

But this place was different. There was a silence about it that was unnerving; a silence not of peace but of fear. It echoed through Castlehold and along Holyrood, down Croker Street and across the misty gravestones of Church Litten where the plague-dead lay.

Marlowe had borrowed a scruffy old cloak from one of Carey's servants so that he blended rather better with people on their way to market. His own Colley-Weston was too flash for a man nipping in to the side door of a house in Quay Street. Mary was waiting for him as she had promised and she shut the door quickly.

'Father's gone,' she said. 'But you'll have to hurry. What is it you are looking for, sir?'

Marlowe looked at her. She was plainer by daylight but nobody's fool, he guessed. 'I am concerned,' he said, 'that something might have happened to Harry Hasler.'

Mary blinked, catching her breath. Clearly, the thought had occurred to her too. 'How do you know him, sir?' she asked, leading the way up the rickety stairs to the first floor.

'In London,' Marlowe told her. 'We shared rooms.' He glanced at the girl's belly again. 'Did you know him well?'

Mary blushed. 'Not really, sir,' she said, her eyes lowered and she opened a low door on the landing.

'Thank you, Mary.' Marlowe smiled. 'I'll call if I need you.'

She bobbed and he heard her clatter downstairs. He was not sure how much time his silver had bought him and Mary's father could be back at any minute. Marlowe had just walked through the market, where the bulls steamed in the morning, shackled by iron to the ground. The man could be here before George Carey's clock struck the hour. He checked the cupboard, the corners of the room. Mary kept a clean house; not so much as a cobweb. He looked under the bed; nothing. The chest in the corner was locked and he guessed that neither Mary nor her father had a key. In seconds, Marlowe's dagger-point was nuzzling the cold metal of the lock and in a few seconds more, the lid was open and he was rummaging inside. Two shirts. A pair of Venetians. An expensive ruff. Unless gardeners were earning a lot more these days, these were not the clothes of a mechanical. Hasler would have hidden these to allay suspicion but kept them in case he had to make a fast getaway. The Sumptuary laws still meant something in the sticks. Rustics took off their caps and stepped aside when a gentleman swept past.

There were no books in the chest but there was a small pile of papers. Most of them were covered in very bad drawings of knot patterns, the plans for Carey's castle garden. But one held the projectioner's gaze and he took it to the small window to read it carefully in the growing light. It was a love letter. '*Tonight,*' it said, '*my darling one. But be careful. He knows, I am sure of it. I long for the touch of your caress, the press of your lips on mine. My heart aches for you and my loins tremble. Three steps back and three steps fore.*' There was no signature – that would be too much to hope for. But the words were there again as they had been in Marlowe's own room the night before – the cryptic poem of the three steps.

'Sir!' Mary was hissing frantically at the bottom of the stairs. 'My father!'

Marlowe shut the chest, taking the letter with him, and looked for a way out. One door, one set of stairs. He could hear the old man's voice grumbling below. Marlowe pushed open the window as wide as it would go. He had done this dozens of times, jumping in and out of the Court at Corpus Christi in the small hours of a roistering night when the proctors were on the prowl. It was nothing. Except that he was fifteen feet above the ground and the ground was cobbled and uneven. He glanced up and down the street. There would be no hope of doing this silently. He would just have to take the leap and brazen it out.

His cloak flew out behind him as he sailed through the air and he landed well. Straightening, he stepped along the road as if it was the most natural way in the world to leave a house.

'Another of Miss Mary's fellers,' grunted a passing swineherd, tapping his porkers into line ahead of him.

'Ar.' His mate nodded, still chewing the blade of grass he had brought with him from the West Wight three hours earlier. 'Old Sculpe had better have a word with that girl. If she was mine, I'd put her over my knee.'

The swineherd paused. 'I think somebody's already done that,' he said and they both guffawed their way to market.

Marlowe had recovered his poise by the time he reached his room at Carey's mansion and he entered with a plan already formed in his head. Bed, a few hours' shut-eye and then a late breakfast. His hunt for Harry Hasler could wait at least a while. Then there was the matter of a dead body in the chapel. He shrugged off his cloak and doublet and left them in a pile on the floor. At home he was rather more fastidious, but here there were servants and he was sure they would prefer to do these little tasks for him than to find themselves at a loose end. He unlaced his breeches and wriggled out of them, boots and all. If they had time on their hands, he knew that Mistress Avis would find them something to do, something much less pleasant than picking up his clothes. He pulled the shirt over his head and jumped on the bed, just for the pleasure of feeling the taught strings beneath him. Sometimes, he thought, he had grown up a little too fast. Where was the carefree boy of the Dark Entry now, splashing through the puddles at the tolling of the bell?

'Were you brought up in a field, Master Marlowe?'

He froze in mid bounce. There was only one person in Carisbrooke who sounded like an old gate creaking when she spoke, but what was Mistress Avis Carey doing in his bed chamber? He hurriedly gathered a couple of handfuls of bedclothes over himself and sat up against the bedhead, ready for anything. Somehow, he didn't think that Avis had the same thing in mind as the dancers he had dallied with so recently. Or at least, he hoped she hadn't. As he hauled on the sheets, a piece of vellum slipped out – Nicholas Faunt's warning note of the cuckoo in the nest.

He gave a cough. Somehow, his mouth had gone very dry. 'Mistress Carey,' he croaked. 'How do you do?'

'I asked you a question,' the woman snapped.

'Erm, no, I was not brought up in a field.' He could tell that sticking to the bare facts would get him further with this woman than most of her kind. 'My mother was very strict, as mothers of sons go.'

'Then why did you drop your clothes on the floor? A gentleman does not behave in such a manner unless he is in drink. Are you in drink, Master Marlowe?'

'No.' He was on firmer ground now. 'No, Mistress Carey. I am certainly not in drink.'

'Then,' the woman was nothing if not persistent, 'are you waiting for an assignation?' She peered through the gloom. 'I understand from my sister-in-law and her friends that you attract them in that way. Have you made some arrangement with one of those drabs? Is that what excites you to such ungentlemanly behaviour?'

'No, no, I must reassure you, Mistress Carey.' Marlowe gave a wriggle that released another couple of yards of linen to use as a cover and he felt all the better for it. 'I am here as Sir George's guest, and I would not dream of abusing his trust.'

She sat back and looked at him long and hard. He could

practically feel her gaze sizzle on the sheets. A smell of airing laundry filled the air and he was reminded for the second time in as many minutes of his mother. Her voice when it came was softer than usual and she sounded a little surprised.

'I believe you, Master Marlowe. I do not take you for a dissembler.'

Pressed against the headboard of the bed, Marlowe almost felt himself blush. For a projectioner, this had to be the highest accolade. He bowed slightly. 'Thank you, Mistress Carey,' he said. There was a silence and then he asked, 'What are you doing in my chamber, if I may ask?'

She looked him up and down as if he were the lowliest kitchen boy. 'You were not in your chamber, Master Marlowe,' she said, as if that explained everything.

He paused again. He knew the answer to his next question, but posed it anyway. 'How did you know?'

'How did I know what?' Avis Carey's voice was just as carrying as ever.

'That I wasn't here. Did you come and look for me for some reason?'

'I did look round the door, yes,' she said. 'I look round everyone's door at some time in the night. Sometimes twice.' She gave a delicate shudder but her solid flesh did not take the hint and there was not even a flicker of an eyebrow. 'I see some things, Master Marlowe, that it would be better not spoken of.'

Marlowe gave a slow nod. A peeping Thomasina, if he were any judge. He clutched the sheet a little closer. 'I see. I didn't mean to distress you, Mistress Carey. I had business in town.'

She leaned forward and hissed at him. 'Business. Business, Master Marlowe. I can only imagine what your business might be.' She wiped her mouth where her venom had caused her to spit.

'No, Mistress Carey, please do not misunderstand me.' Marlowe had faced ravening mobs, men armed in all kinds of subtle ways, but this woman, with her single thought in her head, was scaring him far more than any one of the other threats had had the power to do. 'I was . . . I was arranging for a message to be sent to London. To bring my stage manager down to the Wight. Sir George has asked me to put on an entertainment.' He looked up under his lashes. 'I rather think he was thinking of asking you to do something.'

It was hard to tell what she was thinking, but at least she had stopped hissing at him, so hope could at least creep out of hiding, if not spring eternal.

'I sent a letter with a ship.' He was on shaky ground here. She was a local woman who probably knew all kinds of things relating to seafaring and the tides and the only thing he knew about water was that it could drown a man. 'I had to . . . catch the tide.'

She looked at him and then clapped her hands down, one on each knee with a sound of a small explosion. 'Master Marlowe,' she said, and he heard rather than saw a smile. 'You have gladdened my heart. It has been too long since anyone did anything to make my Georgie happy. Only I care for his welfare; only I am on constant watch to keep him safe.'

'When do you sleep, Mistress Carey?' He had to know if the woman ever closed her eyes. Otherwise he would need to grow two more of his own, in the back of his head.

'I nap.' Her mouth closed like Skeffington's Gyves, that nasty little contraption they kept in the Tower, just in case.

'I see.' He smiled and made as though to move off the bed. She shrieked and covered her eyes. 'Please don't concern yourself, Mistress Carey,' he said. Nothing would induce him to let her see an inch more flesh than she had already; although he was unsure whether an inch more existed anywhere on his body. 'See, I am wrapped in my sheet.'

'My brother's sheet!' she snapped. Then her voice softened. 'Forgive me, Master Marlowe. I am so used to looking after little Georgie that I forget my manners, once in a while.'

A memory forced its way to the front of Marlowe's brain. 'Is this all because of the crossbow incident, Mistress Carey? Because if so, I am sure he has forgiven you after all these years.' He spoke in his most dulcet tone, unsure how she would take it.

She leapt to her feet and he wasn't sure whether she was planning to hug him or fell him where he stood. In the event, she did neither but what she did do was far more disconcerting. She burst into noisy tears, not the kind of elegant, silvery tears cried by her sister-in-law when the occasion demanded it, but huge, fat tears, snot bubbling from her nose, her mouth set in a hot, red circle of pain.

'I am so lonely, Master Marlowe, looking after Georgie all by myself.' She gave an enormous sniff and, picking up the edge of Marlowe's swaddling, blew her nose with a sound to wake the dead. She put a hot, wet hand on Marlowe's arm. 'I feel much better for our little chat. You are not the Devil incarnate after all.' And she stumbled to the door, almost colliding with a small maid, carrying a pitcher of hot water along to George Carey's chamber.

The woman recovered herself at once and slapped the girl round the head. 'Is that water hot?' she asked.

'Yes'm,' the girl said, holding it out.

Avis Carey dipped what on another woman would be called her little finger in the water and slapped the girl again. 'Have you no sense?' she yelled at her. 'Sir George could have severely scalded himself in water as hot as that. Go and get some hot water that is . . . not so hot.'

The maid was not a brave woman, but she knew the drill. 'Where shall I take this very hot water then, m'm?' she asked.

Avis Carey looked around and met the startled eyes of Christopher Marlowe, still standing wrapped in linen in the middle of the chamber floor. She pointed. 'Give it to Master Marlowe,' she said. 'But . . .'

The maid turned, sensing another instruction. 'Yes, m'm?'

'Tell him to be careful. It's hot.'

The maid couldn't wait to get down into the kitchens and soon had a rapt audience.

'And there he stood – ooh, he's got lovely legs. In the altogether he was, the bed all mazzled up and that and there she stood in the gallery and told'un to be careful!'

The cook gave the poor girl yet another slap, to balance the ones she had already received. The story had sounded quite believable until that last bit. She could tell a tale, could Ester, and no mistake. Mistress Avis, worrying about anyone but her brother! It would be a cold day in hell before that ever happened.

Diego de Valdez was not a happy man. For days now, his Castilian galleons had wallowed in the troughs south of Biscay, the wind against them and the rain lashing the slippery decks. He stood on the quarter, the helmsman wrestling with the wheel beside him. His orders, decorations and armour lay below and he was huddled under a rough cloak of the type the shepherds wore in the high Sierra del Escudo, cursing the wind, the rain, his cousin (whose fault, of course, all this was). He did it softly, however, because His Majesty had given implicit instructions that there was to be no blasphemy on board the ships of his great crusade against England.

The *San Cristobal* battled through the grey, foam-flecked waters, groaning and shuddering every time she hit a large wave. It had taken the Armada two days to make fifteen sea miles and already the stench in the ship's hold was unbearable. His notary had told him that the Candia wine had gone off and somebody must have miscalculated; they were already running low on chickpeas. Today was Thursday, so the admiral had six ounces of bacon and two ounces of rice to look forward to. Every inch the professional, he refused to eat anything his men did not. He chewed his pine kernel and watched the ships of his squadron ploughing the churning waters behind him, their sails and flags bright with the heraldry of Spain and the Papacy. The castles and lions of Castile flew proud and defiant, on every spar and every strut in his squadron. There they were, the *San Juan Bautista*, the *Santiago el Mayor*, the *Trinidad* and the *Santa Ana*, their decks crammed with soldiers hurling their half-digested rice over the side, longing to be on dry land again. Well, Valdez thought to himself as he turned back into the wind, their day would come. Just as his would when he blew El Draque out of the water. If only the damned wind would turn. If only spring would come.

SEVEN

The *Bowe* rocked gently in the harbour along the Medina. The day's market was almost over and Henry Skirrow had places to be. He hurried up the rope ladder, his pattens clattering on the swaying boards, and disappeared below decks to where Master Vaughan sat with his companions. Skirrow took off his hat, passed the letter to Vaughan and waited.

The man slit the seal carefully and read the contents. He passed it to Thomas Page who in turn passed it to Edmund Denny. Both men shrugged.

'It's all about a play,' Page said, helping himself to another goblet of Rhenish. 'No mystery there.'

'All that's on top,' Vaughan muttered. 'What's he *really* after?'

'John, you're dreaming,' Denny said. 'You'd swear your bloody anchor chain was out to get you. Some people have other fish to fry. I've heard of this Marlowe. He's a scribbler, poet, playwright, university wit, pain in the arse. He's no threat to us.'

'That's as may be,' Vaughan said. 'But I've met the man. At the castle the other night. He watches your every move. And his eyes . . . it's like he can see into your soul.'

Denny gave Page an old-fashioned look. He took the letter back. 'It's just asking this fellow . . . what's his name? Tom Sledd. It's just asking him to come down and put on a play at the castle. Mind you, that's typical, isn't it? The most powerful navy in the world is on the way to crush us and the Captain-General of the Wight is going to the theatre.' He shook his head. 'Be afraid,' he murmured. 'Be very afraid.'

'It's too pat,' Vaughan said, taking a longer swig of his wine than was strictly necessary. 'First Hasler, now Marlowe. They're on to us, gentlemen.'

Denny sighed. 'Tell him, Tom, will you?'

Page leaned forward and patted Vaughan's arm. The man could patronize for England. 'We took care of Hasler, didn't we?'

Vaughan was not placated.

'So Marlowe won't be a problem either.' Page went on regardless. 'Trust me. I've seen his type before.'

'Have you?' Vaughan said, gnawing his lip. 'I'm not so sure. Skirrow, when you get to London, be sure and find out all you can about this Sledd. Who he knows. What he does. You have Sir George's writ?'

Skirrow patted his doublet. 'And his expenses, Master Vaughan . . . Not that they go very far these days, of course.'

Vaughan sighed and rummaged in a drawer in his bureau. He threw the man a purse which he caught with all his years of experience. Henry Skirrow had been a servant of two masters for more years than he cared to remember.

'What are Sir George's instructions? Are you to bring this Sledd down in person?'

'If possible, sir.'

'Good.' Vaughan's mind was racing. 'Good. But when you do, bring him to the Hole and send me word. On no account is he to meet Marlowe until one of us has had a little chat with him. Clear?'

'As St Thomas's bell, Master Vaughan.' Skirrow bowed. He reclaimed Marlowe's letter and was gone. He could reaffix the seal later.

Francis Walsingham was at Placentia that Sunday. He had taken divine service with the Queen and was walking in the garden watching the ladies at their archery.

'Her Majesty not shooting today?' Nicholas Faunt was strolling with him, wearing his Sunday best in case Her Majesty should suddenly turn a corner and come upon him.

'Gout,' Walsingham said. He glanced around quickly. 'And you didn't hear that from me. Thanks for coming, Nicholas.'

Faunt smiled. When the Queen's Spymaster called him by his Christian name, there was always trouble in the wind. It had to be said that Walsingham was not quite his old self. His legs were stiff with rheumatism and he was having difficulty seeing sometimes by candlelight. He had caught a glimpse of himself in a mirror the week before and thought he looked older than Lord Burghley, who in turn was older than Methuselah.

'Is something amiss, Sir Francis?' Faunt asked him. He would walk through fire for the Spymaster, but he was not about to let him know that.

Walsingham again checked the grounds. The laughter of the ladies and the soft thud of arrows hitting their mark were fading in the distance and no breeze disturbed the hedgerows, clipped and trimmed into obedience by the royal gardeners. 'You remember Fenner's dispatch from Lisbon?'

'An Armada of four hundred sail and fifty galleys, provisioned with more bacon, fish, cheese and rice than we have in the whole of England. Oh, and God's on their side, of course.'

The Puritan in Francis Walsingham wanted to reach out and grab his subordinate by the fancy-ruffed throat, but he knew Faunt was just trying to make light of a bad situation.

'Well, we've heard from our man in Finisterre since then.'

'Oseley?' Faunt chuckled. 'He's usually reliable.'

Walsingham nodded his agreement. 'Only four galleys, apparently.'

'Oh, that's good,' Faunt said, but saw that his master's face was as thunderous as usual. 'Isn't it?'

'They won't be able to use their galleys until they're in the Thames anyway, so the number they bring is irrelevant. I've told Oseley to get himself back home and get on the *Revenge*.'

'With Drake?' Faunt raised an eyebrow. 'Is that wise?'

Walsingham stopped in his tracks. 'Are you saying there's something . . . sinister . . . about Francis Drake?' he asked.

'Heaven forfend!' Faunt raised his hands. 'You know my views, Sir Francis. The man isn't just a peasant; he's a rogue and a scoundrel. I don't envy the Lord Admiral trying to keep him in line.'

Walsingham let that go. 'Anyway, there's more news. Reading.'

'What about it?'

'The mayor and corporation have found a cache of Popish books.'

'Ah,' said Faunt, straight-faced. 'The enemy within.'

Walsingham nodded. 'The question is, how far within? Get yourself there, Faunt. Usual discreet enquiries.'

'Very good, sir. Oh, by the way, any news of Kit Marlowe?'

'Machiavel?' Walsingham said coldly. 'No, nothing. That man is on his own.'

'Must you go?' she purred, stretching out to stroke his chest.

'One of your husband's field days, Bet,' he said, smiling at her. He took her hand in his and kissed her fingertips. 'I *am* a centoner, after all; you know, responsibilities?'

'Oh, you boys,' she scolded him, breaking away and sitting up in bed. 'Why can't you live for today? Tomorrow will take care of itself.'

He sat next to her, still naked as the dawn flooded the chamber. 'It won't take care of itself. We have to take care of it.'

She pulled his pillows over to her side of the bed and plumped them up behind her, flopping back on them and looking up at him through a tangle of curls. 'Now you're beginning to *sound* like George,' she said with a pout.

'What about tonight?' he asked her, rummaging in the press for his clothes.

'I can't. I'm due at Cecily's. You know what a bastard Henry is.'

'Yes,' he sighed, 'and I've got to face him in an hour.'

'Oh, Matt,' she said and heaved herself off her nest of pillows and rolled out of bed, crossing the room to him. 'Couldn't you delay, just a little?' She ran her hands over his arms and shoulders, grinding her hips against him. He looked down at her and smiled, kissing her full on the lips. 'Just a little,' he said, stroking her breast. 'You're a wicked, wicked woman, Bet Carey.'

The sky was bright to the west but it had rained during the night and the canvas of the tents was sodden and dark. Two hundred damp, dispirited soldiers had been turfed out of their slumbers by the bugle call and now did their best to look like a fighting force. They were pikemen from the flat marshes of Essex and had been in the Wight for a week. They had passed to the command of Sir Henry Meux of Kingston who sat his horse that morning on St George's Down, watching them form up.

'Not exactly the London Trained Bands, are they?' he grunted to Robert Dillington. The master of Knighton had to agree. He had seen the London men at the funeral of Philip Sidney a couple of years before and had to admit, they were impressive; tall men in white coats stitched with the scarlet cross of St George and the upright sword.

In front of these gentlemen today the Essex men looked a sorry bunch. Their doublets and Venetians were heavy with the night's rain and only their sergeants had backs and breasts; the rest wore no armour at all. At least each man had a pike, a twelve-foot pole of ash topped with murderous iron. The thing was six feet shorter than the weapons of Spain, but it would have to do.

'Oh, Holy Mother of Our Lord, look at that!' Meux jerked his head to his left. 'Georgie-boy's dressed up today!' Trotting over the rise on a tall bay gelding came the Captain of the Wight, gilded armour from his neck to his thighs that could have bought the Essex contingent twice over. The ruff he usually wore was replaced by a linen collar and his head was encased in a Spanish-style burgonet, complete with nodding scarlet plume. A brace of wheel-locks bounced at his saddle-bow and a rapier hilt twinkled in the morning's brightness.

Dillington looked down on his own buff coat and plain breeches and felt decidedly outclassed. 'I'm sorry I bothered now,' he said. 'Matilda said, "You've got to look the part, Robbie. Dress like a soldier." What does she know, eh? Oh good,' he muttered, 'Georgie's brought his band with him.'

Marching behind Carey came a solid phalanx of musicians, drums beating and fifes trilling, their uniforms bright with coloured ribbons and streamers. Beyond that came the feudal levy, the men of the West Wight and the south, the Militia of Yarmouth and Richard Turvey's men from Cowes.

'Does your heart good to see it, doesn't it?' Meux said out of the corner of his mouth. 'The king of Spain must be shitting himself.' Then he looked up, pinned on a smile and waved. 'Good morning, George!' He doffed his cap and half bowed in the saddle. Dillington did the same. George Carey halted his horse alongside them as his units stood still and the music, mercifully, stopped.

The governor leaned forward. 'Salute, gentlemen,' he reminded them quietly. 'This is a field day. We're not at Court now.'

Meux and Dillington exchanged glances. George Carey was insufferable at the best of times, and never more so than when he was playing soldiers. They both sat to attention and raised their hands to their hats. Carey smiled. He was a stickler for protocol.

'Where's Matthew Compton?' the governor asked. 'I specifically requested his presence today.'

Matthew Compton was buckling on his sword and looking for his hat as Bet Carey lay back on the bed, tired but happy and glowing after the hectic round of the last few minutes. She watched him rummage in a chest for his wheel-lock and waited while he opened a window and yelled at his man to saddle his horse.

'Why don't you drink smoke, Matt?' she asked him, looking around for a pipe and tobacco in case he had taken up the habit.

'Can't abide the stuff, Bet,' he said, checking his sash in the mirror.

'Pity,' she said. 'It's very relaxing at times like these.' Her smile vanished. If there was anything she liked more than writhing on a bed with Matthew Compton, it was teasing him. 'I think he knows,' she said.

Compton turned to face her. 'Who?' he said. 'Knows what?'

'George, of course,' she smiled. 'Knows about us.'

For a moment, Matthew Compton's heart stopped beating. He was standing at the end of a long, dark tunnel. There was no sound, just the quiet drip of his own blood hitting the ground, seeping from the wound made by George Carey's sword.

'Nonsense!' he said, shaking himself free of it. 'How could he?'

Bet Carey slid off the bed, still naked, and crossed to the

window. 'This is George's island, Matt,' she said. 'That's
Holyrood Street down there. And every single one of its
inhabitants acknowledges him as their lord. And some of them,'
she tapped his codpiece playfully, 'are observant and very
loyal to him.'

'Are they?' he snapped. 'Well, that's where you're wrong.'
He sounded like a petulant child as he grabbed his hat. 'I happen
to know that George Carey is the most hated man in the Wight.
And anyway,' he turned to her, now kitted out like the centoner
he was today, 'no one knows you come here.' He looked her
up and down and let his temper show. 'And, for God's sake,
cover yourself up!'

She stepped back from the window but didn't make a move
to cover herself. She stood there, displaying herself to him,
one hip thrust out and a hand brushing her nipples. She smiled
and said, 'While we are on the subject of no one knowing I
come here, perhaps you could call my maid as you pass your
kitchen boy's door. He has more stamina than you and keeps
her in bed betimes.'

The door slammed behind him and he did not hear her
laughing as he clattered down the stairs, aiming a vicious kick
at the little door into the kitchens as he went. The front door
shuddered on its hinges and Matthew Compton was gone.

'Have a care!' George Carey roared and three hundred pikemen
extended their right hands and rested their left fists on their
hips. 'No thumbs!' he bellowed. 'The swine array of Spain
won't be impressed by a bunch of catamites, however patriotic
you may be.'

A few furtive thumbs hooked inside clenched fists.

'Porte your pike!'

The pikes came up to the vertical and everyone waited.
Apart from the snorting of the horses, there was silence on
St George's Down.

'Handle your pike!'

The pikes fell to the diagonal, men leaning in and gripping
their staves with both hands.

'Advance your pike!'

The pikes probed forward, like a bristling hedgehog.

'And . . . have a care!'

The pikes came up and everyone relaxed.

'Well, Henry?' Carey turned to the man beside him. 'What do you think?'

'You're the expert, George,' Meux said. 'I'd say it needs work.'

'Robert?' Carey looked across to Dillington.

'It's good to see our local lads aren't much slower than the Essex boys,' he said. 'But all in all . . .'

'Yes, I know.' Carey was irritated. For weeks now he had been working with pikemen, demilancers, calivermen and musketeers. The Essex lads were sloppy, but the Hampshire boys two weeks ago were no better. His eyes blazed as he looked around the field, the drummers waiting for the word of command. His eyes fell on his nephew a hundred times removed.

'Remind me again, Martin,' he said. 'You are here because . . .?'

'It's a tedious job, George,' the man said, as much under his breath as possible. 'But somebody has to count the pennies. In a minute you're going to have artillery practice, aren't you? Get the Shott moving?'

'Of course,' Carey said. 'Can't have a field day without guns.'

'Well, guns cost, George,' Martin said. 'And so does roundshot. I have to keep accounts.'

Martin Carey had had a special saddle made, one with a wooden lectern that swung across the pommel. It had an inkwell, a quill and a ledger. George Carey knew he should be impressed. But he was not. He sighed. 'You're a sad, sad man,' he said. 'Ah.' He caught sight of a horseman galloping across the front of the Essex Bands. 'Watch carefully in the next few minutes, gentlemen. I believe I have some entertainment for you – Martin, you brought the candles?'

'Yes,' the comptroller said. 'Here in my saddlebag; but I don't see . . .'

'No, of course not.' Carey beamed. 'That's why I'm Governor and Captain-General of the Wight and you are an accountant. Master Compton,' he called to the rider, 'good of you to call.'

Compton reined in his lathered horse and saluted. 'Sorry, Sir George,' he said, 'I got a little delayed, I'm afraid.' He suddenly smelled the Governor's wife on him, the scent of civet, and turned a little pale. Looking down, he saw a long dark hair on his cuff and felt his breath catch in his throat. He dropped his hands and held the reins low, hiding the tell-tale filament.

'You see, gentlemen,' Carey beamed, returning Compton's salute, 'a centoner who knows how to behave. Splendid.' His smile suddenly vanished and he scanned the line of his levy standing at ease behind the band. 'Sergeant Wilson, if you please.'

Three men broke from the ranks, their pikes passed to others and they stood to attention before the Governor.

'Dismount, sir,' Carey said to Compton.

The man was a little surprised by the order but he obeyed and someone took the animal's bridle, leading it away. Carey eased himself in the saddle. For all his martial bearing, his thigh boots were agony and his gorget much too tight. 'Tell me about yourself, Matthew,' he said, as though conducting an interview.

'Sir George?' Compton frowned. Had the man gone mad? Meux and Dillington were equally confused and even Martin Carey had no idea where this was going.

'Humour me.' Carey smiled.

'Er . . . well, I was born in the County of Middlesex and attended John Lyon's new school in Harrow . . .'

'And then?'

'Well, I am of private means, Sir George. A gentleman.'

Carey snorted. 'You may be of private means, sir, but you are no gentleman.'

Compton wanted the ground to swallow him up. Bet had been right. George Carey *did* know and now he was to have his revenge in the most public and humiliating way possible. He felt the long, dark hair stream from his cuff in the wind on the Down's top, flying like a pennon, like a lady's favour.

The Governor leaned forward over his horse's neck. 'You are a lawyer, sir,' he said as though the words were choking him. 'Specifically, a Bencher of Lincoln's Inn.' He sat upright again and looked down his nose at the man before him. 'My views on lawyers are well known,' he shouted. 'I will not tolerate a lawyer on my Island. They are crawlers, hypocrites, liars and parasites.' He looked at the speechless Compton. 'Did you think you could fool me, sir? Gentlemen!'

The two pikemen dashed forward and pinioned Compton's arms. The sergeant whipped the man's sword from his scabbard and broke it over his knee. Martin Carey shook his head. That weapon would have paid for two dozen calivers and the matches to go with them.

Compton found his voice, the one he used, not in bed with Bet Carey, but across the floor of a London courtroom. 'This is an outrage!' he shouted.

'It is,' Carey agreed, 'but I have the solution.' He clicked his fingers and the sergeant collected six candles from the Governor's comptroller. He quickly cut the loops of Compton's Venetians and tied their dangling ends to the wicks. Then he collected a small bell from a pikeman's satchel and hung it on a rope around the lawyer's neck.

'Ready, sir,' he said.

Carey was smirking. So were most of the men in the ranks and the musicians. The Governor spoke to them. 'For the rest of the day, gentlemen,' he said, 'you will run a foot race, in full pack, to test your mettle. You will accompany this . . . gentleman . . . to the quay. And there you will put him on a boat. If the boat takes him to the mainland, all well and good. He can practise his black arts over there. If not, and he drifts with the tide . . . who knows but that he can offer his services to the Armada of Spain.'

There were hoots of laughter and the sergeant lit the tapers that smouldered and spat, dripping hot wax on to Compton's boots. Carey leaned to the man as the pikemen held him fast. 'Bell, book and candle, Master Lawyer,' he hissed, 'the way we drive out evil hereabouts. The bell will tinkle round your neck all the way into the Solent. The candles will roast your balls if you're not careful. And as for the book; I've just thrown it at you!'

The band struck up a merry tune and the sergeant led the way, the smouldering, clanging Compton being dragged behind him. All the way to the quay, dogs barked and children spat. This was better than a holiday and all thanks to good old George Carey.

When he had ridden away to make sure his orders were carried out and the field day had descended into a leaping, laughing rabble on a picnic, Henry Meux still sat his horse alongside Robert Dillington. They watched a bewildered Martin Carey trot after his kinsman. 'Something will have to be done about George, Robert,' Meux said.

'You don't like lawyers any more than he does,' Dillington reminded him.

'That has nothing to do with it. The man thinks he's God rather than the Queen's servant as we all are. Today, it's Compton. Tomorrow, who knows? You? Me? Something will have to be done.'

'Well, it isn't likely to be me,' Dillington said, rather on his dignity.

'How can you be so sure?' Meux asked.

'I am neither a lawyer nor am I making him wear the horns.'

Meux turned in the saddle and stared at the man. 'You mean . . . Compton and Bet?'

'Has Carey another wife?' Dillington asked archly. The man could gossip for England. And often did.

'No . . . but . . . *Compton*?' Meux was scandalized.

Dillington looked after the laughing mob that was accompanying Compton on his long journey to the quay. 'I would say the women find him attractive enough,' he said. 'He seems to be quite well set up, as far as a man can judge.'

Meux was lost in thought.

Dillington, that most perspicacious and tenacious of gossips, being a man, sensed a story in the air. 'So,' he probed. 'Tomorrow, as you say. It could be you or me.'

Meux tapped his heels on his horse's flanks and rode away.

Dillington watched him go through lidded eyes, still as a lizard on a wall. This might come in useful. He would bide his time.

'You must tell me all about Christopher Marlowe.' Cecily Meux was at her drawn-thread work but her mind was not on the job in hand. She was known for her delicate reticella lace and the rumour ran that the Queen herself wore Cecily's trimmings on her nightgown, but she could never do her best work when Bet Carey was visiting – her stories were not conducive to accurate weaving.

'Well, you've danced with him, Cecily.' Bet Carey's fingers flew over the cloth. Her work was simpler than Cecily's, whipping some edging to something filmy that Cecily would not even recognize, let alone wear.

'Well,' Cecily's eyes shone brightly. 'He cuts quite a dash, doesn't he? *And* he has the legs for it.' She blushed, as Cecily always did when more risqué ideas entered her otherwise empty head.

'I'm more interested in codpieces,' Bet said, smiling wide-eyed as though discussing the weather.

'Bet Carey!' Cecily scolded her, but a little shiver ran up her back. Her Henry had long ago lost all interest in that sort of thing and she hardly liked to bother him, what with the cares of running Kingston and now this wretched Spanish business. After all, he *was* a centoner in the Militia and a man could not be everywhere at once. But Bet, now . . . Bet was different. She and George went to the court – in London, that is – and they knew *everybody*. The last time Bet had been, she had danced with the gorgeous Henry Wriothesley, the second Earl of Southampton, and he had whispered things in her ear that even Bet could not repeat. Not even to Cecily.

'And the man's a poet. They say he was called Machiavel at Cambridge and has had dark dealings with Dr Dee.'

'Yes,' Bet mused, staring for a while into the middle distance. 'I would imagine Master Marlowe has many dark dealings.' She winked at her friend. 'One to watch.'

'And talking of watching.' Cecily, feather-headed as ever, had changed tack. 'What is the mystery of Walter Hunnybun?'

Bet's face hardened. 'There's no mystery, Cecily; he's dead.'

'Yes, of course,' her friend gabbled. 'But murdered, they say. Did you have a look at him?'

'A look at him?' Bet looked askance. She would rather remember the man when he was alive, riding her in the bedroom of his farmhouse. What he lacked in elegant technique he made up for in stamina and enthusiasm. She had no interest in death. Unless of course . . .

'Well,' Cecily went on, 'I mean, he was laid out in your chapel, wasn't he? Who could have done such a terrible thing?'

But Bet had no time to speculate because the dogs were suddenly barking and there was the clatter of hoofs in the courtyard outside. Servants were scurrying in all directions.

'That'll be Henry.' Cecily put her needlework down. 'He's been out at his war games all day, Bet, with that husband of yours. I warn you, he'll be in a foul mood.'

EIGHT

Tom Sledd was sitting on the wall of Master Sackerson's Bear Pit, throwing his breakfast leftovers to the great animal, who lay on his back, all four paws in the air. Were it not for the lack of an enormous ball of wool, he could have been a kitten lying there. A stale bread roll hit him on the nose and suddenly, there was no kitten, just a moth-eaten old bear with one tooth clinging resolutely in its gum. The growl was low in his throat and shook the wall, vibrating up Tom's leg and into his bowel.

'Sorry, Master S,' Tom said, and threw a ham hock with some shreds of meat still clinging. His Johanna was a dear girl but cooking was not one of her talents. Master Sackerson rolled over and mumbled on the bone, licking into the end for the marrow.

Tom sighed and rested his elbows on his knees, his chin in his hands. In a minute, he would have to go into the theatre and start trying to wring a performance out of the few actors who remained. Alleyn had stormed off in a huff and was holed up in the grand house of an even grander lady in Greenwich, at least until her husband came back. Burbage, given the lead in Alleyn's absence, had taken umbrage and had also stormed off in a huff, flinging over his shoulder comments along the lines that he would be damned if he was so desperate as to take Ned Alleyn's leavings. Shaxsper alone remained, but, losing more hair by the day, had decided that he was a playwright, not a player, and was skulking in corners with an inky face where he kept sucking the wrong end of his quill. Tom Sledd really did not want to go back inside.

'Master Sledd?' The voice at his shoulder made him jump and he turned on the newcomer, glad to have someone to shout at.

'What in the name of God do you think you're doing, idiot, to shout at a man who is sitting on the wall of a Bear Pit? I could have fallen in!' Sledd swung his legs over the parapet and stood up on the pavement.

The speaker stepped back and then, drawn by his own inquisitiveness, stepped forward an extra pace. 'Is there really a bear down there?' he asked, looking over the wall.

'Of course there is,' Sledd said sharply, pointing to a sign on the wall. It said, in rather shaky capitals: 'BEAR PIT'. 'Can't you read?'

Skirrow shrugged a shoulder. 'Rather flea-bitten, but a bear nonetheless. I never thought to see such wonders,' he said, trying to sound as though he meant it. Then he turned a rather unsavoury smile on Tom Sledd. 'I can read, indeed I can, Master Sledd. That is how I could read your name on this packet here and also your description, written by Master Marlowe himself.'

'Kit sent you?' Tom Sledd felt his heart lift. If Kit was coming back . . . Then a horrible thought struck him. 'Kit is well, isn't he?' Why would he write a description of him; why wouldn't he come himself? He was lying, dead or dying, he knew it. Poisoned by hemlock. Skewered by a rapier. Drowned in the outer deeps. He should never have let him go.

If Tom Sledd had a failing, it was that he wore every thought on his head across his face, flickering and flashing light and shade as though the pictures themselves moved there. Skirrow laughed and clapped him on the shoulder. 'Master Marlowe is well,' he said. 'My master, Sir George Carey, has asked him to get up a little entertainment for his guests, and Master Marlowe said there was no man in England who could put on a show as well as Thomas Sledd, of the Rose.'

Tom Sledd grew two inches and puffed out his chest. 'Kit said that?' he whispered.

Skirrow nodded and held out the package. Sledd tore it open, taking scant notice of the seal, which was just as well. Skirrow made a mess of it when he resealed it aboard the *Bowe* and had been picking at it absent-mindedly as he rode – it was a poor thing by now. But Sledd was reading, paraphrasing for Skirrow as he read, punching him on the arm every couple of words.

'It's true,' the stage manager said. 'It's true. Kit wants me to go down to . . . a castle?' He turned huge eyes on Skirrow, who sketched a bow. 'And help them put on a play . . . with music . . .' His eyes skimmed down the page. 'He has enclosed some expenses . . .' He weighed the little oiled silk bag which had been packed with the letter and then peered inside, raising his eyebrows. Little did he know it was now only half as valuable as it had been. Kit wanted him on the Wight and that was enough for him. He quickly did some calculations. An angel or two for Johanna and the rest for him would be enough. Skirrow meanwhile had taken the opportunity to step out of punching range.

'So,' he said, looking down on the bear again, which had now dropped off to sleep, tongue resting wetly on the bone. 'To cut a long story short, are you able to come down to Carisbrooke and put on the ladies' little amusement?'

His tone was bored and flat. He made it clear that he cared little about Tom, the ladies or their entertainment. Tom was of a mind to send the fellow packing. And yet . . . and yet, Kit had asked for him. The theatre was going to the dogs. Henslowe was on his back to get this atrocious play of the Spanish Tragedy up and earning. Alleyn was away . . . Kit was away . . . Johanna was proving not quite worth the indigestion . . .

'Yes!' Sledd said. 'I just need to get some things.' He heard a door slam in the theatre. 'But not from there. We will just go past my home, if that is on the way.' He paused. 'Which is the way?'

Skirrow threw an arm behind him, pointing roughly south and west.

Sledd linked an arm with his. His step was light and he gave the man a tug down the lane into the muddy thoroughfare beyond. 'We won't be passing my house, sad to say,' he said, with a smile. He could always send word later. 'Horse or carriage?' He so hoped it would be a carriage, but horse would do as well. He had covered the length and breadth of the country with Ned Sledd's travelling players in an old cart with wooden wheels and a broken-down horse to pull it. Whatever this man had at his disposal, it would be a cut above that.

Skirrow laughed. 'Horse.' It was almost too easy, but

Vaughan need never know. 'The stables are down this way.' And the two men walked off together, Sledd's head full of dreams.

Inside the theatre, Philip Henslowe was in full cry. You can take a dyer out of Bermondsey but you can't make him like stage managers.

'Tom! Tom Sledd!' The echoing rafters mocked him but that was all.

One of the lads looked up from his nest in the costume corner. He was trying to learn his lines. His lisp gave him an almost insuperable problem with them and he was working hard to make himself understood. He didn't need all of this noise and bellowing. He had been promoted to Isabella from a lowly Page and this could be his big break. 'See,' he cried, 'where his Ghost solicits with his wounds revenge on her that should have revenged his death.'

'Shut up, you loathsome little scullion,' Henslowe roared. 'If you don't get that lisping tongue of yours sorted out, you're back to the spit-turning, you little runt. Now, where is Tom Sledd? Have you seen him?'

Choosing his words with care, the lad enunciated. 'No, I haven't . . . been near . . . anywhere where . . . he may be.' How much easier to have said *No, Master Henslowe, I haven't seen Master Sledd this morning*, but a lad had to think of his career.

'Imbecile!' Henslowe threw a random piece of rotting vegetable missed by the cleaning crew that morning and went off up the stairs to his office. By the time he had opened the window and yelled for Tom Sledd out in the street, he and Skirrow were cantering towards the road that led south through the marshes.

'She said you'd be in a foul mood.' Bet lay back on the pillows, puffing softly on Henry Meux's pipe.

'With her I usually am,' Meux was washing his face in the water jug on the night stand. They were both talking in whispers.

'You *are* beastly to her, Henry,' Bet said, watching the smoke drift up to the velvet hangings of the bed. 'She loves you, you know.'

He looked at her. 'Yes, I'm sure.' He threw himself down next to her and tickled the soft flesh around her navel. 'But she doesn't have your charms, Bet. It's like swiving a barn door.'

Bet chuckled. 'What was all that nonsense with Matthew Compton?' she asked.

'Hmm?' He was watching her skin prickle under his touch.

'You were telling us over supper, before Cicely retired. That business with the bell and the candles.'

'Oh, that,' Meux chuckled. 'Well, it *was* rather amusing, I suppose. But it doesn't do much for George's popularity, Bet, not among the Island gentry, anyway. Of course, the riff-raff lap it up. Did you know Compton?'

Bet set her mouth in a rueful half smile and shook her head a little, her curls whispering on the linen of the pillow. 'No, I don't think so.'

'Dillington.' He chuckled again, reached for the pipe and sucked on it hard until the tobacco reddened and there was a roar from the stem, like a fire in a distant chimney. He handed it back and blew smoke to mingle with hers in the hangings. 'Dillington said that you and he . . . well.' For an adulterer Henry Meux was very nice about the words he used, and baulked at this one. 'That you and he . . .' He turned her face towards him and looked into her eyes. 'Were you?'

She laughed and moved his hand back to her belly. 'I may have met the man once,' she said, her gaze not wavering. 'He turned a handsome calf as I recall.' She moved his hand further down and smiled. 'But why did George see him off like that?'

'He was a lawyer, by all accounts. I didn't know.'

'I had no idea he was a lawyer,' Bet said, then hurriedly added: 'That once I met him. Still, I suppose it's hard to tell.' She started to move rhythmically. 'Whether a man is a lawyer or not. Not from his calves.' She reached to one side and put the pipe down, wriggling down on the pillows as she did so.

'Well, we'll need a new centoner now, of course, in the Militia.'

She half turned to him. 'Are you up to this?' she asked.

'Twice in one night. And you having tramped all over St George's Down all day.'

'I am if you are,' he said. 'But not so much noise this time, please, my lady. Cecily may be stupid and her room may be in the east wing, but she's not deaf.'

Bet laughed, then covered her mouth with her free hand. 'Your trouble, Henry,' she said, rolling over into his arms, 'is that you've lost all interest in this sort of thing.'

It had to be said that Tom Sledd was not much of a sailor. He was fine in the river with the water slipping like silk past the skiff's sides. He even found the gentle roll restful. Then suddenly, they were out into the open sea and the wind hit him like a wall. Sledd was used to the rattle and lurch of wagons on the road as Lord Strange's men had rumbled from town to town in search of a stage. He was even used to roughing it on dark and deadly nights when he was rowed across the Thames under a guttering, spitting flame. He knew all of the watermen and whilst it would be madness to trust them with your purse or anything that glittered in the moonlight, he trusted them not to send him down to the river bed. But this was different and he had never felt anything like it.

The skiff's bows churned into the whitecaps before butting skywards again, spraying the occupants with wet salt. 'That's Spit Sand.' Henry Skirrow was keeping a running commentary. 'Horse Sand over there.' Since Sledd could see neither horse nor sand he found the whole thing a little baffling. 'That's where the *Mary Rose* went down in good King Harry's day.'

'I'm not surprised,' Sledd managed.

'What?' Skirrow looked at him askance. 'Don't tell me you admire the accuracy of French naval gunnery.'

'Gunnery?' Sledd frowned. 'No, I was talking about the sea. The place must be littered with the wrecks of ships.' He suddenly didn't want to know about how much water was between him and the bottom and he swallowed hard.

'This is nothing, lad,' Skirrow assured him, swinging easily with the movement of the ship, shifting his weight from one foot to another to compensate. 'You want to be back o' the Wight in a north-westerly.'

Tom Sledd could not begin to tell him how much he did not. His life flashed before him as the bows came round and the little crew began to haul sail. Ahead of them, against a dark canopy of trees, masts of all sizes bobbed above a little armada of ships. There must have been fifteen vessels crowded into a bay along the margins of which a shanty town of wooden huts clustered at rakish angles to each other, smoke drifting up through the branches overhead.

The canvas was hauled down at the end of the worst two hours of Tom Sledd's young life and oars were slid rumbling into rowlocks as the skiff began to snake its way between the ships moored farthest out. The London man had rarely seen so many foreign merchantmen in one place, even along the Queen's quays at Rotherhithe. Their sterns were emblazoned with exotic names from France, the Levant and the Barbary Coast. Outlandish flags fluttered from the halyards and bright parrots, green, blue and red, flapped and cawed on their perches on the decks.

Tom Sledd was never so glad as when the keel slid up the wet sand, dragging seaweed with it and slicing through the debris on the beach. His legs felt like blancmange as Skirrow helped him ashore. There were people everywhere, buying and selling; well dressed gentlemen in earnest discussion with stallholders of every colour of the rainbow. A dark-skinned beauty with painted lips swayed seductively over to the new arrivals. She draped a length of coloured silk around Sledd's neck. 'Welcome to the Island,' she said, looking at him under her eyelashes.

Sledd found himself grinning from ear to ear but an even more voluptuous girl wound herself close to him and whispered in his ear.

'How much?' The stage manager's purse was longer than most, but he had never heard anybody charge that, not even in London.

'You girls get lost now,' Skirrow grunted. 'Bothering young gentlemen with your whiles.' And he shooed them away but not before one of them turned her back and flicked up her tattered gown to reveal a naked arse, which she waggled at them both.

'Where are they from?' Sledd asked, his heaving stomach forgotten. 'I couldn't place the accent.'

'The Indies,' Skirrow told them. 'The flotsam and jetsam of the high seas, Master Sledd. Coming over here, taking our girls' jobs. This way.'

He led Sledd through the maze of people where the stall-holders cried their wares, up a gentle slope that led through a grove of silver birch. Ahead wound a twisting road along which carts grumbled and there was a grey manor house on the rise of a hill. Skirrow stopped at a shack, larger and set apart from the others, outside of which two sailors in their wooden clogs and red trousers sat on barrels, roped and tarred. Sledd had seen the dress before along the Thames, so he knew these men's calling. Their coats were long, almost down to the ground, and they made no pretence at all of lacing up their breeches which flapped around their ankles. They wore shapeless caps of blue wool, but Sledd could not help staring at their faces. Each man had blue swirling patterns across his forehead and rows of painted dots down his cheeks like tears.

Skirrow held open the hut's front door. 'Welcome to Mead Hole, Master Sledd,' he beamed.

Tom Sledd did not have time for his eyes to get used to the almost total darkness inside. Somebody rammed a boot into his calf from behind and he went down, sprawling on the floor. The dagger was gone from his back and he was spreadeagled over an upturned barrel, one large sailor grabbing one wrist, another large sailor grabbing the other. There was a scrape and spark of a tinder and a flame burst in front of his face, to be passed, seconds later, to a candle.

Holding the candlestick, an expensive piece of French silver gilt, a bearded man sat on an equally expensive chair, carved and inlaid with ivory.

'Are you Thomas Sledd?' the man asked, cocking his head to one side.

'Who wants to know?' the stage manager asked. If this was the hospitality of the Wight, he was not impressed.

He felt a stinging slap across his upturned face and as he dropped his head he felt blood dripping from his lip,

'We ask the questions here, sonny,' one of the sailors

growled, pulling harder on Sledd's right wrist so that he thought his arm would leave the socket.

'Now, Jacob,' the man with the candle said. 'Where *are* your manners? I am Thomas Page, Master Sledd, captain of the *Bowe*. What brings you to the Island?'

'Master Skirrow's skiff,' Sledd said, his lip already swelling to make his speech difficult.

'Jacob,' Page smiled, leaning back. 'I do believe we have a wit among us.' His smile vanished and he nodded at the sailors. Both men put their feet against the barrel and tugged. Sledd screamed. Those human racks would dislocate his shoulders any minute.

'You can make as much noise as you like here, boy,' Page assured him. 'Nobody's coming to your rescue. Now.' He leaned forward like a conspirator. 'Let me put my question another way. Why have you come to the Wight?'

Sledd sensed that another flippant answer would break his bones so he craned his neck to look into Page's expressionless face. 'I was sent for,' he said.

'Who by?'

'Master Christopher Marlowe.'

'And what is this Marlowe to you?'

'He's a friend,' Sledd told him. 'A playwright. I am stage manager at the Rose.' He saw the lack of comprehension on Page's face. 'In London,' he said. Then an inspiration came to him. 'Master Philip Henslowe knows I am here. So does Ned Alleyn, the tragedian. Then there's Will Shakespeare . . . he's a playwright too.'

Page's left hand caught the man's collar and he pulled his head up towards the candle flame. The sailors held him fast. 'I don't give the Pope's arse about playwrights,' he said. 'This Marlowe, what else is he?'

Sledd thought quickly, cursing himself for every kind of idiot for walking into this trap. The candlelight burned bright in his eyes until even when he shut them, the circles of blue light danced and flashed and he could not see shadows any more. 'A poet,' he said, as though he were breaking every confidence in the book. 'A university wit . . .'

'And?' Page lowered the candle and ran his left hand through

the lad's hair. Then, with his fingers tangled in his curls, he
suddenly jerked his head back so that Sledd heard his neck
click. The bright light had gone now. That was because the
candle was out of his direct eye-line and burning just beneath
his chin. In fact, as he became aware of the smell, it was
burning him. The hairs of his skimpy beard were curling still
further in the flame that Page passed slowly to and fro under
his chin. Sledd was screaming, trying to shake his head free
of the grip and his arms free of the sailors. Singed hair was
curling back to its roots, reddening his skin before it crisped
to a bloody brown. 'And?' Page repeated.

'He works for the government!' he screeched. The candle
was gone from his face and the fingers from his hair. He let
his head fall, blowing desperately to extinguish any burning
hairs still clinging to his skin.

'Now, you could have said that earlier, couldn't you?' Page
asked. 'That would have saved you a lot of pain and me a lot
of bother.'

Sledd shrieked again as the sailors yanked hard on his wrists
and Page was once again shining the candle into the man's
face. He could see the flickering reflections in his terrified
eyes. 'How, works for the government?' he asked.

'I don't know,' Sledd sobbed, dreading the pain if that flame
reached his chin again. 'As God is my witness, I don't know.
I just came to put on a play, that's all.'

'A play?' Page chuckled. 'Well, how nice. Has it got a clown,
Master Sledd? And a pig's bladder? I *do* like a good comedy.'
He jerked his head and the sailors let go of the man's
wrists. He groaned and sagged forward over the barrel. His eyes
were stinging with tears and he didn't know which hurt most,
his shoulders or his face. Page snuffed the candle out and stood
up, brushing past the shattered man on his way to the door.
'See yourself out, Master Sledd,' he said as one of the sailors
helped himself to Sledd's purse. 'Oh, and give my regards to
Master Marlowe, won't you?'

'Damn this rain,' Sir George Carey muttered out of the side
of his mouth to his wife, as they stood under a dripping yew
in the churchyard. 'It's gone right down my neck.'

'Rain seems the right weather for a funeral, George,' she replied tartly. She was glad her black clothes were old ones because the persistent drizzle would have ruined anything nicer. 'Besides, and I am sure you won't mind my reminding you, there is really no need to be here. We hardly knew . . . what's his name again?'

'Hunnybun. And of course I had to be here. He lay three days in my chapel before anyone claimed his body.'

Bet Carey shrugged a slim shoulder and took a step back further into the shelter of the tree. 'He had no family, the maids were saying.'

'Widower,' her husband muttered. 'No children.'

'He lived alone, then?'

'Lived alone, yes. But the gossip goes . . .' Carey stopped himself. The man was dead, after all. Time to bury the gossip with his body.

Bet inclined her head and her eyes sparkled. 'Do go on, George.'

'This is according to Dillington, mind you, so probably not to be trusted.'

'Tell me and then I can decide.'

'According to Dillington, there were often lights seen out in Hunnybun's fields at night. Shrieks. Howls.'

'Spirits walking out on the meadow?' Bet asked. She had never seen a ghost herself, but presumably a field was as likely a place to meet one as anywhere else.

'That's what the maids thought at first. Then, one night, one of them was going down Hollow Lane to meet her young man – a groom in Newport, I believe, and . . .'

'George!'

'Sorry . . . where was I?'

'A maid. Hurry up, they will be here with the coffin in a minute.'

'Yes, a maid going down Hollow Lane saw her master, breeches down round his ankles going at it something awful, if I may repeat her actual words . . .'

'According to Dillington,' she reminded him.

'According to him, yes, something awful between the thighs of a lady, who was shrieking and howling fit to raise the Devil.'

'How common,' muttered Bet.

'Indeed,' her husband agreed. She was always very quiet on the rare occasions he was called upon to go it something awful. He sighed and wiped the rain off his face with his cuff.

'Shhh,' his wife hissed. 'Here they come.'

The small crowd rustled to attention as the vicar led the cortège across the sodden grass from the church towards the grave. The sexton, never one to stand on ceremony, was leaning on the wall to one side of the grave, his pipe glowing as he drew on it thoughtfully. Another one down, he thought to himself; another one gone to a better place. The sextons of St Thomas were of two kinds: introspective and morose or introspective and miserable. Today's was of the latter kind and he was enjoying every minute of this funeral. Rain, hardly any mourners, another lonely soul going under the sod. If it wasn't so against his nature, he would have laughed out loud. As the vicar's drone got louder, the sexton leaned down and twitched the sacking from across the grave mouth. He personally preferred to have the corpse approach the yawning grave, something of a reminder of mortality in his opinion, but he knew it could sometimes upset the ladies. He wouldn't forget in a hurry the fuss and bother of hauling the Widow Buckett out of her husband's grave when she came over unnecessary. And a waste of time as it turned out, for she was in it again not six months later. He turned and spat before looking down.

Marlowe, watching the proceedings from the back and making mental notes to use this gravedigger in a play should the occasion ever present itself, saw the man's face change and his knees buckle just a little before he recovered himself. He looked up at the approaching vicar and held up his hand, his mouth working. Marlowe took a step forward. There was clearly something very wrong.

'Vicar, vicar,' the sexton said. 'You'm got to stop this burial.'

The vicar sighed. He had worried about this man for some time now; he seemed to enjoy the whole process of burying people far too much. His heart stopped whenever he heard of an unexplained death in the parish for fear that the sexton was rustling up more business on his own account. In his turn, the vicar held up his hand and the pall-bearers stopped and waited patiently. The Urry brothers were at the head, their sons, like peas in a pod, holding up the feet. The linen cross over the coffin lid hung limply in the rain and one of the men stifled a sneeze.

The sexton edged round the grave and, leaning still on his spade, reached up to whisper in the vicar's ear.

The man jerked away and said loudly, 'No!'

Marlowe stepped nearer still. Bet Carey clutched her husband's arm convulsively and stopped him moving forward. 'What is it, George?' she asked, her voice taut with anxiety.

'I won't know if you don't let me go,' he said and, shaking her off, joined the little group of the sexton, the vicar and Kit Marlowe.

'What is it, Vicar?' he asked, in ringing, Governor-like tones.

The vicar whispered something, with a vague gesture to the few mourners.

'What's that you say?' Sir George Carey never could abide whisperers.

Marlowe leaned forward. 'There is already a body in the grave, Sir George,' he said quietly.

'Well, there's nothing new in that,' the Governor said. He turned to the sexton, leaning heavily on his spade, the blade cutting into the turf. 'Surely you find bones all the time, fellow. Did you dig this grave yourself? Why didn't you just ferret them out and put them in the charnel house with the rest?'

The sexton was suddenly overwhelmed by his proximity to greatness. He knew that Sir George Carey was a conniving jackanapes who was out to bankrupt the Island for his own evil ends, but even so, he was the Governor and he had never stood this close to a nob before. He touched his hat and dipped his head. ''T'ain't an old 'un,' he explained. ''Tis a new 'un. Look.' He turned and pointed down into the grave and the vicar and Marlowe craned over to see.

'I am afraid I don't know the gentleman.' The vicar hurriedly looked away, turning pale.

Marlowe looked at Carey. 'Sir George?' he asked.

Carey looked down and then looked again, eyes bulging. 'What in the name of all the saints is he doing there?' he spluttered. Perhaps he could be forgiven for the rather Papist outburst in the circumstances.

The vicar thought that perhaps Sir George had missed the point. 'We know he shouldn't be there, Sir George,' he said gently. Perhaps it was the shock . . .

'I saw him off the Island,' Carey said. 'I had my Militia turn him off in an open boat. Damned lawyer. What's he doing down there?' He couldn't take his eyes off the man in the grave, who lay there, one arm bent over his head, one knee drawn up and his eyes open, oblivious to the raindrops falling on them, giving them an almost lifelike brightness.

Marlowe touched the Governor's arm. 'Who is this man, Sir George?' he said.

'Compton. Matthew Compton. Damned lawyer.' Carey kicked a sod of earth which crumbled wetly into the grave, landing on Compton's body. 'I'm going back to the castle until you sort this out, Vicar. If I were you, I'd change your sexton. The man doesn't know his job.' And he turned back to where Bet was sheltering under the arms of the yew.

But his wife had gone.

Sledd had no memory later of how he got to Carisbrooke. He remembered the jolting of a cart and whimpering a lot and some fool of a carter not understanding how the gen'leman from London could have got his injuries. Still, the carter knew, it was dangerous stuff, fire. And he should know. He'd been to school from time to time and had learned about that Master Prometheus who had stolen fire from the gods. And that was a true story; the carter knew it for a fact, certain sure.

There was a flame playing tricksily in Tom Sledd's gaze. Could he actually see it, he wondered? Or was it burned on to his brain? But more than the light, there was a face behind it, glowing now bright, now pale and he could not make it out. He screamed.

'It's all right, Tom.' It was Kit Marlowe's voice, gentle, kind and puzzled. It was Kit Marlowe's face beyond the candle.

'Do you mind, Kit?' the boy said, and lifted an arm that weighed like so much lead to wave the taper away.

'What happened to you, man?' Marlowe was looking horrified at his friend's face. Below his swollen lip, his scanty beard had all but disappeared and there were blisters, filling and taut with pus, all over his chin.

'A trio of gentlemen welcomed me to the Wight,' Sledd told him. 'After Master Skirrow disappeared, that is. They wanted to know all about you.'

'Me?' Marlowe frowned. 'Who were they?'

'The one who was handy with a candle called himself Thomas Page. Said he was captain of the *Bowe*.'

'The *Bowe*?' Marlowe repeated. He had seen that name somewhere before. 'What did you tell them?'

'Nothing,' Sledd lied, a little too quickly for either of their liking. 'Just that you were a playwright and I was here to help put on a play with you. That *is* right, isn't it, Kit? I mean, that *is* why I'm here?'

'Of course, Tom,' Marlowe said soothingly. 'Of course.'

There was a tap at the solar door and Marlowe put his finger to his lips, urging Sledd to stay quiet and stay where he was. The boy looked around him, taking in his surroundings for the first time. He was lying on a tester, high in the bed, and the heavy brocade curtains to either side were embroidered with the Queen's *Semper Eadem*. It was night and a soft glow of torchlight flickered through the latticed window from a passageway outside.

'Who is it?' Marlowe was still holding the candle but his right hand held the dagger hilt at his back.

'It's me, Master Marlowe. Avis Carey. I heard a cry.'

Marlowe hesitated, then slid back the heavy bolt and let the woman in.'

'Oh,' she said, raising her candle to peer at the forlorn figure sprawled on the bed. 'I didn't realize you had company. Who is this?'

'Mistress Carey,' Marlowe said, 'may I introduce Thomas Sledd? A finer stage manager never drew breath. He is from the Rose and has come to put on a play for us.'

'Oh,' she said again, a smile breaking over her large, square face. '*You* are the young man who has come to help Master Marlowe and Georgie.'

Sledd was staring open-mouthed at the apparition in her voluminous nightgown. He looked at Marlowe, who nodded.

'Yes,' he slurred, his mouth more painful by the moment. 'Yes, I am.'

'You poor dear.' Avis closed to him, setting her candle down and sitting on his bed. 'What *have* you been doing to yourself?'

She took one of his hands in her meaty one and stroked the back of it with her thumb. It was strangely comforting and Sledd smiled as best he could. 'Oh, it's nothing,' he winced.

'A slight altercation with a candle, Madam,' Marlowe explained.

'Ah, these things will happen,' she said. 'Now, you wait there, Master Sledd. I have a poultice receipt that I can make up in a moment and it will put you right in a trice.' She laid his hand down tenderly and picked up her candle, turning to go.

'Mistress Carey,' Marlowe stopped her. 'Does the name *Bowe* mean anything to you?'

'*Bowe*?' she repeated. 'No. Not a thing.'

'What about Thomas Page?'

Avis paused, frowning and thinking. 'Oh, yes,' she said with a sneer. 'That snivelling rogue is a pirate. And yes, now you mention Page, the *Bowe* – I remember now. It is his ship. It – and the dreadful Page creature – work for John Vaughan. You will find him moored in the quay at Newport.' She closed to the playwright. 'Georgie will hang that man one day; you mark my words.'

And she hurried off to make her sovereign remedy for Thomas Sledd.

The Lord Admiral was not in the best of moods that evening in Plymouth. He paced to and fro in his rooms over the White Hart, arms locked behind his back, white beard shaking along with his head. At fifty-two he was too old for this game, chasing dangerously headstrong captains along the south coast. And he had not even started on the Spaniards yet.

'Up and down, she says, Faunt,' he snapped, his voice trembling with fury. 'Up and down. Does she know what it's like? Taking a ship to sea? Still less an entire fleet? I know for a fact the only time she's set foot on the deck of a man of war is when she laid her sword on the shoulder of Francis Drake. And then the damn thing was safely tied up at Deptford.'

The Spymaster's right hand thought it was time to play God's advocate. 'She *is* the Queen, my lord,' he said softly.

Howard of Effingham stopped in his tracks and his narrow eyes flashed fire at the man. 'I know exactly who she is, sir,' he hissed. 'She is my bloody cousin. My point,' he tried to calm himself, staring at the untidy heap of charts and maps that cluttered his desk, 'is that she doesn't know a bowsprit from her elbow. And yet she proceeds to send me orders. Up and down! God, give me strength!'

'I *am* just the messenger, my lord,' Faunt reminded him.

Howard looked at the man. The time was he would have slit his throat and thrown his carcase to the fishes. But they were different days. Now, he had responsibilities. He made do by grabbing the projectioner by his braided sleeve and dragging him across the room. 'You see these?'

Faunt did. There were forty letters if there was one, each one sealed with the Privy Seal and dangling with the Queen's ribbon.

'These are just *some* of the missives I have received from Her Majesty last month alone. And there are others. Those are, as Martin Frobisher never tires of saying, the tip of the iceberg. I am drowning in parchment. Can she give me more guns? Powder? Men? Ships?' Howard did not wait for an answer. 'No, Faunt. She can't. All she can tell me to do is to use the ships I have and sail up and down the bloody Channel. Do you know what the odds are doing that? And finding a single Spanish galleon, I mean?'

'No, sir.'

'Nearly sixteen thousand to one. I had my comptroller on the *Ark* work it out for me. Preposterous!' The man crossed to the latticed window and looked out on the inn's courtyard, flickering with torchlight. It was full of soldiers, standing to, lying down, trying to find somewhere to sleep for the night. Beyond the inn, Howard knew, the entire town was bursting at the seams and the night rang to the rumble of cannon, the shouts of arriving quartermasters and the whinnying and stamp of horses.

'You know they'll make for the Wight, don't you?' The Admiral had not moved from the window, watching his reflection dance in the glass. 'The dons.'

'Sir Francis Walsingham thinks not, my lord,' Faunt said. 'He believes the target will be London.'

Howard spun to him. 'Does he?' he said with contempt. 'Not what he was, is he, old Francis?' There was concern on his face. 'When last I saw him at Whitehall, he seemed drawn, distracted.'

'These are trying times, my lord,' Faunt said, though he too had noticed the changes of which the Lord Admiral spoke.

A silence passed between them. 'Wind,' Howard said quietly.

'My lord?'

'Wind. The Queen can keep her ships and her guns and her men. We'll manage. What I really need is wind. I've got eighteen ships of the line out in the Sound and more arriving by the day. The point is that once they're in, on present showing, they can't get out again. If things don't change I'll have the whole fleet riding at anchor while Medina Sidonia turns England into a colony of Spain.'

Another silence.

'No,' said Howard, turning back to the window. 'Mark my words, Faunt, the dons will make for the Wight first. They'll take it and use it as a base for the invasion of the south. Then Parma will come. *He* will take London and Francis Walsingham will claim he was right all along.' He half-turned to the projectioner. 'And it'll be the last claim he'll ever make. Tell me, Faunt, have you ever been to the Wight?'

'Never, sir.'

The Admiral closed to him. 'I don't want to interfere with your orders, but get over there, will you? See how my cousin George is doing? He's not the brightest apple in the barrel.'

'My lord.' Faunt bowed as Howard's mind and Howard's body drifted across to his charts again, praying for wind.

In the passageway outside the projectioner nearly collided with a florid-faced man with a neatly trimmed beard. He was dressed in scarlet velvet with a Colley-Weston thrown back over his shoulder.

'Faunt.' The man nodded, the west country burr unmistakable even in that single syllable.

'Drake.' Faunt nodded back and neither man turned as Drake called, 'That's *Sir* Francis to you, pizzle!'

NINE

The mist was still wreathing the quay at Newport the next morning and the bell of St Thomas's was tolling the faithful to prayer. The weather was still hardly that of summer, still being dull and cold, but the fine, soaking drizzle of Walter Hunnybun's funeral had gone and the people of the Wight were making the most of the dry and were parading in their best. The market stalls had gone now and sharp-eyed Puritans were everywhere, making sure that the good citizens of the town were obeying God's laws.

Kit Marlowe was not one of them. This time he had borrowed one of George Carey's horses, a tall black that caracoled along the High Street, past the Audit House and along Holyrood. Here, Marlowe found a ragged urchin to hold his horse and paid him handsomely, but not so handsomely that the boy did not wait for the rest of his retainer when the gentleman came back.

The *Bowe* rode at anchor, where the warehouses crowded with their cranes and gantries. Her sides were new-pitched and smelling to high Heaven, her sails furled. Marlowe knew enough about ships to know that it was etiquette to ask permission to come aboard, but he was in no mood for etiquette that morning. There was no one on the dog watch and he hauled himself up the creaking rope ladder, feeling the hemp sharp and rough under his fingers. The deck was deserted, coils of rope and barrels scattered the length of it. To Marlowe's left the stern castle reared up and the helm was lashed with more rope. There was a gun here, a saker lashed in place and another one at the bows. The *Bowe* was too small for a man of war with guns along its hull to fire a broadside but there were stands of halberds and pikes in racks below the poop.

The ship was swaying slightly as a little breeze shivered down the river and seagulls wheeled screaming overhead. On dry land knots of the faithful were trudging up the hill to the church and George Carey's Militia wandered the streets, trailing their pikes with the town watch.

Marlowe looked at the door that led to the cabins. He could open it silently, there was no doubt of that, but he could not do it without letting in light down the stairs and that would defeat his purpose. He pattered up the stairs to the poop deck and found another stash of small barrels. He slipped the ropes on these and threw them on to the main deck one after the other.

There was a bellow from below decks, a sudden rush of cursing and the clatter of pattens on planking. The door below Marlowe crashed back and a large, bearded man stood there, frowning at the smashed kegs and spilled salt that littered the deck.

'I am terribly sorry,' Marlowe said. 'I didn't wake you, did I?'

The man on the deck was squinting up to the pale sun trying to break through the low cloud. All he could see was a figure lounging against the ship's helm. Then, realization dawned. 'I know you,' he said. 'You're Kit Marlowe.'

Marlowe smiled and bowed, without taking his eyes off the man. 'And you must be Thomas Page . . .'

'Master of the *Bowe*,' the man finished Marlowe's sentence for him, something a sensible man would not have done. 'What are you doing on my ship?'

Marlowe sauntered down the steps so that he was nearly on the same level as the man. '*Your* ship?' he said. 'Now, why did I think the *Bowe* belonged to Master Vaughan and you were just his boot boy?'

Thomas Page may have had a clever answer ready, but he had no time to give it. Marlowe's right boot lashed forward, driving into the captain's face and he fell back, bleeding and groaning. The next thing he knew, he was lying face down on his own main deck. And the next thing after that, he was staring down towards the bows, his hair gripped like a vice in Marlowe's left hand, while Marlowe's right hand held a dagger blade horizontally across his throat.

'I understand you've been asking after me,' the poet said. 'Being rather persistent in your enquiries with a friend of mine.'

'Don't know what you mean,' Page could just about grunt, what with the pressure on his windpipe. He tried to move but Marlowe's knee was in the small of his back and Marlowe's full weight was behind that.

'Oh, I think you do,' Marlowe breathed in his ear. 'So, just to reiterate . . . that means to say again, should you be wondering . . . I am a playwright. I have come to this demi-paradise to gain inspiration for my writing. In the process, I have agreed to put on a play for Sir George Carey. And Master Thomas Sledd has come to help me stage it. But I feel sure that he told you all of this when you met, did he not?'

Page just gurgled as he felt Marlowe's blade graze his skin above his epiglottis.

'Now, I don't have the wherewithal at the moment to repay your hospitality to Master Sledd – no candles on me, as we speak – so what would you say if I just slit your throat and have done?'

'Marlowe!'

The poet did not move but he heard the click of a wheel-lock behind him.

'Let him go.'

For a split second that seemed to Thomas Page like a life-time, Marlowe contemplated finishing the job anyway. Then he changed his mind and got up, bouncing the captain's already bruised and cut chin on the deck.

'Master Vaughan.' Marlowe sheathed the dagger at his back. 'How nice to see you again.'

'You had better have an explanation for this, sir.' Vaughan had not lowered the pistol. Page lay stunned and moaning on the planking.

'Does this,' Marlowe tapped him with his boot, 'work for you?'

'He is the Master of my ship, yes.'

Marlowe walked slowly towards the man. 'So, when he interrogated my friend Thomas Sledd, burned his face with a candle and stole his purse, he was acting on your instructions?'

Vaughan looked horrified and released the catch of his gun. 'Thomas,' he said, frowning at the man. 'Is this true?'

Whatever Page said, it was not comprehensible, what with the swelling and the pain; both the men still standing chose to ignore it. Vaughan crossed to his captain and aimed a hearty kick into his ribs. 'I will not have this, you rogue,' he snarled. 'You are herewith deprived of your livelihood. You will collect your belongings together and be off my ship within the hour. Do I make myself clear?'

Page nodded and sighed. This was the old routine and he had lost count of the times that John Vaughan had sacked him. He looked forward to the evening when the merchant's bag of silver and nod of reinstatement would make up for the pain now spreading down his side.

'Master Marlowe, how can I make all this up to you? Will you take some wine with me? That's my house over there.'

It *was* a little early for Marlowe but the wine was excellent and the house vast, its fittings easily outshining those of George Carey up the road. It spread up Quay Street and along Sea Street, commanding an imposing view up the river. Servants bustled in and out preparing the food for the midday meal. Vaughan clearly liked to live well in all respects – all his maids were comely and Marlowe was sure that he saw at least three suckling pigs on spits before the enormous fire in the kitchen as Vaughan took him on a tour of his property. Like all men revelling in new money, he liked to flaunt it and he felt that this playwright – if such he be – would probably be impressed. As a Customs man he would no doubt see it with different eyes, but letting him see there was nothing to hide at this early stage would probably be all to the good.

'This is Spanish wine,' Marlowe said, but he could not place the origin of the silver-gilt goblet he drank from.

'It is,' Vaughan smiled. 'Oh, I know it's a little unpatriotic of me to stock it at the moment, with the way the political wind is blowing; but that's the marvellous thing about trade, Master Marlowe – it is universal, isn't it? Whoever wears the crown, whoever rides the high seas, people will always buy and sell. It's in our blood.'

Marlowe heard the bell of St Thomas signalling the end of another service. 'So you worship Mammon, Master Vaughan?'

The merchant looked outraged. 'I am a Christian, sir, as I am sure you are. If I do not attend church today, it is because I have weightier matters on my mind.'

'Oh?'

Vaughan leaned forward in his chair. They were alone in the chamber, but it paid to be careful. 'I will be blunt, Master Marlowe. You are sleeping under the eaves of a traitor.'

Marlowe blinked. 'You had better explain that, Master Vaughan,' he said.

'In pursuance of my business,' the merchant told him, 'I am often at sea. The *Bowe* rests here for the moment, given the impending news from Spain, but usually I am in Calais or Boulogne. The River Scheldt is particularly pleasing at this time of year.'

'Your point?'

'I hear things.' Vaughan leaned back in his chair, sipping his wine.

'Things about George Carey?'

Vaughan nodded. 'The man is Captain of the Wight, Marlowe,' he said solemnly. 'Governor, coroner, cousin to the Queen herself.'

'So I understand,' Marlowe said. 'But . . .'

'I have it on good authority,' Vaughan went on, refilling the cups for them both, 'that he is in touch with Spain.'

'With Spain?' Marlowe repeated. 'How?'

'That I don't know,' Vaughan conceded. 'But not long ago a man named Hasler came to the Island.'

'Oh?'

'He claimed to be a gardener – no, more than that, a designer of gardens. Claimed to have worked for the Earl of Leicester at Kenilworth.'

'And?'

'Have you seen that so-called knot garden he planted?'

Marlowe shrugged. 'I am not much of a gardener myself. It looked quite . . . unusual, I will concede.'

'You are right. He was no more a gardener than ex-Captain Page out there.' He jerked his head in the direction of the *Bowe*. 'That was a front.'

'What for?' Marlowe asked. It was not every day that Francis

Walsingham's system was exposed, but Francis Walsingham seemed to have been particularly careless in his choice of Harry Hasler.

'I thought you might tell me,' Vaughan said, smiling over his cup.

Marlowe could fence with this man all day and he shook his head. 'I am a playwright, Master Vaughan. Gardens and whatever skulduggery you have in mind are beyond me.'

Vaughan let the silence fill the room. Then he said, 'I believe he was an intelligencer, a spy.'

'Really?' Marlowe had the innocent face of an angel and he knew exactly how to use it. 'Working for . . .?'

'Her Majesty's Customs.' Vaughan had cut to the chase at last. The bonhomie had vanished and there was a sudden chill in the chamber. 'Isn't that who you work for?'

Marlowe burst out laughing. 'I didn't know Her Majesty had any Customs,' he said, 'other than those of course that might stale her infinite variety.'

'What?'

'Never mind. What happened to . . . Hasler, is it?'

Vaughan shrugged. 'Your guess is as good as mine. He lodged around the corner from here but was last seen up at the castle. After that, no one has seen him,' Vaughan leaned forward and patted the man's dagger hand. 'I suppose what I am saying is, be careful, Master Marlowe. There are things not right about George Carey. I would hate to see you come to harm.'

'So would I, Master Vaughan,' Marlowe said. He finished his wine. 'And now, I must thank you and be on my way.'

'Of course.' Vaughan stood up with him. 'Shall I have a few bottles of Bastard sent to you at the castle?'

'That's kind,' Marlowe said. 'But I'd prefer a little Rumney if you have any.'

'Aha,' Vaughan chuckled. 'I like a man who knows his wines. Because he is a man to trust.'

Tom Sledd was glad to be back in action, if only to take his mind off his chin. He popped dutifully into the chapel of St Nicholas for morning service, just in case Sir George Carey was a stickler for the recusancy fines, and then got on with it. His stage manager's eye had worked out that the best place for a Masque was in the courtyard outside the governor's mansion. They could set up raked seats on three sides like galleries at the Rose and use Sir George's front door for exits and entrances. They could hang lanterns in the trees because it would be a novelty to stage the piece at night. The carriages of the nobs in the audience could be brought through and left on the Militia ground below the keep and the groundlings would have a chance to marvel at the architecture of the governor's mansion should the Masque have any boring bits. Not, Sledd told himself quickly, that there would be any of those, because this one would be written by Christopher Marlowe, the Muse's darling. There would not be a dry eye in the castle.

Sledd had been introduced to Lady Elizabeth Carey that morning and her eyes had burned through him. Tom Sledd had always found conquests easy and he read a very easy one in the smile of Bet Carey. But Tom Sledd also knew his place. His Johanna was neither here nor there, but the fact that she was actually there and not in the Wight made life easier for him. No, Tom Sledd's problem was the social chasm that yawned between him and the Careys. Climbing on to a lady like that took breeding or at least a fatter purse than a stage manager possessed. All the same, he worked with more of a spring in his step that day as he saw her in the upstairs windows smiling down at him.

It was Avis Carey who proved equal to the hour and Sledd wondered if he might engage her back at the Rose. Assuming, that was, that an angry mob of disappointed theatre goers had not even now burned the place down. Assuming that Philip Henslowe had not already given Tom Sledd his marching orders *in absentia*. The stage manager stretched ropes and jotted down figures on his vellum pad with his treasured pencil, just a short stub now but a gift from Kit Marlowe, so he would use it to its last stroke. Avis hauled and dragged timbers into place at his bidding, smiling at the boy but in a completely different way from her sister-in-law. Two labourers were carrying the wood for the platform from the storehouse, but

Avis casually lifted their load, lifting three to their two and standing to attention like a militiaman with the thickest pike in the world while Sledd noted the alignments.

'Do you really need all this timber, Master Sledd?' Martin Carey asked. He was following the man around with a vellum pad of his own, his quill scratching over the surface as a lackey bobbed behind him with an open inkwell. Tom Sledd stopped and looked at him. 'I am stage manager at the Rose, Master Martin,' he said. 'I *do* know what I am doing.'

'I'm sure you do,' Martin said. 'But I have to watch the pennies, sir. Sir George is not made of money.'

'Tosh and fiddlesticks, Martin!' Avis scolded, tucking another beam under her arm. 'This was Georgie's idea and it's a good one. Cut this boy a little slack.'

'I don't know what slack is.' Martin scowled at his aunt several times removed. 'And I have people to cut things. I am a Comptroller. I do the sums.' He walked over to Avis who looked him squarely in the eye. 'I'm surprised at you, Avis,' he whispered, pretending he was out of Sledd's earshot. 'I always thought you were of the Puritan persuasion. Are you really happy with this play nonsense?'

'It's not a play, it's a Masque,' she explained as though Martin Carey were the castle idiot. 'Something different altogether. Besides,' she suddenly became a snob, 'all the best people have them performed at their houses nowadays. To have one specially composed by Christopher Marlowe is a particular honour. Thomas,' she called to the lad, 'where are you going to put the orchestra?'

Martin Carey groaned. He should have realized. A Masque meant music and music meant money. Bandoras, orpharions, virginals, citterns, shawms and sackbuts, they all added up to one thing in Martin's view: expense. A brief thought rushed through Martin's mind, trailing money-saving opportunities like a comet leads its tail, but he dismissed it instantly. Sir George Carey's band of three fife players and a drum would not constitute an orchestra, no matter how forgiving the audience. And what with the rumours from Spain, there was no chance that the Earl of Southampton would be lending *his*

men any time soon. He sighed. He really would have to tackle
George about it.

George Carey was in his solar that night, pacing with a
stately tread and one hand on his hip. The other was holding
a piece of parchment that had been scribbled on by
Christopher Marlowe. He cleared his throat and declaimed
in his best Governor's voice, '"And here, the Isle doth dance
and shine, So far beyond this wit of mine, Encased in silver
of the sea, A haven and a home to me. May sun shine on
her all her days, And God above protect her ways, And 'ere
the world be clothed in night, Send Heaven down to
warm the Wight."'

There was a knock at the solar door and Carey crossed to it
in one and a half strides. 'Christopher, my boy!' The Governor
clapped the man on the back. 'This opening of the Masque.
Superb! "May sun shine on her all her days." Immortal. No
wonder men speak so highly of you.'

Marlowe chuckled. 'It's not my usual style,' he said. 'It's
not even iambic pentameter. The feet are all over the place.'

'I don't care, I don't care. It's riveting. Shall I give you my
rendition of it now? See if you think it's all right? Trinity was
many years ago, I fear.'

'I understood you wanted to talk to me about the late
Matthew Compton, Sir George.'

'Did I? Oh, yes, of course.' Carey put the script down.
Frivolity left his face and he was the Captain of the Wight
again, with cares weighing him down.

'I don't see how I can help,' Marlowe said, accepting the
governor's offer of a seat.

'Martin tells me you were useful in the Hunnybun business,'
Carey said, pouring a stiff claret for them both. The candles
glittered in Sir George's eye and in Sir George's windows.
Outside them, torches guttered in the June breeze. Tom Sledd
had had them placed there so that the unwary did not kick
over his stage foundations.

'I have seen sudden death before,' Marlowe conceded.

'So have I,' Carey said. 'But that's because I am the bloody
coroner, to add to my woes. Difficult to say, in this instance,

who the First Finder was. The sexton, blind as a bat? That miserable old Puritan of a vicar? Me? It's complicated.'

'Suppose you tell me about the deceased,' Marlowe suggested.

'Well, he was a lawyer, Marlowe,' Carey explained, as though that said it all.

'And?'

'And I won't tolerate them in my Island. It's that simple. The damnable fellow posed as a gentleman of private means – you'd be amazed how many such people retire here. They claim the sea air does them good. Well, he introduced himself to me and we got on like a house on fire. I even made the man a centoner in the Militia.'

'And what is your objection to lawyers, exactly?' Marlowe wondered.

'I'm not a naive man, Christopher. I realize we need laws and that we need people to enforce them. But that's not what a lawyer does, is it? They batten on to honest folks, bleed them dry with their obscene charges. No, the Wight is better off without them, believe me.'

'So you sent him packing?'

'I did. At our last muster on the Down. Made such a thorough spectacle of the man I was sure he would never show his face here again.'

'I don't think he intended to show his face, Sir George,' Marlowe murmured.

Carey was silent for a moment. 'Such men must make a lot of enemies,' he said.

'I'm sure they do.' Marlowe nodded, mentally adding that George Carey must be at the top of the list. 'Where is his body now?'

'In the charnel house alongside St Thomas's,' the governor told him. 'I can arrange for you to take a look, if you like, in the morning.'

The storm hit hard that night, driving the white horses of the spray crashing into the rocks around La Coruña. The Duke of Medina Sidonia's *San Martin* and thirty-five of the ships of the Captain-General of the Ocean Sea had already reached a safe haven in the harbour. But the huge vessels of the Levant Squadron, Juan de Recaldé's Biscayans, the hulks and the galleases, still wallowed out to sea, water washing their decks and their canvas threatening to tear itself to pieces in the wind. Sailors hauled sail in the total darkness since the torches had all blown out and they clattered and slid their way along the decks, making sure the guns were secured and trying to keep the powder dry. No one was shinning up the rigging on a night like this and in the hold, thousands of men who did not know the sea lay crammed like herring in a kreel, fingering their rosaries and listening to the urgent prayers of their priests.

When the grey morning dawned, the sea beyond the harbour looked like a battlefield. It was as though El Draque himself had sailed among them, driving in on the Devil's wind to crush the Armada of Spain. Medina Sidonia trotted along the beach with his staff and his keen-eyed sailors. They had an impossible job – to see what was not there. To identify which ships had not found the gentle lee of Coruña. Not for nothing did men call this place Finisterre, the end of the world. There was timber everywhere, drifting wood that had once been, perhaps, the *San Nicolas Prodaneli* or *La Concepcion de Zubelzu* – there was no way of telling. He did not need his comptroller to give him the final tally – twenty-eight ships of the line had vanished without trace, the artillery train and some six thousand souls. They may not be lost forever but Medina Sidonia had no way of calculating that.

That night, cold and shivering with the enormity of the setback, he wrote a letter to Philip of Spain. 'At any time,' his quill flew over the vellum, 'it would be remarkable; but since it is only June and since this is the cause of Our Lord, to whose care it is being entrusted, it would appear that what has just happened must be His doing, for some just reason.'

The last four words came to Medina Sidonia as an after-thought. He had been to the Escorial. He knew King Felipe. The man was half-monk himself, with a passageway that probably led to God's right hand itself. Medina Sidonia knew, as the galloper raced south across Spain with his message, that he had already offended his king with its contents. No sense in offending his God too.

'It was a city, Kit.' Tom Sledd was demolishing a hunk of fresh bread in the kitchen, 'or at least a town. I saw workshops, blacksmiths, stalls without number. Ladies and gentlemen of quality were buying there. And stews like I haven't seen anywhere but Southwark.'

'You must have felt at home, then.' Marlowe had eaten earlier. 'Tell me, this Skirrow, the man who took you there . . . what was it called?'

'Mead Hole. Don't ask me if I could find it again, because I couldn't. Well, Skirrow *said* he was Sir George's man. Had your letter to me with him, so he must have been.'

'Oh, I'm sure he was,' Marlowe said. 'It's just that no one's seen him, apparently, from that day to this. Fancy looking at a body today, Tom – when you've finished your breakfast, of course?'

'Well . . .' The stage manager was reluctant. 'I *do* have a stage to build.' Tom Sledd had seen some sights in his short life, some of which could still bring him awake and sweating in the small hours of the morning and he had promised himself some time ago that he would try not to see any more.

Marlowe looked out on to the courtyard from the Great Hall to where Avis Carey was giving orders, barking and braying at a variety of smocked and jerkined labourers who ran backwards and forwards to do her bidding. 'It looks as though Mistress Carey has that well in hand,' he said. He picked up Tom Sledd's hat from where he had lain it down beside him at the table and crammed it on the lad's head. 'Come on, Tom. Don't tell me you're squeamish.' And he was gone, leaving Tom to follow reluctantly in his wake.

Matthew Compton had been a good-looking man once. Now he was an unpleasant shade of grey and lay on a hurdle in the cold of the charnel house hard by St Thomas's Church. Tom Sledd's experience of the dead had included the recently deceased – if men run through with his own blade could be described thus – or the decently laid out, but this was a departure from all that. He realized now what was so unsettling about the dead. They stared back at you with an unblinking gaze that never wavered. Compton's eyes bulged in his head and above the linen collar, smeared with the clay of Walter Hunnybun's grave, there was a clear mark of a ligature around his neck. Someone had hooked a rope around it, twisted with a stick to one side and had turned and turned it relentlessly so that the rope tightened and choked the life out of the lawyer who was not supposed to be there.

'Any number of people saw him off at the quay.' Marlowe's breath snaked out in the chill of the charnel house, for all it was June and warm outside. The damp had soaked into these thick walls for so many years that winter always seemed to rule inside. 'Apparently he was put into a rowing boat and towed to the mouth of the Medina. Half the Militia seem to have run along the bank taunting him.' Marlowe checked the man's clothing. His Venetians were scorched by the candles that Carey's sergeant had tied there, but there was no sign of the candles now. The bell had gone too, the one that the same sergeant had draped around the man's neck as they ran him off the Island. He was a centoner of the Militia, yet there was no sword, no armour, not even the scarlet sash that was his badge of rank.

'What does an open boat do when it reaches the sea, Tom?' Marlowe asked.

Sledd shrugged. 'Buggered if I know. The last time I was on one it was all I could do to keep my breakfast down. I would imagine that there are quite a few obstacles out there. Skirrow kept pointing out horses and things, but I wasn't really paying attention, what with being scared of dying and all.'

Marlowe shrugged. He had had quite a pleasant crossing but even then there had been a bumpy bit in the middle – he was almost certain that these were not the proper nautical terms, but they would suffice. 'He would have had no sail.' He was thinking aloud. 'They would have given him oars, though. Carey wanted to get rid of him but I think that even he doesn't hate lawyers enough to want to drown them wholesale.' He picked up a cold, dead hand and turned it palm up. 'Look, there, see – blisters.' He put the hand back and gave it a pat. 'Which way did he row, though, that's the question.'

'North,' Sledd said after a moment's thought. 'Away from this place.'

'You would think so, wouldn't you?' Marlowe mused. 'But I think you're wrong, for two reasons. The first is that the coast of the mainland is a long way for a man unused to rowing and, as you say, there are obstacles out there, though for the life of me I can't see where the horses come in. The second is that he is a man of some wealth. He has clothes, books, valuables. And he's told to go. Now. At once. No ceremony. So . . .'

Sledd was with him. 'So he doubles back,' he said, clicking his fingers, 'to pick up his stuff.'

Marlowe nodded. 'Let's have a look at Holyrood Street,' he said.

Matthew Compton's house along Holyrood Street was locked and bolted so while Tom Sledd stood whistling and picking his nose on what passed for a pavement, Kit Marlowe broke in. Two clicks of his dagger point and all the secrets of the late lamented lawyer were revealed. Well, not quite all. While Sledd ransacked, very carefully, the downstairs rooms, Marlowe went to work on the upper storey. There was a chest, its lid open, its contents the wardrobe of an officer of the Militia. There was a useful-looking rapier, a wheel-lock pistol, a burgonet and breastplate, a pair of spurs. A pile of books teetered precariously in a corner. They had once stood, Marlowe could tell by the slight impressions in the dust, on a shelf on the wall. They were law books, learned tomes leather-bound and all bore the same legend on the fly: 'Ex Libris Matthew Compton'. A pair of boots stood on their own in the far corner and a cloak and hat still hung from a peg.

The bed was cold. He smelled the pillows. Civet. Either Master Compton was not as other Benchers of Lincoln's Inn or . . . And the 'or' came to him in a moment. There was a long, dark hair on the pillow and a yellowish stain on the satin. The lawyer had been entertaining a lady friend and not that long before he died. The books, the boots, the cloak and hat, all looked as if Compton had been about to leave and take them with him.

Marlowe knelt on the hard boards and looked under the

tester. Cobwebs and not a little dust, but nothing . . . He almost missed it at first because it was half hidden by the chamber pot. It was a piece of parchment. More than that, it was a note, written in an untidy hand and in haste. It read: 'Church Litten. Midnight. I must see you again, dearer than life.'

Dearer than life. That was a good line. He might be able to use that somewhere. This was not the same hand as the letter he had found in Harry Hasler's room in Quay Street, but letters were fluttering around this Island like the flags of the Armada, somewhere out to sea.

'Anything up there, Kit?' he heard Tom Sledd call. 'There's bugger all down here.'

'Nothing much, Tom,' Marlowe said. 'Nothing much,' and he tucked the letter into his doublet.

TEN

George Carey's bay was saddled and waiting alongside Tom Sledd's makeshift orchestra pit by midday and the Captain of the Wight was surprised to find a second animal tethered alongside, the black he had bought from William Oglander, of Nunwell. On its back sat Christopher Marlowe, the poet and university wit.

'Mind if I tag along, Sir George?' the playwright asked. He was dressed for the road with his Colley-Weston slung over his shoulder and Tom Sledd's shapeless Picadill on his head.

'Er . . . no,' Carey said, waiting until the groom had held his knee and hoisted him into the saddle. 'Are you sure you can keep up? It's a long ride to the West Wight.'

'I'll manage,' Marlowe said. 'I'm nearing completion of ideas for my play, but I must get the feel of your Island beyond its centre. Mead Hole, I understand, is well worth a visit.'

'Mead Hole?' Carey scowled. 'Stay wide of that place, Christopher. Anyway, we're not going that way. We're bound for the Needles. Are you armed?'

'My dagger,' Marlowe said.

'All right.' Carey took up the reins in his gloved hands. 'I have my trusty rapier and a brace of wheel-locks. Stay with me and you should be all right. But I warn you, we're riding into the West Wight.'

'Where the anthropophagi live, I understand.' Marlowe smiled. 'The headless men with their faces on their chests.'

Carey looked at him for a moment, then burst out laughing. 'The anthropophagi?' he said. 'In the West Wight, they'll be the least of our worries, believe me.' And he hauled his rein and clattered away under the arch of the barbican, Marlowe behind him. The last thing the poet heard was Avis Carey's dulcet roar as she clapped her hands and ordered the set builders back to work.

The wind was blowing from the south-west, unseasonably

strong for this time of year, and long before they reached Calbourne with its water mill and hissing geese, Kit Marlowe owed Tom Sledd a new hat. The original was tumbling away across the high ridge of the land the pair were cantering over. The miller of Calbourne had all his family paraded, from his eldest, a stout lad who might be useful in the Militia in a month or two, to a little girl, all curls and snot, who sheltered behind her mother at the hugeness of the horses that snorted and pawed the ground in front of her.

Caps came off at Shalcombe too and there were three hearty cheers for the governor, God bless him. Then the riders were trotting out along the road that led to Freshwater, the forest of Brighstone dark and gloomy on the sloping ground that led to the sea. All along this stretch, Marlowe noticed that Carey's eyes rarely left the sea. He was as concerned now as he had been that second day of Marlowe's visit, striding his ramparts. He reined in and pointed. 'That's Catherine's Race,' he said, 'and beyond that, Catherine's Deeps.' He caught the mystified look on Marlowe's face. 'Oh, yes, it looks calm enough today, doesn't it, for all the whitecaps. But that's a graveyard you see there, Christopher. Dead men still in their ships' holds, full fathom five and feeding the fishes. Freshwater's over the next rise. We'll eat there.'

Edmund Burley joined the travellers at Freshwater. He was captain of the castle at Yarmouth, one of those fortresses built as a precaution in the days of King Harry of blessed memory. He was a large and jolly man who proceeded to eat and drink Carey and Marlowe under the table, much to the delight of the innkeeper of the Crown, whose establishment nestled in the lea of the church.

'Are you ready, Edmund?' George Carey asked as the three men were preparing for the road. 'For what's coming, I mean?'

'Readier than most,' Burley replied, swigging the last of his ale. He looked at Marlowe. 'The dons will land in one of four places, Master Marlowe. The least likely is Sandown Bay. The bastard French tried that in my dear old dad's day and got a bloody nose there, for all the beach is shallow. This side of the Island they'll try here, at Freshwater, at Brighstone and at Chale. The problem with all those is the Race and the Deeps.

That's our secret weapon. It'll destroy Philip's ships faster than the guns of that old pizzle the Lord Admiral . . . Oh, begging yer pardon, George. Forgot he's your cousin.'

Carey waved the insult aside. With Spain knocking at his gate he had better things to do than antagonize his captains.

'Course.' Edmund Burley timed his parting shot to perfection. 'If the bastards land in all four places at once, then we're buggered.' And all George Carey could do was scowl at the beaming idiot. He had never understood what made Edmund Burley so damned cheerful.

All day Carey and Marlowe had ridden past the beacons, tall masts dotted along the ridge that formed the Island's spine, with ladders lashed to them and iron fire baskets crowning their tops. The faggots lay ready, roped under canvas to keep them dry. Each beacon was actually a pair. As Carey explained, one light meant a state of emergency: 'Handle your pike.' Two flames guttering side by side meant something like 'Prepare to meet your God'. At Freshwater, on the chalky slopes above the bay and again on the promontory men called the Needles, where the white rocks stood sentinel above the roaring surf, there were three. There were three likewise, Carey explained, at the eastern forelands on the high ground of Culver, by Bembridge Ledge. That overlooked the shallow beach that Captain Burley had mentioned. There was a fort there too, Carey had said, but he had no faith that it would hold the Spaniards long.

All that day Marlowe had talked to George Carey, dropped snippets of information, watched the man's reaction. Everyone hated him; Marlowe knew that already. Only Carey's sister and perhaps his wife supported the man. He had no children and no friends. The gentlemen of the Wight and their ladies had no qualms about eating and drinking the man out of house and home at one of his parties. And everyone today had been the epitome of respectful tenants. And yet, something was not quite right about the Carey household and Marlowe was not going merely by the word of John Vaughan. It was something he had noticed himself. Something to do with missing gardeners and murdered lawyers and farmers dead in their own fields.

'Captain! Captain!' a voice was calling from the road and

a solitary horseman was lashing his mount across the tussocks of grass cropped short by the sheep. Carey swung his bay away from the beacons and took the salute of the galloper. Marlowe could not catch much of it, because the wind was rising again and the ridge was exposed. The horseman saluted again and spurred back.

'Marlowe.' Carey walked his horse over to the man. 'I've been called away. Some trouble at Nunwell.'

'Nunwell?'

'The Oglanders. It's probably nothing.'

'I'll come with you.'

'No, no, Christopher, my dear fellow. It's a punishing ride and night's approaching. No offence, but you'd only be in the way. Here.' Carey unbuckled his rapier. 'Take my sword. Unless you want to find lodgings back in Freshwater, you've a long ride back to Carisbrooke. Go that way, to Chale.' He pointed to the south-east. 'Follow the coast. It's an easier road.'

'Very well, sir.' Marlowe took the proffered sword. 'Thank you.' He slid the expensive weapon with its gilt curled guard into his saddle strap and watched the Captain of the Wight disappear into the darkness, his hoofbeats soon lost to the cloak of the coming night.

Marlowe watched the two men canter off in the direction of Newport and suddenly felt rather alone. Carey's instructions, thrown over a retreating shoulder, to take the coast road to Chale and then turn left did not somehow fill him with confidence. A Governor of an island and Captain of the Militia should be a little more precise in his geographical detail, Marlowe couldn't help thinking, but on the other hand, on an island how far wrong could he possibly go? The sun was beginning to sink below the Down which led to the Needles and as he turned his horse's head to the east it was already clear that night would not be long in coming.

Marlowe was a city boy at heart but had spent plenty of nights out in the open for reasons nefarious and otherwise and so was not afraid of the dark. Fear of the dark, he had always believed, came from thinking that there were things at your back more scary than you were and when that thought dug itself into a man's heart, then screaming madness would follow. He touched his dagger lightly, nestling in the small of his back, and the sword hilt at his thigh and knew that he was ready for anything the night could throw at him.

There was no moon yet and the rays of the setting sun still lit the sky behind him. The sea to his right was gleaming in golden ripples and after the wild weather of the last few days, all seemed strangely still and calm. There was a bank of cloud to the south which was picking up the rose tints of the sky, but it had billowing depths that promised – or threatened – some interesting weather in the future. All Marlowe wanted was to get back to the mansion without getting drenched, so he wished the cloud a thousand miles away and spurred his horse into a canter. While there was enough light, he could risk a faster pace; dark would come soon enough and then he would need to walk the animal. George Carey was a generous man, but even he might baulk at a horse with a broken leg. The silence was so absolute that the sound of the hoofbeats on the road sounded like thunder and the clip of the occasional flint being struck by a shoe set the poet's teeth on edge, so after less than a mile, he slowed the animal back to a rolling amble that went very well with the silently lapping sea and the call of a seabird, out too late from its nest down on the cliff below.

As he ambled along on his horse, Marlowe let his mind wander where it would. Although his cover story of wanting inspiration for a play had been just that, a story to cover his darker purpose, he was a playwright first and foremost, a projectioner least of all. The dark around him became peopled with all manner of apparitions and he turned them over in his mind, discarding them when the image was too bizarre. The three witches outlined briefly on the hilltop he dismissed at once as being so far-fetched that not even a Rose audience at their most ale-soaked would swallow them. A beautiful woman with a face of an angel led his horse for almost a mile, her gentle hand on the bridle. Marlowe watched her treading softly alongside him, turning her head from time to time to give him a sad smile.

'Nell?' he said to the dark and with a spark like a bubble

flown too high, the woman disappeared. Dr John Dee's dead wife, the lovely Helene, mourned even now by all who had known her, had come to keep him company for a while and the thought gladdened him, even as he wiped away a tear.

The horse, calm until now, gave a snicker and tossed its mane. Out to sea, just beyond the gleam of the starlight that was beginning to light the waves, strange creatures gambolled, throwing up silver spray and shrieking to the sky. Marlowe shook his curls to match the horse's flying mane and turned his mount landwards. This island truly was a haunted place and even as the thought passed through his mind, a flash of flying fire crossed his path. It dissolved into myriad points of light which flared once or twice and then went out. Risking everything, Marlowe closed his eyes and counted to ten. When he opened them, the points of light had gone, replaced by the steady lamplight of a house ahead of him, on the seaward side of the road.

Marlowe approached the low door and, leaning out of the saddle, tapped on it sharply. The voices he had heard from inside stopped at once and the dark velvet silence of the night rolled back in. His horse shook his head and the bridle jingled, but that was all. Marlowe rapped again and called out. 'Is there any one at home?'

After a few seconds, a voice, from its sound coming from a mouth pressed against the door, said, 'Who is't?'

'My name is Kit Marlowe,' the poet said, trying to sound friendly. 'I think I may have lost my way. Can you tell me where I am?'

There was a storm of whispering from the other side of the door and then a voice, elderly and female from the sound of it, called out. 'If'n you be Kit, us don't want ee here. Begone, back to where you be from.'

'Marlowe is my name,' he said, beginning to get a little testy. After all, to get back to where he was from was just what he wanted to do. 'Marlowe. Christopher Marlowe. The playwright.' He was about to add that he was a friend of George Carey but that might have earned him a pitchfork through his throat.

There was shuffling from the other side of the door and the

sound of someone falling heavily. Then the ancient female spoke again. 'You did say your name was Kit?'

'That's what some call me, yes.'

'Ar, your dark master.'

'I have no master . . . wait a minute.' It was all coming back to him now. He had not been in touch with Reginald Scot for a while but he wished he had him here now. What that man didn't know about witchcraft was not worth knowing. And he had talked of a familiar, what was the creature's name . . .? 'Are you thinking of Kit with the Canstick, by any chance? Mother,' he added, for good measure.

The answer was a shriek.

'I am not . . .' Marlowe leant his head against the eaves above the door and cursed volubly under his breath. 'Goodnight to the house,' he sighed. 'I will ask directions elsewhere.'

As he was turning his horse back to the road, the door flew open and a clod of something he hoped was earth flew past his ear, spraying wetness as it went.

'Get hence, foul fiend!' a cracked voice screamed. 'Get hence, back to the pit of . . .' A racking cough took the rest of the diatribe and the crone hobbled back into the ramshackle house, muttering between hacks.

'Yes, yes,' Marlowe said to himself. 'Whatever you say, you mad old bat.' He pressed his heels into the horse's sides and cantered off towards the next light showing in the gloom ahead.

This time he dismounted and looped the horse's reins over a handy fence. He left Carey's rapier with it, but his dagger was at his back. He walked up to the door and rapped smartly with his knuckles. This time there would be no shilly-shallying about with names. Just directions to Carisbrooke and make it snappy. The door opened a crack and a blast of warmth and a babble of voices came with the narrow beam of light.

'Good evening to you,' he said, in what he hoped was a suitably friendly and yokel-flavoured greeting. 'I was wondering if you could tell me how to get to Carisbrooke Castle from here?'

The door shut and a voice asked a question, to be met with a gale of raucous laughter.

The door creaked open again and the same voice repeated the answer which had proved most popular with the crowd. 'They do say,' there was a spluttering snigger, 'they do say that to get to Carisbrooke Castle, they 'oodn't start from here.' The laughter roared out again. 'Us'd start from up the road aways.'

Marlowe clenched his fist and took a deep breath. 'But always assuming that I was not up the road aways, but had got myself lost here, then how can I get to Carisbrooke Castle?'

The voice gave a cough and a blast of ale came through the door.

'Sorry, sir,' the man said. 'I shouldn't mock them as are lost out in these mazy roads at dead of night. No moon nor glim to light his way. You just goes on down the road . . . you do be come from Brook, do you?'

'I . . . think so. I came from the west.'

'Ar. Well, you carries on down the road aways and you come to an inn.'

'Isn't this an inn?' Marlowe asked. It had all the ingredients: heat, light, loud men and the stench of tobacco and ale.

'Lord no, matey. No inn, this.' The speaker closed the door to a touch and spoke over his shoulder. 'The stranger do think this is an inn,' he cried. The laughter this time made the little window to the side of the door rattle in its frame. 'No, sir,' the man recovered himself eventually and carried on. 'The inn be down the road aways. But she be shut. Not much fer drinking, down here, we b'ain't. Sir?' A grizzled head stuck out from the door and looked both ways. 'Sir?'

But Christopher Marlowe had gone, up the road aways.

The inn appeared to be closed. Not just for tonight, but forever if the smashed windows and board roughly nailed across the door was anything to judge by. But there was a road, heading inland just alongside one wall and so Marlowe took it, as the only option. He had gauged as well as he could how far he had come and he thought he was probably more or less due south of Newport, so as long as he kept going that way, he should soon see something he recognized. The road down here was little more than a track but his horse was a sure-footed creature and he left it to its own devices. A sea mist was curling up from the beach, its stealthy tendrils twisting

round the horse's hooves and swirling in little spirals as it
stepped carefully along the rutted road. Marlowe looked to
his left and saw a gate standing open in a rough wall, enclosing
a churchyard. The graves were flat and the land was higher
so he urged the horse through the gate. Up higher he would
be free of the mist and also he might be able to see more
lights ahead. Although dwellings had not served him well so
far, if he went from hamlet to hamlet, at least he would not
be riding off into the wilds or, worse, off a cliff.

The horse dug its hooves into the moss inside the gate and
turned its head, desperately trying to get back to the rough
roadway.

Marlowe kicked the black in the ribs and urged him on.
'Come on,' he said. 'They're all dead here. Safer than the
people we've met so far on this ride, wouldn't you say? On,
on.' And he pressed with his knees again and dug in his heels.
The black stepped forward gingerly as if every step was agony,
rolling his eyes, his ears back flat to his head. Marlowe bent
over the horse's neck, patting and stroking him, murmuring
in his ear to encourage him on. They took the broad path
round the church, to reach what Marlowe was sure was higher
ground to the north, and came out on a flat area, dotted with
table tombs. Marlowe had never seen a churchyard quite like
it. Either only rich people died here, or the poor were buried
elsewhere. There were no standing memorials or even any flat
to the ground. All around, spread randomly over the space,
were once splendid tombs, white in the starlight. The mist was
only a ground covering here, lapping at the edges of the slabs
of stone where they disappeared into the rabbit-cropped grass.

With his back to the dark flint-pocked wall of the church,
Marlowe looked north and could see a few faint lights. So far
so good. He pulled on the rein to turn his horse's head, but
the animal was now completely spooked and wouldn't move
an inch. The playwright patted the animal's neck and eventually he felt the tight muscles begin to soften and the horse
began its turn. Then it was Marlowe's turn to be transfixed.
Right in front of him, over an empty sward, the top of one of
the tombs was very slowly turning. The noise was only slight
but it chilled his blood. It was the creak of stone on stone, as

the fragments of shell embedded in each piece scratched and ground at each other. It was the cold sound of night, the chink of spade on grit as the gravedigger did his lonely work. The horse gave a nervous whicker and the stone stopped turning for a moment, as if the ghoul beneath was wary of warm-blooded creatures breathing above its head. Then, when no other sound came, the relentless slide of the tomb top carried on. Slowly, slowly, like a glacier calving in Greenland in the Ice Sea at the top of the world, the slab slid on until it finally toppled to the ground at one end, biting into the turf. Marlowe let out his breath in a long silent exhalation and then waited, with empty lungs, for what was to follow.

He had just time to see a cadaverous hand grip the edge of the tomb when the horse, its nerves finally broken, sprang from the shadow of the church and careered down the slope, taking the churchyard wall in one bound. Horse and rider had passed the next two hamlets before either of them dared stop. Marlowe's heart had stopped thumping by the time they reached the plain below the castle and he could see the torches on the battlements. By the time they clattered in under the gatehouse, even the cold sweat had dried on his brow and no one would have known he had seen the dead rise that night.

The house was asleep when Kit Marlowe crept up to his bedchamber, his boots tucked under his arm and a hand outstretched to feel his way. He had forgotten how dark the countryside could be, away from the bustling streets with the torches on busy corners and stalls selling every conceivable edible thing and some it was best not to think too carefully about. He reached his door without encountering anyone and slipped inside gratefully. Presumably, the crisis at Nunwell had been averted and Sir George Carey was sleeping the sleep of the just in his room just along the gallery.

The maidservant had been into the room at dusk and pulled the heavy curtains across the windows and the room was totally dark, but Marlowe had been in the mansion for enough nights now to know exactly where the bed was and that was all he wanted. He slipped off his Venetians and his doublet and crawled into the bed from the footboard, sinking against the pillows gratefully. After a moment, he pulled back the covers and put his cold legs down inside the crisp linen sheets. He turned his head and sighed. When he was really rich, when this spying and dodging and watching his back was all over, when he could finally do exactly as he wanted, he would have a crisp new bed every night of the year. He let himself fall asleep.

Just as he was on the edge, about to drop off, he heard a rustle beyond the bed hangings and a low voice say his name.

'Master Marlowe?'

It was so quiet he couldn't begin to identify it, but there was a precedent.

'Mistress Avis?' he said, not bothering to whisper.

'Avis?' There was a click of a tinder and a candle burst into light on the desk in front of the window. It illuminated the cheek and lips of the mistress of Carisbrooke Castle.

'Mistress Carey!' Marlowe said. 'My apologies.' As he spoke he couldn't for the life of him think what he was apologizing for, but it seemed as good a way as any of starting a conversation, in his bedchamber, at the dead of night.

'Avis?' the woman asked again. She had had some surprises in her life, some good, some bad, but none as unexpected as this.

Marlowe sat up in bed and looked across at her. This was becoming a bit of a habit and he couldn't think of a way to stop these women coming into his room willing, nilling. It was their home after all, but even so, surely the humblest guest deserved some privacy. 'You misunderstand me, madam,' he said. 'Mistress Avis . . .'

Bet Carey held up a hand. 'Please, Master Marlowe. I won't pry. I had heard some gossip from my maid but . . . but that is not why I am here.' She blushed, an unusual response from Bet, known as the boldest woman at Elizabeth's court or anywhere else.

Marlowe could tell that sleep was not to be his lot tonight. He gathered his pillows together and leaned back on them, settling down for a long and probably difficult conversation. He looked at his hostess, dressed in a nightgown under a plain stuff wrap. She had a shawl over her head and although the night was chilly for June, it was clearly more for disguise than warmth that she wore it. She leaned forward, keeping her voice low.

'Master Marlowe, I need your help.'

He leaned forward to catch what she was saying. Then he came to a decision. It might prove his undoing, but he could barely hear her. She was whispering but also her voice kept fading as her will deserted her and he would never get the facts this way. He rearranged the pillows again, slid over in the bed and patted the vacated half.

'If you must whisper, Mistress Carey,' he said, 'then please do it in my ear and not to the air. Blow out the candle and come and sit with me here.' He patted the coverlet encouragingly. 'Look. I will stay under the covers. You can stay above them. All will be quite proper, I can assure you.'

To her surprise, Bet Carey took no offence. It was not often men took pains to observe the niceties and she found she liked it. She looked across at the bed. The man who sat there, patting the empty space beside him, was probably the most handsome man who had ever made such a gesture. His hair was curling round his face from the damp night air, his eyes were large and dark, his mouth carved like a cherub's. There was danger there but she somehow knew it was not anything she need fear. Making her mind up, she blew out the candle and in two strides was at the bedside. She hopped up with the grace of long practice and curled up against the pillows, her knees to one side. Marlowe could feel the warmth of her and her breath stirred his hair.

'That's better,' she whispered. 'I can talk more freely in the dark.'

'The dark makes many things easier,' Marlowe agreed. 'Now tell me, why are you here?'

'I am frightened, Master Marlowe,' she said quietly. 'I am afraid of . . . you will misunderstand me. I should not have come.' She started to get off the bed.

'You have come so far,' he whispered. 'Don't go now. I promise I will jump to no conclusions.'

She settled back and took a deep breath. 'I am afraid of my husband, Master Marlowe.'

Marlowe was surprised. Sir George Carey was a man of sudden enthusiasms and his decisions were not always the wisest; he may even be a traitor, but he had not seen that side of him. 'Does he beat you?' he asked.

'No, no, of course not. He wouldn't raise a hand to me. No, I am afraid he is . . . there is no way of putting this so that it sounds like sense, Master Marlowe. I am afraid he is killing people.'

'Anyone in particular?' As he said it, Marlowe knew it sounded trite. He would certainly not put that line in the mouth of anyone on stage. And yet there was no other way of putting it. As Captain of the Wight, he knew perfectly well that George Carey killed people. He did it with the full force of the law at his back as the Island's chief magistrate.

She was silent and in the dark Marlowe sensed she bowed her head. Her voice when it came was as soft as a breath. 'Men with whom . . . men who have . . . men with whom I have lain in adultery.'

Marlowe was surprised at her mealy mouthed choice of words. He had decided that Bet was Rabelaisian to her core. Perhaps she thought that he was not worldly enough to bear more earthy words. Perhaps she thought he was a Papist priest; he had posed as one before. He contented himself with a querying grunt.

'I do not know whether you have heard the rumours, Master Marlowe, but I fear I am notorious. I am a woman who needs . . . affection. More affection than my husband has had at his disposal for some while. I thought he knew and had no complaints. It is not as though I have ever refused him. Not even when I have spent my day fornicating around the town. But . . . you don't need to know my wicked ways. Only what I fear my husband may be doing. To the men I . . .'

'Have lain with in adultery.' Marlowe could not keep the smile out of his voice.

'Exactly so. I see we understand each other, Master Marlowe.'

'Words can say what we want them to, Mistress Carey. Let your phrase stand.'

'I am discreet, I assure you. I never, for example, would

ever lie with a man under this roof. Even if the assignation is made here, I always . . .'

'Go outside, down Hollow Lane, for example.'

'How did you know about that?' She drew back in surprise.

'I had the misfortune to meet with Sir Robert Dillington at the militia camp the other day. That man can impart more gossip in an hour than most men can in a lifetime. It seems to be a favourite story of his; the observance of one of the castle maids, as I understand it.'

'Does he say it is me that the maid saw?'

'No, simply that some cries and shrieks have earthly explanations. I presume it was Walter Hunnybun who was having the pleasure of your adultery on that occasion.' It wasn't a question. Marlowe had already guessed at it when Dillington was boring his way around the Militia camp.

She gave a low chuckle, remembering. 'Yes, indeed, Walter. Poor Walter.'

'That does surprise me a little, Mistress Carey,' Marlowe pointed out. 'Farmer Hunnybun was not . . .'

'Walter Hunnybun was as rough as a badger's arse, if you will excuse the language,' she whispered. 'But he was inexhaustible. He was standing ready at any hour of the day or night and if I felt lonely, I only need go across a field or two and I could be in his bed, in a hedgerow or up against a wall, depending on my fancy, within minutes.' She sighed. 'I shall miss Walter.'

Marlowe's mind was clicking like an automaton. 'So Matthew Compton was another of your inamorata, if I may put it so baldly.'

'Scarcely baldly, Master Marlowe, but I thank you for your politeness. Yes, indeed. Matthew Compton had caught my eye. He was very well set up, you know, for a lawyer. He had . . . well, you don't need to know that. But you may have noticed that he and Master Hunnybun have something else in common, besides my company in their beds.'

'They are both dead.'

She let out a long breath. 'Correct, Master Marlowe. Indeed they are.'

'That doesn't mean much, Mistress Carey, in these uncertain times. Men die every day.'

'They are not the first,' she breathed.

'Oh?' Marlowe had not been on the Island long, but he sensed that Bet Carey had been warming the beds of the townsmen for a while since.

'In the past year, four men of the town have been found dead. That is not counting Walter and Matthew. Three of the dead men were . . .'

'Yes.' It seemed fair to take that as read.

'The fourth one I had considered, but I had not had need of him as yet. He only had one eye and I found it a little off-putting.'

'So, you have concluded that your husband is making away with these men. Do you have any proof?'

'Proof?' Her voice rose and she instantly regretted it. If Sir George Carey really was watching her every move, she would put Kit Marlowe in mortal danger if she let this assignation be found out. 'Proof, Master Marlowe?' she whispered. 'Even you must see that five men dead in the last year, all from around the town and all of them partners in my crime of adultery is beyond any coincidence.'

'I agree.' Marlowe nodded in the dark, rustling the pillows. 'That isn't what I mean by proof. I mean, was your husband near the men when they died? Has he ever spoken to you, a single word, to let you know that he is aware of your behaviour? Has he—?'

'I must stop you there, Master Marlowe. Your first question is easily answered. My husband would not need to be near anyone for them to die by his hand. He only has to say the word and anyone he wanted dead would be dead. It is as simple as that. As for speaking to me about it – well, we don't speak much. Even if we did, I think he would keep his counsel on this. It may be that he gains pleasure from doing it.' She fell silent for a moment. 'Though I don't think he is a cruel man.'

Marlowe didn't think so either. 'How did the other men die?' he asked.

'Throttled,' she said with a sob. 'A horrible way to die. And no attempt to hide the bodies. They were all just . . . left there. For anyone to find. It was very cruel.'

'Hunnybun and Compton were hidden,' he pointed out.

'A blocked drain is dealt with in hours,' she said. 'I can tell you are not a country boy, Master Marlowe. A freshly dug grave is also not much of a hiding place. It is bound to be discovered when the funeral is held, if not before.'

'A fair point,' Marlowe said, but his mind was elsewhere. Could it be that Bet Carey was seeing a link where there was none? Or rather, where there was a link but of another kind altogether? 'Mistress Carey, these five, are they the only ones?'

'The only ones?' she hissed. 'They have nothing else in common. One was a . . . I'm not sure what they are called. Sold oats and things like that.'

'A grocer?'

'No . . . corn chandler, that's it. One kept an inn and the other was a draper. Walter Hunnybun was a farmer of course and you know that Matthew Compton was a lawyer. Five completely unrelated lives. And five is enough for any woman to bear, surely?'

'I am not belittling your pain,' Marlowe said politely. 'I mean, have any of your other . . . men . . . died or gone missing?'

'Not died,' she said. 'Some may be missing, who knows? When it is over it is over, if you follow me. I don't mix socially with most of these men.'

Marlowe made a deprecatory noise in his throat.

'They may be missing. Or they may just be away. Some were merchants, you see. Some were of private means. These men tend to come and go. The Island climate doesn't suit everyone.'

Certainly not Hunnybun and Compton, Marlowe thought. It had proved fatal for them.

'I don't tend to involve my neighbours.'

'Except Hunnybun,' Marlowe couldn't help adding.

'Perhaps I should have said, my equals.'

'Ah.'

'Although . . .'

'There is an exception to every rule, Mistress Carey,' he said.

'Mine is Henry Meux,' she said hurriedly.

'Mistress Cecily's husband?'

'Yes. I do feel very badly about that.' To Marlowe's surprise, the woman did sound genuinely unhappy.

'Have you and Captain Meux been . . . um . . . for long?'

'Yes,' she said shortly. 'Since before any of us married. He is, if there is such a thing, the love of my life, and I am his. But our marriage was not what our parents wanted, so . . . you understand, I am sure.'

'Ah.' Marlowe suddenly realized the reason for this nocturnal visit. 'So you are worried about the health and well-being of Henry Meux. Not the myriad other men who could be horribly throttled.'

She stifled a sob. 'If you must put it that way, yes. But I do love them all, Master Marlowe. Just a little. In my own way.'

Marlowe shuffled to get a little more comfortable and give himself time to think. He was still not sure that Bet Carey was the link between these deaths. It had occurred to him that Walter Hunnybun's land lay in the path of Carey's guessed-at invasion, and that Matthew Compton was a lawyer, with many connections in London. What was such a man doing in the Wight when his business was elsewhere? He turned to the mistress of Carisbrooke. 'Could you make me a list? Of your . . .'

Her hand came up across his mouth. 'I can, Master Marlowe. Lie there and sleep. I will do it now. Do you have ink? Parchment?'

He moved her hand away and whispered, in some dudgeon, 'I *am* a playwright, Mistress. Ink and quill are never far away. Please – use my desk. I will find a way to protect your Henry, if I can.'

She leaned over and took his chin gently in her hand. Years of practice meant that she knew exactly the position of all his body parts, even in the enveloping dark. She put her mouth on his and kissed him, gently but long and lingering, tasting the cold salt from his ride, the sweet flavour of his skin. 'I wish that things were different, Master Marlowe,' she murmured.

He didn't answer, but drew a gentle finger down the side

of her face. 'Make your list, Mistress,' he said. 'And let me doze awhile.'

She slipped off the bed and as he turned the corner into sleep he heard the snick of the tinder and the scratch of her quill.

It was dawn when Lady Elizabeth Carey let herself quietly out of Christopher Marlowe's chamber, nearly knocking over Ester, scurrying along the corridor with a ewer of hot water.

'Who is that for?' her mistress asked, in a peremptory tone.

'Sir George,' the girl replied, holding it up in a world-weary gesture.

Elizabeth Carey dipped an aristocratic finger in the water. 'This is almost cold, you stupid girl. Sir George likes his water really hot. Get rid of it.'

Ester sighed. 'Shall I give it to Master Marlowe, Mistress?' she asked.

'Yes, that is a good plan. I understand he was up late and will probably feel better for a wash this morning. Good girl.' And with that, the lady of the house swept away.

Ester had the kitchen all agog.

'And she came out of his room, bold as brass. So she says, "Take it in to Master Marlowe," she says. "We've been at it all night like a couple of weasels. He could do with giving his tackle a good wash." And so I goes in and there he lays, flat out on his back and as naked as a jay.'

The other maids all leaned in, so as not to miss a word.

'He's got an enormous—'

Just as she approached her denouement, the door to the kitchen was flung back and Avis Carey stood there. 'Do you girls have no work to do?' she said, smacking Ester round the head by force of habit. 'Have you taken Sir George his water? Not too hot now. And Lady Carey? Has she been awoken yet? Get on with it, girls. Come along. Must I do everything?'

And she swept out.

Ester turned to the others and mouthed, 'Jealous,' to them,

and scurried off, with a jug of boiling water held gingerly in front of her.

Kit Marlowe, unaware of how his notoriety had gone up one more notch in the kitchen, woke late. Of Bet Carey there was no sign, just a lingering scent of civet on his pillow. He rolled out of bed and faced the day. The curtains had been drawn back and inexplicably there was a ewer of tepid water on the press. On the desk, there was a piece of parchment, with a row of names down one side, their social standing opposite each one. Bet had been nothing if not thorough. He picked it up and scanned it; even after his short sojourn on the Island, he recognized a few and one or two of them made him raise an eyebrow. Checking these men for their political affiliations and other important points might cost him a few flagons of ale but it should be quite short work. He looked down at the desk and saw another piece of parchment, covered in names, just like the one in his hand. And beneath that another.

He sat down and with a sigh pulled a clean sheet towards him. He would need to rewrite this list, in order of priority, or his hair would be grey before he finished his investigations. And, if he knew his Lady Carey, there would be more names added before the week was out. He headed the sheet 'Merchants'. He had to begin somewhere and this seemed as good a point as any.

ELEVEN

The wind moaned in the Sierra de Guadarrama and rattled the shutters of the Escorial. Little Gonzalillo had been worried for weeks. The king, his lord and master, had talked of nothing throughout that time but the Enterprise of England. The man was dying of overwork and not all Gonzalillo's pratfalls and *bon mots* could shake him out of it. Documents came in from the King's ministers in Madrid by the wagonload and the whole business was making him walk funny.

That night, the candles fluttered and leapt, flashing bright on the gilt Madonna and Child in the Chapel Royal. It was past two of the clock on a wild, wet night. Even the weather stood on its head. By this time, on the first of July, the King's ministers were usually hauling off their ruffs at council meetings and urging their people to fan them with greater vigour. As it was, Felipe el Prudente sat in his closet with his fur stole about his neck, poring over the parchment littered on the table in front of him. To Gonzalillo it looked as if the man had not moved for three months. His face was like a fungus, leprous white and grey, and it was difficult to tell where his beard ended and his skin began.

He looked up at the jester's entrance. The faithful little man was bowing before him, as always. The king had no doubt that all his subjects loved him; the question was, did his God?

'I've worn my clerks out today,' Philip croaked. He had not spoken for an hour or two and his throat was dry. 'Is your hand steady, pequeño?'

Gonzalillo somersaulted neatly, the bells on his knees ringing for good effect and he balanced for a while on his left hand while waving the right in the air. That was good – Felipe was smiling at last. That *was* a good sign.

'Take a letter, then,' the King said and waited while the jester heaped pillows on to a chair and found clean parchment. Philip cleared his throat and reached for his watered claret, taking a careful sip. 'Duke and Cousin,' he began, listening to Gonzalillo's quill scratching as he spoke. 'I have received the letter written in your own hand. From what I know of you, I believe that your bringing all these matters to my attention arises solely from your zeal to serve me and a desire to succeed in your command. The certainty that this is so prompts me to be franker with you than I should be with another . . .'

He paused to make sure that Gonzalillo was still with him. Now he spoke faster, leaving the little jester floundering in his wake. England had no allies. Their army was not an army at all but a rabble of senile serving men and beardless boys. With the wind on their side, the Armada could be in the Channel within the week. If the Captain-General of the Ocean Sea sat on his arse in La Coruña, he was a target for El Draque. And, with the Armada pinned in harbour, the English could go on raiding silver fleets and colonies to their hearts' content.

When Gonzalillo looked up, almost breathless and with an aching wrist, Philip said, 'I have dedicated this enterprise to God. Get on, then, and do your part.'

The dwarf finished with a flourish, blotted his work and passed it to the King for his signature. He would affix the seal himself later.

'And still,' Philip said, pausing with the quill in his hand, 'no news from the Island of Wight.'

Once a week, Sir George Carey dined alone with his sister, Avis. Neither of them could remember when this little tradition had started, but it seemed to Avis that her little brother had still been in his hanging sleeves when it had begun and she had wiped his nose and spooned in the veal pasty she knew he loved. The little mother had grown large now but actual motherhood had eluded her, like so much else in her sad and lonely life.

'Here's to Master Marlowe's Masque.' She raised a goblet that shone in the candlelight.

'Marlowe's Masque.' Carey clinked his cup with hers. 'You're enjoying all this, aren't you?' He had not seen Avis

so happy in a long time. Her eyes sparkled and she had a
spring in her heavy step.

'Thomas Sledd is such a sweet boy.' She beamed. 'Reminds
me of you not so long ago.'

'Did I ever have such disgusting table manners?' He laughed.

'You know what I mean.' She flicked him with her napkin.
'He is honest and good and kind. Actually, Georgie, I wanted
to talk to you about that.'

'What? Sledd's honesty?'

'Sledd's chin. You know he was set upon by ruffians, don't
you?'

'I'd heard something of that.' Carey clicked his fingers and
a lackey refilled his cup with wine. 'Mead Hole, I understand.
That runagate Skirrow took him there.'

'Mead Hole.' Avis held out her cup for more wine too.
'Thank you, Benjamin. They're pirates, Georgie, not to put
too fine a point on it. The riff-raff of Europe washed up on
our beaches. You know that "Mead Hole goods" are synony-
mous with stolen contraband, don't you? It's the talk of
Southampton, apparently.'

'And has been for a while, my dear. When Edmund de
Horsey sat in this chair, he was actually taking a cut from the
bastards. I'm sorry, my dear.' He sketched a bow at his sister.
'Please excuse my language.'

'Degenerate!' Avis scowled as Benjamin retreated dutifully
into the shadows and George Carey's heart missed a beat until
he realized she did not mean him. 'I'm astonished the Church
allowed him burial in St Thomas's.' She reached forward,
squeezing her brother's hand. 'Can't you *do* anything, Georgie?'
she wheedled. 'I'm not a woman to get mad, as you know,
but I do like to get even. For young Thomas's sake.'

'There is a rumour,' Carey said, patting her hand in turn,
'that Christopher Marlowe has already done something on that
score.'

Avis gave a delicious shudder. 'I'd heard that too,' she said.
'He's a dangerous man, Master Marlowe, but I fear nothing
will get to the bottom of our piracy problem short of putting
Mead Hole out of business.'

Carey looked at the woman who had been a mother to him

all his life. He nodded, smiled and threw down his napkin. 'Do you know, Avis,' he said, 'you are absolutely right. I've been turning a blind eye for too long. I'll take the Militia tomorrow – the Essex boys, not the locals. Too many vested interests there, I shouldn't wonder. We'll hit them at first light. Burn the bastards out.'

'Oh, George.' Avis suddenly had a pang of conscience and clutched her stomacher. 'I didn't mean now, right away . . .'

'No, no.' Carey took up his cup. 'No time like the present. Strike while the iron is hot. Benjamin.' He turned in his chair to where the lackey should be standing in the shadows. 'Benjamin? Where is that blasted boy with the wine?'

The blasted boy had left the chamber. He had passed the bottle and the tray to a fellow servant and had run helter-skelter down the hill towards the ford. He had urgent business at the Quay.

The army of Essex was marching steadily over the open ground towards the sea. At their head, riding a tall grey that morning, Sir George Carey looked an imposing sight, his scarlet plume fastened to the blue-gilt burgonet that nodded under the three banners – the scimitars of Essex, the cross of St George and Carey's own roses on their black and white field. There were no shouts of command, no fifes and drums, just the steady tramp of two hundred determined men, their pikes challenging the grey sky of dawn, their calivers at the slope on their shoulders.

Old Arnold Osborne in his manor house on the hill was woken by it nevertheless. His dogs were barking and his horses were whinnying and kicking in their stables. The grounds of his estate were shaking with the solid tramp of four hundred boots flattening his rye and crashing through his orchard. Bloody George Carey! On his endless manoeuvres again, playing his silly bloody war games. Arnold Osborne got back into bed and pulled the covers over his head. Then he sat bolt upright. War games, be buggered! That blasted man was marching on Mead Hole, two and a half per cent of which belonged to him for turning a blind eye all these years. He dived under the covers again, but this time for a completely different reason.

George Carey scanned his lines to left and right. He was quietly impressed. Two weeks ago he had despaired of ever welding an efficient fighting force out of this lot, but now they had a certain look about them. He had placed the best armoured pikemen in the front two ranks with the calivers behind them. He had no cavalry but he was not marching to the field to face the Duke of Parma's men; he was just going to root out a rat's nest that had outstayed its welcome on his Island.

As they neared the beach, a wall of sea mist rose up before them, sudden and impenetrable. The tree tops on Arnold Osborne's estate had no trunks. Mead Hole with its ramshackle huts had vanished. Carey felt the water droplets on his face at the same time as the Essex men faltered. The pikes wobbled; men missed their step.

'Drums!' he roared in an attempt to keep them in step. The thud stuttered at first, then all six drummers were smashing the goatskin for all their worth, the damp giving the sound a dull, deep resonance, and the line found its rhythm again. Carey drew his sword with a flourish, making a mental note to get his second-best one back from Christopher Marlowe at some point. He did not notice – no one did – the solitary rider racing to the right, to outflank the Militia and find the road to Newport.

'It's a little fog!' Carey yelled at the top of his lungs. 'It's nothing. You boys must have seen this before. Your marshes are full of the stuff. Remember, when you come through it and out the other side, there'll be warm work to do. There's a few angels in it for the man who brings me the most prisoners. Charge your pikes!'

There was a roar from the Militia as the murderous weapons came up to the level. The first rank disappeared into the mist, the second hard on their heels. George Carey was first in the fray. He could just about make out the probing pikes on each side of his prancing horse and he kept the animal in check. He actually had no idea what to expect down on those sands. On the face of it, the traders at Mead Hole were just that, honest merchants making a groat the best way they could. Behind that face, though, were cut-throats and killers, the flotsam of all the seas of the world, with murder in their hearts.

Suddenly, Carey and the front rank were through the mist, as though it had been the smoke of a broadside from one of the Lord Admiral's ships of the line. To each side of them, the shacks of Mead Hole stood abandoned and forlorn, like a town of ghosts in the mist. The pikes came down one by one and the guttural battle cries died in a hundred throats. There was jostling and disbelief as the rear ranks came on and the clash of iron as men and their weapons bumped into each other.

But no one was looking at the emptiness of the bay and the derelict shacks and tattered stalls. They were looking at a handful of Spaniards, their weapons thrown to the sand, kneeling in a circle with their hands clasped in prayer.

For a while, no one moved. Then George Carey spurred his horse forward. 'Who speaks for you?' he asked. There was silence, then one of the men got up from his knees and stood before the governor, head bowed.

'You speak English?' Carey snapped, sheathing his sword.

'Sir. Excellence. A little.'

'I am Sir George Carey,' the governor told them. 'Captain of the Wight. Who are you?'

'I am José de Medrano, caballero of Spain.'

Carey looked the man up and down. He knew the type well; England was full of this man's counterpart. Sons of noble houses too low in the pecking order; men who must chance their sword arm if they were to make their way in the world. But this one could not have been much above eighteen; any of the governor's Militia could have him for breakfast.

'How did you get here?' Carey asked.

Medrano half turned and waved behind him. 'My ship,' he said. '*El Comendador.*'

As if on cue, the sea mist rolled back to reveal, not many yards from the shore, a fast-rigged pinnace riding at anchor, its sails furled and its guns at rest. It was small as warships went, the type used for fast communication between the galleons and between the galleons and the shore. Carey counted the portholes – *El Comendador* could fire a broadside of ten heavy-shotted, short-barrelled guns. The vessel was twice the size of John Vaughan's *Bowe* and could blast it out of the water with ease.

'*El Comendador*?' Carey repeated. 'That means commander in our language, does it not? Where are the rest of you?' he asked sharply. 'Where is the Armada?'

The caballero stood to his full height, feeling rather ashamed now at having thrown his sword away. 'Coming,' he said proudly. 'They are all coming. And God is sailing with us.'

Carey snorted and there were sniggers from the Militia. 'Yes, yes,' the governor said. 'Very colourful. Where are your ships *exactly* and what are you doing here?'

'José de Medrano,' the man repeated. 'Capitan *El Comendador*.'

Carey nodded. 'So that's how it's going to be. Sergeant Wilson!' The man stepped forward. 'You were handy when we removed the lawyer. Prove your worth now and tie this rabble together. This one,' he prodded the young caballero with his boot, 'is to be tied behind my horse and they are all to be taken to the Bridewell at Newport. The warden will complain but you will give him this –' he unhooked his chain of office from around his neck – 'and if he still complains you will be so good as to run him through. Am I clear?'

'Perfectly, sir,' Wilson said. He had already set fire to a lawyer; ramming his halberd through the ribs of a gaoler should not be difficult.

'Gentlemen.' Carey wheeled his horse to face his Militia. 'I want twenty of you who know one end of a ship from another. The rest of you will march back to Newport under the sergeant here. Those men,' he waved at the Spaniards, 'are prisoners of war. Any man who abuses them will have to answer to me. But before you go.' He looked around at the shacks and the debris thrown on to the beach, as though a city had suddenly decamped during the night. 'I want this place burned to the ground.'

Christopher Marlowe was wandering around the mansion in mounting confusion. There seemed to be very few people about. Usually at this time in the morning it was hard to hear yourself think for all of the yelling and clashing of metal from the Militia camp just outside the walls, but today it was silent. An odd drift of smoke still curled lazily up from their cooking fires, but as he squinted into the weak sun he could see only a few women moving desultorily about. Tom Sledd was outside still working on the stage for the Masque. It was almost finished now and rehearsals, such as they were, could begin within the week, or so he said. He was to start auditioning singers and musicians soon and Marlowe made a mental note to be elsewhere, especially when the hautboys were doing their stuff. They really set his teeth on edge. But apart from Tom and the odd servant, the mansion seemed deserted.

He wandered outside and was about to call to Tom, who was moodily kicking a flat depicting a formal garden, with exaggerated perspective disappearing in an impossible dot on the fake horizon, and then saw Martin Carey scurrying across the courtyard with a ledger under his arm and a rather haunted expression on his face.

'Martin!' Marlowe called and the comptroller jumped as though shot.

'Oh, I'm sorry, Master Marlowe,' he said. 'I didn't see you there. I must get these books to balance, if I can. There seems to be some discrepancy . . .'

'Never mind a few missing angels,' Marlowe said. 'Where are all the people? The Militia? Sir George?'

'I believe they have gone to attack Mead Hole,' Martin said as though it were the most natural thing in the world.

'What?' Marlowe was appalled. 'It will be a bloodbath, surely?'

'Sir George is certainly rather annoyed,' the man replied. 'I hear that Avis told him last night of the atrocities they wrought on young Thomas over there and for him it was the last straw. He mustered the Militia and off they went, at dawn.'

'I didn't hear them,' Marlowe muttered.

'They were enjoined by Sir George to be quiet, or so I understand.' Martin Carey was keeping a weather eye out for Avis Carey, who was reputed to be on the warpath this morning, crazed with worry for Georgie.

Tom Sledd had ambled over and now put in his groatsworth.

'One of the carpenters sent word a few moments ago,' he said. 'He heard from his wife's brother's neighbour's lad that the Militia went marching off in fine fettle in the early hours and that some of them have been seen on the path through Quarrels Copse, wherever that might be, making their way back to Newport.'

'Casualties?' Marlowe asked.

'Couldn't tell, apparently,' Sledd said, fingering his chin carefully. 'I would imagine so, wouldn't you?'

Marlowe thought fast. 'Tom, stay here. Martin, come with me. We must get to John Vaughan as fast as we can. If there is anyone who can stop this madness, it is him.'

Martin Carey hefted the ledger in his arms. 'I must make . . .'

'The books balance. I know,' Marlowe said, grabbing it from him and throwing it at Tom Sledd. 'But sometimes, believe it or not, Master Martin, there are things more valuable than money.'

And, with incomprehension at the concept written all over his face, Martin allowed himself to be dragged off to the stables.

Tom juggled briefly with the heavy book, tapping the pages straight, and carried it up the seventy-one steps to the keep, counting and cursing all the way, to Martin's inky eyrie against the battlements.

Marlowe and Martin Carey said little on their canter down the hill. The comptroller pulled his horse back all the time, making it slip and slide. Marlowe, giving his its head, had a much less painful ride and ended up at the quay a few minutes before the other animal even made an appearance. It was not hard for the money man to find the poet; he could hear him shouting several streets away.

When he actually came within sight of him, Marlowe had Page's manservant up against a wall, the man's collar twisted in his fist, and he was shouting in his face. 'I said, where is he? Where is John Vaughan?'

The servant, turning an unattractive shade of blue, waved his hands and gurgled incoherently.

Master Martin touched Marlowe's arm. 'Let him go,' he said. 'You'll throttle him if you are not careful.'

Marlowe gave the man a contemptuous look but let go of
the servant's collar and he collapsed on the floor, coughing
and holding his throat. 'I was merely trying to find out what
has happened to your uncle,' he pointed out.

'Many times removed.' Carey was a stickler for facts, no
matter how fraught the situation.

Marlowe looked down and prodded the prone servant with his
toe. 'So, do you have anything to tell me about the whereabouts
of Master Vaughan?' he asked again, in softer tones.

The man still shook his head. Marlowe was frightening, but
he would go away, eventually. Vaughan was frightening too,
but there was the added risk of being turned out in the street
with no character if he were to become annoyed. And that,
especially if you allowed for the broken knees, would be much
worse.

Marlowe turned and slammed out of the house. 'He isn't
on the *Bowe* and he isn't in the house. Where *is* the man?'

'Mead Hole?' The comptroller thought that that had already
been established.

'No, no,' Marlowe muttered. 'Vaughan doesn't do his own
dirty work. Perhaps we ought to look for him at the opposite
end of the Island from Mead Hole. That's where he will be.'

'Chale, then,' Martin said. His geography was as precise as
his figuring.

'That may have to be our next journey,' Marlowe said
reluctantly. Neither he nor his horse particularly wanted to
repeat the experience of the Back of the Wight. He stood on
the quay, looking down into the water under the stern of the
Bowe. 'What now, then, Master Martin?'

'I think I will get back to the castle, Kit, if you don't mind.
Get on with my books.'

Marlowe looked around and saw nothing but the light on
the water and the scutter of a rat in a drain channel. Like the
castle, the quay seemed almost deserted. Where had everyone
gone? The rat plopped over the side, swam to the other side
of the waterway and climbed up a bundle of rags, which
swayed with the faint movement of the tide. The rat was
making heavy weather of it, pausing every few inches and
sniffing, then raising its nose to the wind. Marlowe was

becoming an expert on rat behaviour, living in London, and somehow this one just didn't look right. He focused more carefully on the bundle of rags and it slowly resolved into two legs in canvas breeches and below them, under the water, a wide-sleeved jacket of the same material. The skin showed livid white and gleaming where the jacket was turning itself slowly inside out, stopped by the arms which were tied behind the back.

He hit Martin on the arm and pointed. 'Look. A man, hanging from that groyne. How do I get across to the other side? Look, man. Over there!'

Martin focused his short-sighted, bookkeeper's eyes across the narrow inlet and gasped. 'Oh, God,' he said, raising a hand to his breast. 'Oh, God, Kit! There's a man over there, drowned.' And he leaned over and vomited over the side into the water.

'That's very helpful, Martin, thank you,' Marlowe said, running down the quayside towards the town. 'Hey, you men over there!' He hailed three sailors propping up a bollard on the opposite bank. 'Dead man in the water! Down there!' He pointed back the way he had come.

One of the sailors turned to the others. 'Wass'ee say?' he asked.

'Dead man. In the water. Down there,' Marlowe roared.

The three stood upright, all together, like marionettes on the same string.

'Dead man?' yelled one. 'Why didn'ee say so?' And they took off at a run, matching Marlowe as he headed back towards the *Bowe*, still pointing.

The sailors were not wanting in application once they saw what was needed. Two of them hauled on the dead man's legs, struggling against the weight of his body and the suck of the tide. The third jumped into a rowing boat moored nearby and, untying with a deft motion of one hand, rowed across ferryman style, using one oar off the back, and was across the narrow river within minutes to fetch Marlowe. Martin Carey was leaning against the timbers of the *Bowe*, looking green. As Marlowe got into the ferry, he called to him.

'Go back to the castle,' he said. 'I'll keep trying to find John Vaughan. There's nothing else we can do.'

'Master Vaughan's up in the town,' the sailor volunteered. 'I sin him not an hour since. He'm visiting the shops. T'ain't like him – tis usually the merchants who visit him, if you get my meaning, sir.'

This short exchange had got them across the river and, climbing up a slimy ladder, Marlowe joined the men and the bloated body on the planks of the quay.

The man lay face down, water draining from his hair and clothes and running between the boards and drumming on the timbers below, the ropes undone now from ankles and wrists.

'Do you know who he is?' Marlowe asked the men.

'Ar. He's old man Sculpe, from down Quay Street.' One of the men squinted at Marlowe. 'But you know him, sir. I saw you jumping from young Mary's bedroom winder not so many weeks past, I'm thinking.'

'This is Mary's father? Are you certain? Turn him over.'

One of the sailors put a toe under the man's torso and gave a kick. The body rolled over, one arm flailing out and hitting the echoing boards with a dead crack.

'Ar,' the first speaker said. ''Tis old man Sculpe a'right. 'E must've fallen in at high tide. These planks can be mortal slippy then.'

Marlowe felt someone had to say it. 'His hands and feet were tied. And he had been lowered over the side, surely?'

The three sailors looked at each other and then at Marlowe, shaking their heads. Their spokesman took up his role again. 'No, sir, if we could beg your pardon. We don't see no ropes. And old man Sculpe, 'e be known as a powerful drinker. 'Tis but a miracle he 'aven't fallen in the river long afore this.'

Another of the men leaned forward and said quietly, 'And if you don't mind I saying this, sir, you don't want to be making too much of they ropes. I reckon it weren't just Jem here seed you a-jumping out of Mary's winder.'

Marlowe looked at the men, their weather-beaten faces and pale, far-seeing eyes all turned towards him. A decision had to be made, now or never. He reached into his doublet and brought out his purse. Passing each man a piece of silver, he said, 'My mistake, men. There were no ropes. It was a trick of the light.'

The men smiled between them and at Marlowe. He felt he had been part of justice being seen to be done, even though he wasn't quite sure why. This man had not been on Bet Carey's list and anyway, he would not have thought that even she would fall so far to get some affection. There was one job still to do, even so.

'I will go and tell his daughter,' Marlowe said.

'And we'll fetch a hurdle,' the spokesman said. As Marlowe walked away, the man called after him. 'Least said, soonest mended, sir.'

Marlowe nodded, raised a hand and plunged down the little alleyway that led into Quay Street and Mary Sculpe's house.

'Mother of God!' In moments like these, Captain James Norris found himself reverting to the expletives of his childhood before the Pope became the Antichrist and Philip of Spain wanted to rule the world. He dashed along the battlements of his castle at East Cowes, cursing Winchcliffe again because he still had not cut down that blasted oak tree. The thing was in full leaf now, impeding his view even more, but that was definitely a pinnace curving its way into the mouth of the Medina. More than that, it was a Spanish pinnace.

He turned to the south. There was no beacon, no flame to tell the world that the Armada had come. Yet here it was and from the north, too. Had Southampton fallen? He had heard no guns. Had the bastards raked Portsmouth, sent hellburners into the harbour there? And even now, were Englishmen dying on the beaches to the south of the Island as Medina Sidonia's veterans fought their way ashore?

The others had seen it too; his garrison and his lackeys and everybody was rushing around, clattering up steps, buckling on swords and snatching up halberds, while all the time trying to maintain an air of calm. Stanley had his lads haul the demi-culverin into position, its black muzzle inching out over the ramparts. There was a panic of fuse-lighting, shot-loading. The spongeman rammed the ball into the barrel and the fuseman lit his fuse. The thing sparked and crackled while everybody covered their ears and turned away. The barrel burst into life, a roar of flame from its gaping mouth and the gun bucked and rolled backwards. Choking with the smoke, the gunners grabbed their ropes and held on for dear life in case the demi-culverin rolled off its housing and crashed into the courtyard below.

Norris shielded his eyes against the glare of the sky. A spray of water burst short of the pinnace's bows.

'Shit!' the captain of East Cowes hissed. 'Reload!'

Again, the hauling of the gun into position. The spongeman threw his bucket of water over the barrel, merely warm now but as the shooting went on it would become too hot to handle. The powder was thrown in, black and evil-smelling, and the nine pounds of iron was rolled in after it.

'Damn Richard Turney to Hell!' Norris bellowed. 'Why isn't he firing too? What's the matter with the man? I told him,' he said to his gunners, 'I told Carey that Turney was no bloody good at his job. Now I see him in his true colours – he's in the pay of the bloody King of Spain! Fire!'

The demi-culverin crashed again and this time the pinnace's bowsprit was blown to matchwood, causing the ship to veer sharply as her helmsman hauled on his wheel. A cheer rose up from the ramparts of Norris Castle. This was better. They had found their range now and the next shot would rip a hole in her side that a horse and cart could rattle through.

'For God's sake!' Richard Turney was rushing along his battlements, the telescope that gave him his omniscience thrown to a lackey. 'What the bloody hell is Norris doing? Doesn't he know his flags? That's George Carey out there. He's firing on his own Captain.'

'He's firing on his own Captain!' George Carey fumed on the quarterdeck of *El Comendador*. He looked around at his motley crew. To be fair to the Essex boys, they had done well to bring the ship around the headland, considering there was not a sailor among them, but this was too much. Their faces were white and they were squinting at the dark trees above Norris Castle to see where the shots were coming from. Carey had done all he could. He had struck the Spanish colours and raised his own standard of the white roses.

'Shall we fire on them, sir?' a corporal of Militia asked, seeing this option as one that might keep him alive.

'No, for God's sake,' Carey growled. 'They might be idiots enough to fire on an Englishman, but I won't compound the problem. Anyway, *can* you?'

The corporal shifted uneasily. 'Er . . . I've seen it done,' was the best he could do.

'Yes,' Carey said. 'So have I. I know for a fact the man's only got one cannon on those ramparts. We'll be out of his range in a minute. Shout. All of you, shout.'

'What'll we shout, sir?'

'I'd like it to be "We're going to cut your bollocks off for this, Norris" but it might be misconstrued, what with the wind. God Save the Queen. Shout that – now.'

And twenty-one voices bellowed across the Medina.

'Are they surrendering, sir?' Stanley asked his captain.

'Don't know,' Norris said. 'I can't make out what they're saying. Fire!'

And the third shot sailed out over the water, ripping George Carey's banner to shreds and crashing into the water beyond. And *El Comendador* sailed on into what the Captain of the Wight hoped were safer waters.

The door was leaning ajar when Marlowe found the house and he knocked as he pushed it open. He called out, 'Is anyone here? Mary? Are you here?'

There was no sound from inside the house and he pushed open the door into what he thought he remembered was the kitchen. A fire burned in the grate, a kettle hanging over it starting to sing. If Mary was not there, she hadn't been gone long. He opened the little door in the wall and called up the stairs, but there was not a sound.

He stepped back on to the flags of the kitchen and stepped back into a vice-like embrace, an arm around his neck and a point digging into his kidneys through his doublet. A voice in his ear hissed, 'Don't try and get away. I will skewer you where you stand.'

Marlowe raised his hands and said, equally quietly, 'Let go of me and I won't move.'

'Do you think I am an idiot?' the voice grated. 'Mary!' The voice was loud in his ear. 'Come over here like a good girl and take this gentleman's dagger.'

Out of the corner of his eye, Marlowe saw Mary Sculpe come out from behind a press which did not quite fit the alcove in the corner. It would not be many more days before she would not fit beside it, because the gentle swelling Marlowe had seen when they first met was now frankly visible and she had taken to wearing her apron tied above the bump, with no attempt to hide it.

'Mistress Mary,' Marlowe said, as merrily as he knew how. 'You are blooming, my dear.'

'You know this man?' the voice said in Marlowe's ear.

'Why, Harry,' the girl laughed. 'This is the gentleman I told you about, the one who was looking for you.'

'Who are you?' Hasler asked, his dagger still in the man's back.

'Christopher Marlowe,' the poet told him. 'And I can count among my friends Nicholas Faunt and Sir Francis Walsingham.'

'Marlowe? Dear God!'

The dagger left its place above Marlowe's kidney but the arm was still tight about his throat. 'I have been looking for you. Faunt and Walsingham were getting worried. They thought you might have . . . been hurt.'

'Or gone over to Spain,' Hasler said, releasing his grip and letting Marlowe fall forward.

'Or that, yes.' Marlowe rubbed his throat and turned to his man. The spy was tall and thin, with floppy hair; Marlowe could see how he would be attractive to women. But yet another one not on Bet Carey's extensive list. Perhaps he had turned her down. Marlowe turned to the girl. 'I have some bad news for you, I fear, Mistress Sculpe,' he said formally.

'Oh, if it's just about father being dead, I know that,' she said brightly.

Marlowe blinked. 'But we've only just fished him out of the water, down at the quay.'

'Yes,' she said. 'But we put him there last night, didn't we, Harry? Well, Harry did most of the putting. I can't really do no heavy lifting, just now.' She cupped her growing belly. 'I'm 'aving a babbie.'

Marlowe opened his mouth, closed it, thought and then spoke. 'Congratulations to you both,' he said.

Mary looked at him, confused, and then laughed and nudged Harry Hasler. 'You see what he's done. He thinks you're my babbie's father.'

'Aren't you?' Marlowe said, in some confusion himself.

'No,' Hasler said shortly. 'I am not. But she is coming back with me to . . . Let's just say over in the West Wight. I won't be Faunt's plaything any longer. I have a cottage and a pig and a modest income by way of inducement from John Vaughan – who took me for a Customs man, by the way. Mary can come and keep house for me. The baby will grow up strong on milk and honey . . .'

'Not if all you have is a pig,' Marlowe pointed out. He was no husbandman, but even he knew you didn't usually get milk from a pig, no matter how tame the animal.

'I am speaking in general,' Hasler said impatiently. 'Where was I?'

'Milk and honey,' Marlowe reminded him.

'Yes. The baby will grow up strong on milk and honey and we will all live happily ever after.'

Marlowe looked hard at the man. Had he lost his mind? 'And if the baby's father comes calling?' he asked.

'Then we will call the vicar, with bell, book and candle,' Hasler said. 'The baby's father is dead.'

'Like mine,' Mary chipped in, folding her hands complacently over her stomach. 'Both our fathers is dead. But only one man is dead, if you get my meaning, Master Marlowe?'

Marlowe looked at her. The girl didn't seem to mind that she was an orphan and also carrying her father's child. 'I . . . I'm sorry, Mary,' he said softly. 'I didn't know.'

'No reason why you should do, Master Marlowe,' she said cheerfully.

'If we're being strictly accurate,' Hasler said. 'Mary has lost a father and a grandfather today. It was a fine old family custom, you might say.'

Marlowe knew such things went on in country places, but somehow to meet it in broad daylight and to see the results in this bonny, happy girl was a little disconcerting. He beckoned to Hasler and they walked into the corner. Mary happily turned her attention to the kettle and poured some water on to some gruel in a pot on the side. She stirred it, singing quietly to herself and smoothing her stomach.

'Master Hasler . . .'

'Harry, please. If things had been different, we would have been friends, I think. Colleagues, at least. Sir Francis's golden lads and all that.'

'Harry. You do know she is mad, don't you?'

'As a tree, sadly. Keeping everything in the family will do that after a generation or two. She has been telling me. There hasn't been anyone but an existing blood relation in this family since before Hal was on the throne . . . Hal the Sixth, that is.'

'Did she kill him?'

'She had a damned good try. Last night.'

'Why now? Why not when he started . . . what he started?'

Hasler shrugged. 'I'm not sure. Last straw, perhaps. Her story is a little garbled. From what I could make out, he came past her and stroked her stomach and talked to it. Called it his little maid.'

'I see.'

'I can't tell if she was protecting the baby or was jealous. Either way, she hit him on the head with a skillet. I put the old bastard in the water, tied up in case he was still alive. I couldn't find any signs of life, but you never know. Look, Marlowe, do you really need to talk to her any more? She hasn't got many things of her own, but we were just getting them together to start back to my cottage.'

Marlowe looked over his shoulder to where the girl still stood, stirring and stroking. He made up his mind. 'Go, then. The sailors undid the ropes and hauled the body away on a hurdle. They won't say a word – I would imagine that Master Sculpe won't be missed. But what about you? I understand you are a bit of a one for the ladies. How will you manage, with just a mad girl for company?'

Hasler laughed, a short bark with no humour in it. 'Who told you that, Master Marlowe?'

'I can't remember. It seems to be the accepted rumour of choice.'

'Let it be, then,' Hasler said quietly, laying his hand on Marlowe's sleeve.

'Who sent the letter?' Marlowe asked him.

'Letter?'

'The one in your chest upstairs. I found it.'

Hasler shrugged. He knew such nosiness went with the territory in the Projectioner business. 'I know of no letter.'

Marlowe summoned up his years of learning by rote, of committing passages in Greek and Latin to memory. '"Tonight, my darling one,"' he quoted. '"But be careful. He knows, I am sure of it. I long for the touch of your caress, the press of your lips on mine. My heart aches for you and my loins tremble. Three steps back and three steps fore."'

Hasler looked blank. 'I'm sorry,' he said. 'I've never seen or heard that. I don't know anyone who would write me a letter like that.' He brought his face closer to Marlowe's so the projectioner could feel his breath warm on his cheek. 'My . . . companions are not the kind of lads who are much of a fist with a pen. If you understand me. But,' he added, in unconscious echo of the sailor on the quay, 'Least said, soonest mended. Mary and I will both have to make sacrifices, I think. But it will serve. If you ever get tired of the game yourself, Kit – well, I hope you find happiness.' He smiled sadly and went over to the girl, putting an arm around her shoulder and planting a chaste kiss on her head.

Marlowe watched for a moment, and then saw himself out.

'How can you just sit there?' Pedro de Valdez wanted to know. 'Like frightened children?'

Everybody except the Captain-General of the Ocean Sea was on their feet, screaming and shouting at him. His cousin Diego already had his dagger in his hand.

'Gentlemen! Gentlemen!' the Duke of Medina Sidonia did not

raise his voice often, so when he did, people tended to listen. 'I have not yet heard from His Majesty. It may be we will be going home; that there will be no Enterprise of England after all.'

'You can't believe that, Alonso,' Juan de Recaldé said softly, shaking his head. A moment ago he had been on his feet too, in that little room in the fortress of San Anton overlooking the harbour at La Coruña; on his feet because he was a hidalgo of Spain, and, like all of them, wore his honour on his sleeve. But he was also the first to sit down. He had been at sea for longer than any of them and he knew that Medina Sidonia's caution made sense.

'No,' the Captain-General said solemnly. 'No, I don't.'

'And every day we waste,' Pedro de Valdez said, sitting down too, 'El Draque and his fleet get stronger. This little upset of ours will reach England soon if it hasn't already. They must be laughing in their caps.'

'We're under strength, Pedro,' Medina Sidonia said. 'We cannot cross swords with Drake until the lost ships arrive.'

'What if they don't arrive?' Valdez asked him. 'What if they're at the bottom of Biscay or blown to the Azores? Felipe won't smile on us then. And neither will God.'

Silence hung heavily in the room. Then Medina Sidonia passed forward a document. 'This,' he said, 'is an official minute, urging us to wait. I have already appended my signature. I would like you all to sign it too.'

One by one they scratched their names with a quill – Juan de Recaldé, Francisco de Bobadilla, Diego de Valdez, Hugo de Moncada and the rest. Soon, there was only one signature missing.

'*All* of you,' said the Captain-General.

Pedro de Valdez looked at them under sulky eyelids. Then he snatched the quill and wrote his name, though he would rather have torn the vellum in half. 'War by committee,' he growled. 'Are we ancient Greeks that we fight like this?'

There was a commotion on the fortress walls outside and the rapid thunder of drums. Men were shouting, whooping, running along the battlements and hugging each other. Medina Sidonia threw open the casement. 'What's the trouble, there?' he shouted to an officer on the ramparts below.

'It's the Levant squadron, sir!' the man called back, happiness etched on his beaming face. 'And the Hulks behind them.'

All the officers in the council chamber were on their feet again, the enmity of a moment ago forgotten. They were leaning out of the windows, whooping with everybody else and slapping each other on their backs. All that is except the cousins Valdez, who naturally kept their distance.

'That, gentlemen,' Medina Sidonia said, 'is God's miracle.' He turned to Pedro de Valdez. 'Now, Pedro,' he smiled. '*Now* we can go to war.'

The impetuous commander laughed and leaned far out of the window as the flagship of the Levant Squadron, *La Regazona*, butted its way into the harbour, her sailors hauling on ropes and little boats scattering out of her way.

'Hola, de Bertendona,' he shouted to the ship's commander, although he knew his voice could not carry remotely that far. 'Nice of you to drop in!'

And the hidalgos of Spain laughed.

TWELVE

Howard had at last given Drake his head. The Lord Admiral had one of the most brilliant and the most insubordinate officers of Her Majesty's Navy as his second in command and the fiery West Country man had been badgering his master to let him out of Plymouth for weeks.

The latest missive from the Queen had reminded her cousin that he ought to be aware of an attack launched from Ireland. On that occasion the Lord Admiral had lost his patience altogether. He had slapped the luckless messenger around the head and did not bother to send the usual courteous written reply. 'Tell Her Majesty,' he bellowed after the retreating lackey, his ears still ringing, 'that there is no such place as Ireland!'

So Drake, with the wind turned, had hoisted sail and led his ninety ships, still only half-stocked, out into the Channel and on to a raid against Spain. One of the letters the Lord Admiral had been pleased to receive, this time from Francis Walsingham, was that a storm had pinned the Armada into La Coruña and could Sir Francis Drake be sent with his hellburners. The Spaniards could not believe that El Draque's lightning could strike twice in the same place. And in any case, it was not the same place. Last year Drake had singed the King of Spain's beard at Cadiz. This time he'd burn the rest of him at La Coruña.

An exhausted trio threw themselves down in the captain's quarters on the *Bowe* late that morning. Since darkness had fallen on the previous night, all three of them had been at Mead Hole, sounding the alarm and emptying the place of contraband. The tide was with them so those smugglers who could get away did so, striking east along the Hampshire coast, making for the inlets of the Itchen, *anywhere* away from the wrath of the Captain of the Wight. Denny's *Rat* was safely moored in the creek at Wootton and Vaughan and Page had commandeered every wagon and pack horse they could find to bring the goods back to Vaughan's wharves and warehouses, locking doors and stashing valuables under piles of sacking.

One or two of the livelier inhabitants of the Hole had refused to budge at first. Men like that did not frighten easily and they were no strangers to the insides of gaols from there to the Indies. Let George Carey come calling; they would give him a bloody nose for his pains. John Vaughan had pointed out that there was always a time to cut and run. Now was that time. Give him a week, he said; ten days at most. After that they could all get back together again and it would be business as usual. Governors of the Wight had other things to worry about than a little smuggling and piracy.

Edmund Denny poured them all a large Bastard and sank back on the *Bowe*'s cushions, grateful for their softness. For the last two hours, he and Vaughan had been rushing around the town, having various casual words with the shopkeepers, assuring them that whatever they heard in the coming days, it would be business as usual as soon as humanly possible. Most of them had taken it well, but Hallett the butcher stood outside his stall and yelled at Vaughan, 'You rascal, you rogue, you knave, you thief.' Vaughan had been too tired to remonstrate with the man. He just swung back his fist and knocked him out.

'We've got a little problem.' Thomas Page clinked his cup against the other two.

Vaughan groaned. 'I thought we had covered our backs pretty well,' he said.

'Marlowe's been sniffing around. Asking after you.'

'Oh?'

'And that's not all. He found a body.'

Vaughan and Denny paused in mid-swig. 'A body?' Denny said. 'Where?'

'Just out there,' Page said, nodding towards the stern. 'In the water.'

'Anyone we know?' Vaughan asked.

'Old Sculpe.'

'Drunk, was he?' Vaughan continued to sip his wine, looking around for his pipe. 'It's been a long time coming, if you ask me.'

'No, he was murdered,' Page said.

Vaughan looked at the others. 'And Marlowe found him?'

'So my man Edwards says.' Page shrugged.

'Sirs!' a panicky voice sounded from up on deck. 'You should come and see this. You won't believe it.'

All three got to their feet, aching and tired. Vaughan led the way up the steep steps and out on to the quarter deck. Edwards was pointing wordlessly now up the river. People were hurrying to the bank, chattering excitedly. Sailors, fishermen and bargees were standing in their boats or on the jetties as though frozen in some Ice Sea, unable to move. A Spanish pinnace was churning its way towards them, the men on board furiously shortening sail and throwing a heavy anchor over the bows and another from the stern. The rattle of the chain was deafening and coming closer at an alarming rate. Standing on the shattered bowsprit and holding on with only a casual regard for his safety, his hand on his hip and his head held high, was Sir George Carey, the Captain of the Wight. The Captain of *El Comendador*.

'Oh, and by the way,' Page said quietly, 'I forgot to tell you. There are twenty dagos in the Bridewell. Makes you proud to be an Englishman, don't it?'

'Edwards,' Vaughan snapped, 'can you write?'

'Yes, sir,' the man told him.

'Come with me. I want you to take some letters to some gentlemen of the Wight.' He scowled at the crowds cheering and clapping as the pinnace came to a stop on the bend of the river. 'It's time we all did something about Georgie Carey.'

'What the bloody 'ell's been going on 'ere?'

Nobody could miss the arrival of Martin Frobisher. He swept in to the Lord Admiral's quarters at Plymouth like a hurricane, throwing his sword to one lackey, his pistol to another.

'Good evening, Sir Martin,' Howard of Effingham sighed. He had been dreading this moment for weeks and it came as no surprise at all that Francis Drake was on his feet already, scowling at the bluff Yorkshireman and taking the man's mere presence as a personal insult.

'Drake.' Frobisher ignored the Lord Admiral completely. 'I've just heard you've been on a damn fool reconnaissance.

Have a nice sail out to Biscay, did you? Got some fresh air,
I shouldn't wonder.'

Drake crossed to the man and they stood almost nose to
nose, the man from the north and the man from the west.
'What's your point?' Drake asked.

'My point,' Frobisher said, as though to the fleet idiot, 'is
that you risked losing ninety ships of the line for no bloody
purpose whatever.'

'I could have sunk their Armada in Corunna,' Drake grated,
his Devon vowels more obvious the more annoyed he got.

'Yes, and I could 'ave flown t'moon if I'd got wings!'
Frobisher bellowed. He was becoming more Yorkshire too.
The pair were almost speaking different languages.

'Gentlemen! Gentlemen!' Howard thought it time to assert
his authority. 'We are not engaged in privateer work here. We
are Englishmen all and we must pull together. Sir Francis,
will you shake Sir Martin's hand?'

'I will not!' Drake was adamant.

'I'd rather eat my own shit!' Frobisher snapped.

'Well.' Howard's smile was frozen. 'I think I have the ethos
of the meeting.'

'You 'ave what you like,' Frobisher growled. He snatched his
wheel-lock and his sword and strode for the door. 'I'll be on
board the *Triumph*,' he said. 'When the dons are sighted, let me
know.' And, as suddenly as he had swept in, he swept out again.

'And I'll be on the *Revenge*.' Drake followed suit.

The other commanders watched them go and there was an
awkward silence. John Hawkins cleared his throat. 'I was very
pleased, my lord,' he said to Howard, 'with the performance
of Francis's expedition. The ships held up well, despite the
weather. I have the figures here, if you're interested. Leaks,
repairs and so on.'

'Later, John,' Howard said, still looking at the door and listening
for the clash of steel in the passageway outside. Nothing. 'Our
priority now is to get the fever cases off the ships. I have sent
letters to the local Justices of the Peace asking for more men. I
don't know how much good it will do.'

'I'm not sure it matters that much,' Hawkins said. Everybody
looked at him. The man was a legend. He had designed the

race-built ships that were all that stood between England and
Spanish servitude. He had fought the Spaniards all over the
world and seen shores no one around that table had. He was
not a blusterer like Frobisher. He was not a pirate like Drake.
When Hawkins spoke, men listened.

'How so?' Howard asked him.

'Look at the weather, my lord,' Hawkins said, jerking his
head towards the window against which the rain lashed. 'The
Armada has already had a drubbing at its hands off Corunna.
I think Philip the Wise will wait until next year. I'm not sure
we're needed just yet.'

They came in open rowing boats to the island of San Anton
in the harbour of La Coruña, all the thousands of the Armada;
the arquebusiers and petronels, the lancers and hargulatiers,
the calivermen, the bill and pikemen. Every man came
unarmed. Every man came bareheaded. Their commanders
stood on the platform: the Duke of Medina Sidonia, the High
Admiral Diego de Valdez and the others, glittering in their
gold finery, shining in their blued steel. The bishop of La
Coruña blessed every man, the censors swinging in the morning
and the Te Deum echoing across the harbour. The great embroidered standards shifted in the wind – the flags of Castile and
Leon, of Asturias and Galicia, the banners of Portugal and
Aragon and Andalusia.

Each man knelt before the bishop, who made the sign of
the cross over him, and a priest gave each crusader a pewter
medallion with Christ on one face and His Holy Mother on
the other. 'God keep you,' the bishop intoned.

Diego de Valdez whispered out of the corner of his mouth,
'God keep us all.' Earlier that day he had sent home four hundred
new recruits from Galicia. They had brought their women and
children with them, crying and whimpering. The men did not
know one end of an arquebus from another and he had sent them
home. Desertion was in the wind, but the wind was vital.

And now it would blow them all to England.

'So Drake went off to burn the Spaniards out,' Nicholas Faunt
told Kit Marlowe, 'but it didn't quite work out that way.

Halfway into Biscay the wind changed and Drake's squadron was obliged to turn back. They're in Plymouth now, twiddling their thumbs.'

'That's to the good, surely?' Marlowe asked, passing the goatskin of wine to his fellow projectioner.

'If you want to fight a defensive war.' Faunt took a swig. 'What's the mood here?'

'Here' was Newtown, a wild and desolate place beyond Hamstead Ledge where the sea kissed the pebbles. There were reeds swaying and whispering above the salt marshes and moorhens fought and bickered with the bitterns over their old nesting grounds.

'Funny you should ask that,' Marlowe said. 'There was a town here once, before the harbour silted up. The French sacked it, I'm told.'

Faunt looked at the fields, curiously straight and narrow where the old streets had run. 'Before my time.' He shrugged. 'And I didn't come all the way over to this arse-end of the universe to talk over ancient history. What news of Hasler?'

'There are no further worries on that score.'

'Oh?' Faunt raised an eyebrow. He knew his Marlowe only too well. And yet he did not know him at all. The man was Machiavel; the Devil incarnate, some said. 'No further worries' to him might mean a wagonload of woe to someone else.

'If he was on your payroll, take him off it.'

'Dead?'

'In a manner of speaking,' Marlowe told him. 'Don't press me further on this, Master Faunt. We have other fish to fry.'

'Do we?' Faunt said. What he *did* know about Kit Marlowe was that the man was like an ox in the furrow. He doubted whether even Richard Topcliffe's rack in the Tower would get much out of him. He hoped it would never be put to the test.

'Murders,' Marlowe said. 'Three of them, to be precise. But they're my problem too.'

'Marlowe!' Faunt bellowed at him. A pair of moorhen rose flapping noisily from the water and Faunt checked to make sure that his waiting boatman was out of earshot. 'I have come here, at considerable difficulty and not a little expense, largely, I agree at the bidding of the Lord Admiral, but I have come to find out what the Hell is going on. Your task was to find Hasler.'

'And I've found him.' Marlowe nodded. 'Forgive me, Master Faunt, if I remark that this conversation is going round in circles.'

'The murders,' Faunt persisted. 'Tell me about them.'

Marlowe looked at the man and produced papers from his doublet. 'What do you make of this?' he asked.

Faunt looked at the documents. Not a hand he knew, certainly. He held them up to the sky where the weak July sun hit them. 'No lemon juice,' he said, sniffing the parchment for good measure. 'Where did you get these?'

'They were hidden, rather too obviously if you understand my meaning, in books in my chamber at Carisbrooke.'

'What books?'

'George Carey's. I'd borrowed them from his library. Specifically, they were tucked inside a copy of Ralph Holinshed's *Chronicles*. Does any of it make sense?'

'Lord Thomas,' Faunt murmured, reading the lines again more carefully and looking at the meaning of the words themselves rather than for some hidden cipher hidden within them. '*And Lord Thomas delighted in the girl's body and would chase her through the knot garden and slap her backside bare. She would howl withal but seemed to enjoy it and never more than when the Lady Catherine held her down.*' It had been a long time since Nicholas Faunt had been able to read a piece of writing without looking for the other meaning, the one that lay beneath. 'Lord Thomas . . . hmm. That narrows the field but it still gives us upwards of four hundred people. But this . . . this poem, if that's what it is. *Three steps back and three steps fore.* Can I take these with me?'

'Of course,' Marlowe said. 'I have looked at them until my head ached. Perhaps someone else can make sense of them.'

'It could be a code,' Faunt told him. 'One for Thomas Phelippes. You know how he loves this sort of thing.'

Marlowe did. Francis Walsingham's code-breaker was a genius. If anyone could decipher the thing, Thomas Phelippes could. 'Are they still on their way to us?' Marlowe asked. 'The Armada, I mean.'

Faunt shrugged. 'Who knows, Kit,' he said. 'Our Intelligence changes from day to day.'

'It's just that . . . I think we have a spy in our midst.'

Faunt sat upright, in mid-swig from the goatskin. There seemed to be no one about; just the boatman dozing at his oars and Marlowe's horse cropping the lush grass of what once had been Silver Street. 'How typical of you, Master Marlowe, if I may say as much, to keep the most important news until the last. The cuckoo in the nest, as my all-too-brief brief said. Anyone in mind?'

Marlowe shook his head. 'I *am* a playwright,' he said with a smile. 'I can't let my best plot line out too soon. But, to be serious, there are whispers about George Carey.'

'Carey?' Faunt was aghast. 'He's the Queen's cousin, man.'

'And Cain was Abel's brother,' Marlowe reminded him.

'Point taken.' Faunt nodded. 'But still . . . George Carey?'

'Or his wife.'

'Ah.'

Was that the faintest of blushes that Marlowe saw flit across the marble face of Nicholas Faunt?

'Elizabeth,' the man went on. 'I've met her at court a few times. You think she might . . .?'

'I know she does,' Marlowe smiled. 'The question is, is she sleeping with the enemy? Take it from me, Nicholas, this Island is like a kettle, bubbling and seething with hatred and hostility. Men rise from the grave and towns disappear. Something will crack soon. And one of us had better be ready.'

Faunt stood up and called to wake the boatman. 'There's a rumour in the west that Carey took a prize, a Spanish ship of the line.'

Marlowe nodded. 'News travels well,' he said. 'A pinnace. Landed on the Island.'

'Lost?'

'Lost, be damned,' Marlowe said. 'It was invited here, at a specific time and a specific place. The question is, by whom?'

Faunt looked confused. 'But . . . surely if George Carey invited the bastards, he'd hardly take them as a prize?'

'You are doubtless familiar with the wooden horse of Troy, Nicholas,' Marlowe said.

'Doubtless,' Faunt nodded.

'There are twenty Spaniards languishing in the gaol at Newport, brought into the heart of the town on the orders of Carey himself. He now owns the only fighting ship the Wight possesses. Everybody tells me that George Carey does not have a friend in the world, but what if that isn't true? What if the men of the Wight are merely waiting for his signal, to release the Spaniards and hoist the flag of Spain over Carisbrooke? Medina Sidonia will sail in, a conquering hero.'

'Our understanding,' Faunt countered, 'is that they're all rabid Puritans here, dyed-in-the-wool, watered-down Calvinists.'

'*Your* understanding,' Marlowe reminded him. 'There are more things in Heaven and earth, Nicholas . . .'

'Yes,' the projectioner sighed. 'I'd heard that too. Well, I must away, Kit. See what Phelippes makes of these letters. In the meantime, watch out for yourself, old lad. Oh, and one thing I was asked to ask you – this comes from the Queen herself, mind, so although I am charged to say you are under no obligation, you must understand that if you don't do it, you may end up in the Tower . . .'

'It sounds intriguing. What is it?' Marlowe's imagination, always fertile, swam with possibilities, some of which turned his stomach.

'The Queen is at Placentia, near Leicester's troops along the Tilbury marshes. She will soon have to make a speech to stir the country, or at least Leicester's men in the field. There is no doubt that the Spaniards are coming, Kit, and it won't do if she stumbles over her words. Do you think you could . . . well, could you run something up? No rush. But when you can . . .'

'I'll do my best, Nicholas. Blank verse?' The poet raised an eyebrow.

'Just a speech, Kit,' Faunt said. 'Nothing fancy. After all, she only has the body of a weak and feeble woman. I'll send a messenger if we need it urgently. Well, goodbye. I will see you soon, I'm sure.'

He shook the man's hand and clattered out along the board-walk, towards his boat, not liking at all the sigh of the reeds and the way the clouds were building to the west.

Marlowe watched him go and turned over a thought that was frequently in his head. Did Nicholas Faunt see him as often as he saw Nicholas Faunt? Or, as he suspected, far more often than that?

William Edwards had painful feet but they were not hurting him anything like as much as his hand was hurting him. And that was as nothing compared to his wrist. He had written out what had seemed like hundreds of copies of Vaughan's letter to the great and the good of the Wight and now he was having to deliver them, too. With his worn-out writing arm tucked inside his doublet to try and give him some ease he couldn't ride, even if his masters had seen fit to provide a horse, which they hadn't. With the newly renamed *Commander* blocking the exit of the river, Vaughan and Denny had delivery problems of their own. Edwards carried a canvas bag from his shoulder and delved awkwardly in it from time to time, shuffling papers around to find the right one for the right address. He sighed; the wages were adequate, the food was acceptable, the lodgings not at all uncomfortable, but William Edwards was thinking of changing his employment. Using his shoulder, he pushed open a gate and plodded up a puddle-pocked path to the front door of the house which was the next one on his list. He stepped in a pothole and fell sideways, too tired and too disadvantaged by his arm to break his fall. He rolled over and sat there, wet and fed up to the back teeth.

He drew in his legs at the plash of an approaching horse. The animal was pulled up in front of him but he couldn't even bother to look up.

'Will?' A voice came from overhead. 'Will Edwards? What are you doing here?'

Edwards looked up and saw a huge black horse looming over him and on his back a man he knew from around the town. James . . . James . . . he just couldn't bring the man's name to mind.

The horseman sprang down from the saddle and offered Edwards a hand. 'It's James,' he said. 'James Currier. You must remember me, I . . .'

It was all coming back to Edwards now. This man worked

up at the castle. Hence the horse, he thought, sullenly. He hauled himself up using Currier's weight as a counter. 'Of course I remember you. The Crown.'

The man laughed. 'Amongst others. But I have my orders. No ale or any spirits until I have all these delivered.' He patted a bag slung across his chest. 'There's hundreds of the bloody things. Invites to this Masque thing they're having. You wouldn't believe the to-do.' He peered round under Edwards' arm. 'You delivering too? Not more invites, surely?'

Edwards lied. 'I dunno what they are,' he said, although every word was engraved on his brain. 'I just got told to go and hand them out.'

'You hurt your arm?' Currier asked.

Blasting him for a nosy coke, Edwards lied again. 'Fell off the *Bowe* the other night. Knocked it on the way down.'

'Talk at the castle is that old devil Sculpe drowned t'other night.'

Edwards shrugged. 'So I hear. Well, I must get on. These letters won't deliver themselves.' He started plodding on up the path again.

'Wait,' Currier said. 'I have a thought. You can't ride because of your knock. I'm getting fair tired of upping and downing off this horse at every house. Why don't you deliver my invitations in the town and I will do them in the country? Half the work, same result.' He beamed into Edwards' face. 'What do you say?'

Edwards had more to lose than Currier did if things went wrong. His life, for one instance. Odds and ends of body parts if he was a little luckier, but his feet did hurt him and his arm was aching. He came to a decision. 'All right. But don't open any of these letters. They are private from Master Vaughan and if he finds out you know what's in there . . .'

Currier didn't need Edwards to fill in all the gory details. The rumour mill ground hot and strong up at the castle and what wasn't known for sure, you could rely on Ester to embellish. He held up a hand. 'As God is my witness,' he said. 'I won't even peep around the seal.'

'As long as I can trust you, Master Currier,' Edwards said. 'We will need to divide these up. Where can we go to do that?'

'There must be an inn near here.'

'I thought you couldn't drink while you were delivering.'

'Not while I am *delivering*. I can drink when I am *sorting*. Completely different job, sorting.'

Edwards sighed and agreed. He could probably spare the odd finger, or foot when he got found out. After all, all they did was ache, so why not risk it? The two men, one hobbling and the other leading a horse, wandered off in search of an inn.

Robert Dillington's house at Knighton Gorges lay in the valley below the ridge where the Armada beacons stood ready against the sullen grey of the sky. The man had spent a fortune on it. The gardens were more intricate in their knots than any Marlowe had ever seen and peacocks strutted there, their azure necks bright even on a dull day like this one. They shivered their tails and displayed the feathers shimmering in green and gold like the Queen's banners at Whitehall.

'What news of Whitehall?' The master of Knighton was checking his cherry trees as he walked with Marlowe in the orchard. The river tumbled and splashed its way over the rocks below them.

'I know little of Whitehall, Sir Robert,' Marlowe lied. 'I am a poet, a playwright.'

'Yes,' Dillington said, extending the syllable into a sentence. 'What of the Curtain, then? The Theatre?'

'Alas,' Marlowe smiled. 'I am with the Rose at the moment.'

'The Rose.' Dillington rubbed his hands together. 'Yes, of course. Henslowe's Folly. South of the river. Does he keep a bear there? I have heard it said.'

'He keeps a bear nearby, yes.'

'And, tell me.' Dillington checked under the trees to make sure they were alone. 'The Winchester Geese, are they still . . . gaggling?'

Marlowe laughed. 'I've never heard it called that before, Sir Robert,' he said. 'I think I am wasted here. Philip Henslowe could use you on the Spanish Tragedy.'

'Ah, yes, the Spanish tragedy,' Dillington's face darkened. 'We may yet be caught up in that. But the Geese.' The Lord of Knighton was a persistent man. 'Is it true they do it in the street? Bare themselves shamelessly?' He was almost salivating.

'You'd have to ask my stage manager, Tom Sledd,' Marlowe said. He stopped walking. 'Is that why you have asked me here, sir, to discuss the whiles of London whores?'

'No, no,' Dillington flustered. 'Heaven forfend, no. It's just that we don't get many from the capital here, other than the people George Carey invites, of course. I myself have not been for a while. In fact, the last time I was there, there was a panic in the city. I was attending to a matter of law in the Inns of Court and we got the news of the massacre at Paris. Shocking. Quite shocking. Do you remember it?'

'I was eight, sir,' Marlowe told him. 'At school in Canterbury.'

'Oh, quite. Quite. Ah, here we are.' He led Marlowe into a little dell with stone seats arranged in a circle around a fountain. 'My inner sanctum. My chance to escape from the world.' The look on Robert Dillington's face earlier had made it clear that it was not so much the world he wanted to escape from but Matilda Dillington. Marlowe had met her briefly and understood the man's point of view completely.

'I understand,' Dillington became conspiratorial, 'that the Queen has freaks about her at court.'

'Freaks?'

'A female dwarf called Thomasina. A little black boy – but everyone's got one of those these days, haven't they? And Ippolita the Tartarian.'

'I'm afraid to say I have never met the Queen,' Marlowe said. 'Or been to her court.'

'That's a pity.' Dillington was deflated. 'There's talk of swearing, whoredom, carding, carousing, gluttony and so on.'

'All good clean English vices, Sir Robert,' Marlowe assured him.

'Oh, quite, quite. So, the story of the monkey . . .?'

'I was more intrigued by Island stories,' Marlowe interrupted.

'Really?' Dillington crossed one gartered leg over the other and rested his elbow on one knee and his chin on his fist. 'What, in particular? Not that I'm one to gossip, you understand.'

'Of course not.' Marlowe frowned. 'Well, for instance, this wretched murder business.'

'Murder? Oh, Lord, yes. You mean Matthew Compton.'

'Among others.'

'Others? Oh, Walter Hunnybun. That was the Urrys.'

'It was?'

'Oh, yes. Long-standing feud, Marlowe, long-standing. Those families were at each other's throats in my grandfather's day.'

'I'm not sure it's that simple,' the playwright said.

'Well, if it involves the Urrys, it must be. They don't come much simpler.'

'How well do you know Bet Carey?' Marlowe asked.

The Lord of Knighton dropped his casual pose and sat up, tugging his doublet and running a hand over his sparse hair. 'What do you mean?' he asked.

'Er . . . how well do you know Bet Carey?' Marlowe repeated. As a poet he had a thousand ways to say it, but this one was by far the most direct.

'Well,' Dillington said, 'not Biblically, I assure you. Though –' he glanced towards the house before he spoke – 'there are those who do.'

'For instance?'

'Well, my old friend Henry Meux, for one. But he hardly counts. They have been together, if I may put it politely, since they were hardly more than children. Hmm, Matthew Compton, of course . . . I've heard it said that even Walter Hunnyb— Oh my God!' Realization had hit the Lord of Knighton Gorges. 'You think Bet Carey is doing it? I've read of spiders that do that. And Doctor Percival of Oxford University has told me, in the strictest confidence, that it is not uncommon in the more remote parts of Cumberland, apparently.'

'No, Sir Robert,' Marlowe said. 'I do not suspect Mistress Carey.'

'I have heard it said that there is a suspicion of Popery around Carey, but of course I am not one to believe tittle-tattle.'

'Sir Robert!' A voice called from the cherry orchard and a galloper stood there in the colours of George Carey. Dillington beckoned him forward. 'It's a letter from George,' he said, ripping the seal and reading the contents. 'A Masque. We're invited to a Masque.' His beam vanished. 'Oh, Lord, I suppose that means Matilda will have to . . .' He refixed his grin. 'Tell Sir George that Sir Robert and Lady Matilda Dillington will be delighted to attend.'

The messenger bobbed his head and, reaching into a bag slung across the other shoulder, passed over another letter.

'What's this?' Dillington said, extending his hand but less enthusiastically this time. 'Two letters in one day. What *is* going on? Militia business, I imagine.'

The messenger was a little disconcerted to see Marlowe there, watching him with that all-seeing eye. 'I am delivering this for a friend, Sir Robert, if you will forgive the intrusion. The poor fellow is laid up and his master . . .'

Robert Dillington flapped his hand to silence the man and ripped open the seal, frowning as he recognized the spurious coat of arms embedded in the wax, the one appropriated by John Vaughan. He did not beam this time but nodded solemnly as he read the contents. He looked up to see the messenger still standing there. 'Thank you, my good man. I shall reply to this by messenger later. That will be all.' The messenger bowed and doubled back through the orchard. He had appointments to keep and many miles to go before he slept.

'Urgent news, Sir Robert?' Marlowe could read neither the man's mind nor his letter, crane his neck though he might.

'Hm?' Dillington seemed to be elsewhere. 'Oh, no, no,' he said. 'Just one of the thousand little things that are sent to try us country gentlemen. Look, Marlowe, it *has* been fun, to catch up on all the London gossip, I mean, though as you know I do abhor it. We must do it again, some time, before you leave the Wight, I mean. But now . . .'

Marlowe knew a heavy hint when he heard one. 'Of course,' he said. 'Many thanks for your hospitality, Sir Robert.'

'I'll see you to your horse.'

'One more thing, though, if I may ask it before I go,' Marlowe said as they walked. 'Is this Island of yours haunted?'

'Haunted? Why do you ask that?'

'Oh, nothing. It's just that I was making my way back to Carisbrooke the other night and I happened upon a churchyard.

A gravestone seemed to move, one of those table tombs. I could swear the top slid open.'

'Chale.' Dillington kept walking. 'Devils, they are.' He was chuckling.

'They are?'

'Smugglers, Marlowe. Chale is rife with them. There's a rabbit warren of tunnels under that churchyard and the tombs are the gates to them, so to speak. The tunnels are natural, put there by God and not for smuggling purposes, I feel sure. But the Islanders being what they are, especially down there at the Back of the Wight, have found other uses for them. Terrifies innocent folk, of course, and your horse too, I daresay. It looks as though the graves are giving up their dead. It's quite effective, really.'

'So smuggling is not just confined to Mead Hole, then?' Marlowe asked.

'Lord love you, no; it's everywhere. Why, John Vaughan himself . . .' He waved the second letter in the air and then thought better of it, tucking it into his doublet. 'Well, here we are.' They had reached Marlowe's horse tethered outside the stable block. 'No, no,' he chuckled as Marlowe mounted. 'There's nothing haunted about this Isle, I assure you.'

Marlowe walked his horse around the corner of the house and was about to spur him into a canter when a pale hand snaked out from the shadowy porch and grabbed the bridle.

'Master Marlowe,' a harsh voice whispered. 'Not going so soon, surely?'

'I . . . I must get back to the castle,' Marlowe said to the figure. He had after all just been assured that there were no ghosts here.

'Come in, come in and dine with us,' the figure rasped. Then it coughed, a sound so like the gravestone moving that Marlowe started. 'I am sorry about that,' the creature continued, in a light and cultured contralto. 'I have just recovered from a quinsy.'

Marlowe peered closer. 'Lady Matilda.' He laughed. 'I didn't recognize you there for a moment. I won't come in, thank you. Your husband has business to conclude, or so I understand.'

'Nonsense.' The woman's voice was fully recovered and

would brook no argument. 'If he is busy then your presence
at supper will be all the more welcome.' She stepped out of
the shade, a splendid figure of a woman, with breasts that
parted all before them, like the prow of the *Revenge* or the
Triumph. 'Let me walk you back round to the stable with your
horse and as you go you can tell me all the London gossip.
Tell me, is it true what I hear about the court? Carding?
Whoring and worse? And what about that monkey, eh?'

THIRTEEN

The night was thick and dark when Kit Marlowe eventually left the Dillington mansion. A groom brought his horse up to the door and gave him a knee up into the saddle, then scuttled back round to the stables as if the hounds of Hell were after him. The wine had flowed freely during the meal, which had seemed to consist mostly of rabbit in all its guises, but apart from that it was tasty enough. Marlowe wondered whether perhaps the Dillingtons were as rich as the mansion suggested. Matilda Dillington certainly wore very little jewellery and Marlowe was sure he could see darns in the brocaded pattern of her gown. Sir Robert had contained his disappointment with fortitude when he saw Marlowe at his table and all had gone splendidly. Now, all the playwright had to do was find his way back to the castle. Matilda Dillington had recommended that he aim for high ground. From there, looking west, he should see the castle on the hill. The couple wasted no time at the door, but shut it hurriedly as soon as he was through it and he heard the bolts ram home.

His horse picked its way along the driveway that led from the front door to the road. It skirted thick woods, with the orchards off to the right. Through the serried ranks of cherry trees, Marlowe could make out the lights of a town, but he could not tell which. To his left, the old oaks were twisted and gnarled and seemed to shift and turn to follow him as he rode along. Although Sir Robert had been adamant that the Wight was not haunted, the conversation throughout supper had turned to the uncanny and the couple had an insatiable appetite for gossip about Dr Dee, about whom they had heard so much, but could always do with hearing more. Their house wasn't haunted – no, no, they had chuckled. But the castle was, so folk did say, and as for Hollow Lane . . . well! Lady Matilda had repeated Dillington's scurrilous tale with a blush on her cheek and a good time was had by all.

Marlowe had seen some things that he never spoke of to
another living soul. He had been where no man should be
asked to go, usually in the service of Francis Walsingham.
He was glad that this charade was almost at an end. Just see
the Masque through and he and Tom Sledd could pack up
their traps and head back to London, to see if Philip Henslowe
would still give them the time of day. He felt a pang of longing;
he didn't think he could be so homesick, after all his wander-
ings, but he could hardly wait to get the smell of the crowd
back in his nostrils.

He heard the horse's snicker first of all, then felt it shy and
check. His hand went down to its neck without another thought,
smoothing it, stroking it. Soft words came from his mouth, the
tone was important to a horse, not the words, he knew this. 'I
love thee not for sacred chastity. Who loves for that? Shhh,
shhh, there's nothing there. Nor for thy sprightly wit: I love
thee not for thy sweet modesty . . .' Marlowe looked up from
between the creature's ears and saw what had frightened it. In
the middle of the path ahead, two figures strolled, hand in hand.
One was a slight young thing, a girl with head bowed modestly.
One was a man, thickset, running to fat even, and even as
Marlowe looked, he pulled the girl into the wood. She opened
her mouth and screamed, but there was no sound from those
phosphorescing lips. She stared into Marlowe's eyes, extended
a hand and fell to her knees. The man, silently cursing,
pulled on her arm and then, not able to move her, clubbed her
once on the head with his heavy stick and she lay still. Then
he too saw Marlowe and his horse, both transfixed with horror,
and made for them, mouth wide and foaming, wider than any
mortal mouth could be. But before he could reach them,
Marlowe spurred his horse on and rode through the apparition,
and was on the road and heading for the high ground, his
horse's hooves throwing sparks as he went.

A curtain twitched at the front of Knighton Gorges and
Matilda Dillington turned back to her husband, lying in the
bed with the covers pulled up over his eyes.

'Robert,' she said sharply. 'You can come out. He has gone.'

'Who?' Dillington said, his voice muffled.

'Both. I couldn't see who it was this time, but Marlowe

rode him down, in any event.' She climbed into bed and blew out the candle. 'When can we ever see an end to this, Robert?'

'When they make me Governor,' Dillington said. 'And we can live in the castle.'

'I don't think I can wait until Hell freezes over, Robert,' his wife said peevishly.

'Ah, but you don't know what I do, my dear,' Dillington said smugly. 'It won't be long before I have as good a chance as everyone else, mark my words.'

And soon, Knighton Gorges slept.

Francis Walsingham was up to his waist in papers. Missives from the Queen, complaints from Lords Lieutenant of the counties, whinges from Justices of the Peace. And always, coming in with exhausted gallopers most days, demands from Howard of Effingham. 'For the love of God and our country, let us have some speed, some great shot sent out and some powder with it.'

'For the love of God, indeed!' the exasperated Spymaster bellowed, unconcerned who heard him. 'Does the Lord Admiral think I don't know what makes his bloody guns work?'

'Bad day, Sir Francis?' Nicholas Faunt had appeared in the chamber at Whitehall like the shadow he was. The fortress had yet to be built that could keep Nicholas Faunt out of it. And Her Majesty's Palace of Whitehall was not a fortress; it was a cracking shell that contained all the concentrated panic of the moment. 'I could call back.'

'No, no, Nicholas.' The Spymaster threw down the latest letter from Plymouth and leaned back in his chair. Nicholas. It *was* a bad day. 'Find a seat, will you? This wretched business will be the death of me. But at least here is one honest face.'

Faunt laughed. Not many people who knew him would use that description. 'I'm afraid I have more paperwork.' He pulled some sheets out of his satchel. 'From Kit Marlowe.'

'Really? Any news of Hasler?'

'He says that's resolved.' Faunt took the Spymaster's proffered chair.

'Resolved how?' Walsingham wanted to know.

'He didn't say.'

'Nicholas . . .' The Spymaster looked over his spectacles at the man who might one day succeed him.

'I know.' Faunt raised his hand. 'But you know Marlowe, Sir Francis. He said let it be. I did.'

This was not exactly music to Walsingham's ears. Projectioners who did as they liked when Philip of Spain was knocking on the door were not to be tolerated. And Marlowe had started out so well.

'God preserve us!' Walsingham was suddenly on his feet, Marlowe's pages in his hand. 'Where did he get this?'

'He found it in a book,' Faunt told him, 'borrowed from Sir George Carey's library.'

'What book?'

'Er . . . Ralph Holinshed's *Chronicles*, I believe. Is it a code? I couldn't see anything there. Nor could Marlowe. I thought perhaps Thomas Phelippes . . .'

'There's no need to bother Master Phelippes.' Walsingham sat down heavily. 'The meaning is hidden in plain sight.'

Faunt looked confused. 'No,' he said. 'I am sorry, Sir Francis; I am not with you.'

'Holinshed,' Walsingham explained. 'The book was published last year.'

'It was?'

'Oh, of course,' the Spymaster remembered. 'That's right. You were in the Low Countries at the time. It caused a hoo-ha. Holinshed was arrested – on my orders as a matter of fact. He spent a mesmerizing half an hour with Richard Topcliffe before the Queen relented and decided it was better to let sleeping historians lie and leave him with both arms intact.'

'I don't understand.' It was not like Faunt; he was annoyed with himself.

'Ralph Holinshed is one of those annoying people, an honest chronicler. He wrote his chapter on the Queen warts and all, as it were.'

'So?'

'So . . .' Walsingham became introspective, tight-lipped.

'What I am about to tell you is for your ears only, Nicholas. It is not to go beyond these four walls.'

'Marlowe will want to know,' Faunt warned.

'Marlowe can go hang,' Walsingham snapped. 'We had to expunge various passages from Master Holinshed's opus – *these* passages, to be precise. Obviously someone thought they should go back in.'

'To what do they refer?' Faunt asked.

Walsingham hesitated. 'They are all about the Queen,' he said. He and Elizabeth were of an age and Francis Walsingham had a mind like a razor; he forgot nothing. Ever. 'There were some . . . difficulties . . . with the Princess Elizabeth,' he said in a hoarse whisper. 'She was slim, boy-like, late to develop. Some said . . .'

Faunt leaned forward to catch it.

'Some said that her father was so determined to beget a son that her mother provided him with a child who was neither male nor female. Or both.'

'Not possible, surely.' Faunt frowned.

'No, of course not,' Walsingham assured him. 'But they were different days, Nicholas. When she was thirteen, a clutch of doctors examined her apparently. Under her clothing. All was well.'

'Oh, good.' Faunt liked happy endings. 'And the spanking?'

'Yes.' Walsingham sighed. 'Malicious tittle-tattle. The story went that Lord Thomas Seymour would come into her bedroom when she was still a girl, with or without the connivance of Queen Catherine, whose third husband he was.'

'You don't believe it?' Faunt asked.

'The story came from the Princess's governess, Cat Ashley. Need I say more? Now there's someone I would cheerfully have introduced to Master Topcliffe. And now, this is odd.' Walsingham took off his spectacles and sucked the earpiece. 'This is not Holinshed. Or at least, the story is, but not the poem. "Three steps from door to floor . . ."'

'What does it mean?'

Walsingham checked the door again, just in case. 'Amy Dudley,' he said quietly.

'Lord Leicester's wife?'

'The same. She fell to her death one day while he was out hunting.'

'Now that *is* a story I've heard,' Faunt said.

'She broke her neck,' Walsingham went on.

'Tragic,' Faunt nodded.

'Impossible,' Walsingham corrected him.

'What?'

'Three steps, Nicholas; "three steps fore and three steps back". Amy Dudley tripped and broke her neck falling down just three steps. Try it on your way out. The most you'll get is a grazed knee.'

'So . . .?'

'So.' Walsingham was irritated. His right-hand man was usually more perspicacious than this. 'She was pushed, Nicholas, and from a greater height than three steps. And Lord Leicester . . .'

'Was not there at the time.'

'No,' the Spymaster growled. 'He was riding the Queen at the time, at Nonsuch if my intelligence is correct.'

Faunt sat with his mouth open.

'So you can see why this cannot get out,' Walsingham said. 'Not even to Marlowe. Whoever wrote this verse is out to blacken the name of the Queen, in the most insidious way. Holinshed did not go this far. The poem implies that our gracious sovereign, our Gloriana, is not only an adulteress; she is complicit in murder.'

Kit Marlowe scratched a line through the final name on Bet Carey's list and leaned back in his chair, chewing the end of the quill. Then he folded the paper and tucked it into his doublet, stoppered the ink bottle, laid the quill down, spat out a few fragments of feather and prepared to go in search of the lady of Carisbrooke. He looked briefly at the pile of notes he had made during his weeks at the castle. Although his writer in residence status was not genuine, he could not help himself and an idea was taking shape – a storm, an island, full of noises, of strange lights and devils; all the stuff that the audiences at the Rose lapped up as though it was their mothers' milk. Even so, he couldn't see it going anywhere. It all seemed a little too far-fetched somehow. Old habits dying hard, he hid his notes underneath a book from George Carey's library. It was refreshing not to have to hide his writing from the depredations of Gabriel Harvey and his myrmidons, but even so, no need to make his thoughts too accessible. Taken the wrong way, falling into the wrong hands, some of his allegories could easily be misunderstood.

She was not in the solar with her sewing, nor in the long gallery taking a walk in the sun streaming through the windows. Marlowe went out into the courtyard and looked above him; he knew that Lady Elizabeth Carey often strolled on the battlements and an evil imp suggested that it was from there that she spied out her next conquest, peering through the arrow slit along with the ghost of Philip de Heynoe. He was smiling at the thought when a soft hand on his arm made him turn.

'Madam,' he said, sketching a bow. 'I was just looking for you.'

Her curtsy was just as perfunctory and she took his arm. 'Walk me round the knot garden, Master Marlowe,' she said loudly, for the benefit of the listening carpenters, coming to the end of their work now on the stage. Tom Sledd was sitting on the edge of it, oblivious to splinters, making notes on a piece of much-folded parchment on his knee. A line of anxious-looking people were standing in a wavering line under the gate. He looked up and waved at Marlowe.

'Auditions!' he called merrily. He was enjoying this. All the fun of a play but with no egos to batter his way through. No Philip Henslowe breathing in his ear. And in the sun, with ample food and no heavy lifting. That was all being done by Avis, who clucked around him like a mother hen.

Marlowe waved back but did not offer to join him. Unlike the stage manager, his work was done long before auditions. His golden words on the parchment would then be turned to garbage in their mouths and he would rather not be there to witness it. He raised a hand to Sledd and let himself be led away.

It was not easy walking around the knot garden. Some walks were so narrow as to not even admit the gardener with his hoe and his barrow and here the weeds were taking over, bindweed spreading its hearts along the tops of the hedges, brambles, acid green with sap, making a break for the sunlight overhead. Other walks were fortunately wide and edged with sweetly smelling herbs and low hedges which whispered against Bet's dress as she walked her swinging walk alongside Marlowe, holding his arm with both hands and leaning in to him every once in a while. Anyone watching would have taken them for two lovers out for a stroll, a pretty sight to cheer an unseasonably chilly July morning.

'Have you been through the list, Master Marlowe?' she whispered, peering up into his face.

'Yes, Mistress Carey. Every last one.' His playwright's sense told him to keep the denouement hanging for a while.

'And?' she said softly, clutching his arm convulsively with sharp-nailed fingers.

He prised her fingers looser and gave them a reassuring pat. 'All present or accounted for,' he told her. 'A few have died, it is true – age is no bar for you, is it?'

She looked down, dimpling, and shook her head.

'Some are not in the Wight any more or are away temporarily, but they are well. So, I wonder if you might have . . . well, perhaps you have worried for nothing.'

She shook her head, but adamantly this time, with her head held high. 'No, Kit, I know that my husband has had these men killed. Out of jealousy.'

They walked a few more steps before he spoke. 'A lady likes to think of men dying for love of her, I expect,' he said. 'I certainly have made it happen, in some of my plays. Duels, poison, wars – all for the love of a lady.'

'You think it is my vanity, then?' she said, but without rancour.

He shrugged. 'Perhaps.'

'Have it your own way, Master Marlowe,' she said, and dropped one of her hands from his arm, moving away. 'I know what I know.'

'Indeed, Lady Carey,' he said, bowing and disentangling himself from her other arm. 'I would never have it otherwise.' An eldritch screech made them both cover their ears. '"Sometimes a thousand twangling instruments Will hum about mine ears" – I think Tom has begun his auditions. I must go.'

'Twangling?' she said, with a smile.

'I believe that is a word,' he said. 'Or will be, at least.'

She curtsied low. 'Master Marlowe.'

He reached and kissed her hand. 'Lady Carey.' With a flourish of his cloak and both hands back over his ears, he followed the ear-splitting sound to help with the auditions for the Masque.

Before he reached the stage, the noise stopped. It had resolved itself finally in Marlowe's head as a very amateur rendition of 'Greensleeves' on an hautboy, rather slow and in no key known to man. Even when it stopped it seemed to ring in his head and so he hailed Martin Carey, whom he had spotted making his way up to his room on the keep, rather more loudly than he intended. The comptroller hurried over.

'Is something amiss, Master Marlowe?' he asked politely, for the benefit of passing carpenters.

'No.' Marlowe shook his head, smiling. 'I just had that sound in my head. It made my hearing a little off balance for a moment. I don't seem to have seen much of you. Hardly a moment since,' he dropped his voice, 'the body in the quay.'

'Hmm, yes, the body. Sir George brought it in in the Inquest as death by misadventure,' Martin said.

Marlowe nodded. 'That seems like a fair summation.'

Carey looked at him out of the corner of his eye. 'You saw the ropes, Master Marlowe,' he chided.

'Trick of the light,' Marlowe assured him. 'When I got there, there were no ropes.'

'And you should have appeared as First Finder.'

'The sailors pulled him out,' Marlowe said.

'Well, Sir George was content enough and I have enough to do here, what with the money Lady Avis is throwing at the Masque. So we let it pass. I wonder, though, could you help me with something now?'

'If I can.' Marlowe was aware that he had let this friendship cool, through lack of time rather than anything else. For a man with no specific task to do, he seemed to be busy from morn till night and often night till morn as well.

'Master Sledd –' and Martin managed to inject a note into

the word so that it sounded like 'slime' – 'has asked for a donkey.' He saw Marlowe's eyes widen. 'For the Masque.'

The light dawned on the playwright's face. 'Oh, yes. That's my fault. I wrote a donkey in the lovers' scene.'

'Well, that is of course up to you,' the comptroller said. 'And to save spending good money on hiring one, I thought we could use Old Adam. He turns the wheel in the well-house and as long as we make sure there is a bucket and a good long rope at the other well up in the keep –' he waved a vague arm – 'then I think we'll manage.'

'How can I help?' Marlowe asked.

'Old Adam can be a bit . . . difficult.'

'Mulish,' Marlowe remarked.

'Indeed.' Martin measured out an ounce of smile. 'So I could do with an extra hand, if you have a moment.'

Marlowe looked across at the line of hopefuls wavering away into the distance. He could see from the way Tom Sledd's hair was standing in a cockscomb on the top of his head that he was near breaking point. Adding an accountant and a donkey at this point might be all he needed to throw a rare but spectacular temperament. He put his hand on Master Martin's arm. 'I think the donkey can wait and I'm sure you must have plenty to do. I will sort the donkey when the time comes.'

'Really?' Carey's eyes shone. 'Only, Avis did say . . .'

'I can deal with Avis,' Marlowe said. 'I have a special treat for her.' And he patted his left breast.

Martin raised an eyebrow. He wasn't one to listen to gossip, but there was clearly more to it than met the eye. With a grateful wave to Marlowe, he ran up his steps and, with a creak of a door, was gone.

'Tom!' Marlowe called, his voice now back to normal and his ears no longer ringing.

Sledd spun round and almost hugged the playwright in relief. 'Kit,' he muttered. 'Thank the Lord you're here. I put out some feelers, in the taverns, you know, like we do at home, to say I needed some extras for the Masque, a few musicians, the usual thing. And this is what I get.' He forced his face into a rictus grin before he faced the crowd, waving his arm.

'Good turnout, Tom,' Marlowe said, trying to keep a straight face.

'Well, I've thinned them out already,' he said. 'After that noise from that hautboy player, I had to just dispense with them.'

'You might have sent away some good ones,' Marlowe said reasonably.

Sledd sighed. 'He said – and I *am* quoting now, Kit – he said, "I do be the best ought-boy player on this'n Island."'

'He might have been lying.' Marlowe was still grinning.

'He might, he might,' Sledd conceded. 'But all the others, all carrying their bleeding ought-boys over their shoulders all agreed, if that's what "oh, ar" means.'

'We can do without them,' Marlowe said, patting his friend on the arm. 'What are all the others?'

'A few singers, some actors, or so they say. Some musicians.' He caught Marlowe's eye. 'Mostly strings, I am happy to say.'

'Well, let's do this thing,' Marlowe said. 'I'll split the queue halfway down and we'll both go at it. How many do we need?'

'Say a dozen actors, nothing special needed. That footman Benjamin is really good and can sing as well. He's the girl in the love scene. Not too happy about it but it seems he is on his last warning with Sir George and so he'll do anything, more or less.'

'And the boy?'

Sledd blushed. 'I rather thought I would give that a go myself,' he said.

Marlowe laughed. 'What a good idea, Tom. And why not? Are you sure you don't want to play the girl, though?' Sledd's days of playing the wench were behind him, but a little dig now and then did not harm. Before the stage manager could find a missile, Marlowe had skipped off down the queue to find some likely lads to tread his boards.

It wasn't long before a dejected line of instrumentalists and would-be thespians were wending their way down the hill back to Newport. They were muttering, as only rejected actors can, and heaping curses on the Masque. If the god of thunder had been listening, the castle would be burned to the ground on the Great Day.

Marlowe and Sledd were sitting on stage making a list of names of the chosen ones when there was a delicate cough off to Stage Right. Marlowe glanced over and saw Avis Carey gesturing to him to come over. He passed the list to Sledd, pointing out a few in the jostling crowd who would not turn milk if put near the front, and went over.

'Mistress Avis. How can I help you?'

'Are the auditions over, Master Marlowe?' she asked.

'Indeed they are. At last and not a moment too soon. We rehearse for the next three days and then we're On.'

She looked a little crestfallen and turned to go.

'Is there something the matter?' he asked her, with a smile.

'No, no, not at all. It's just that . . . I saw there was a song in the first half, with no name against it. I wondered . . . But . . .' She forced a smile on to her bland, blank face. 'I do see it would have been unsuitable.' She put a tentative hand on the man's sleeve.

Marlowe was a playwright, but he was an actor too. He used all his skill now. 'Oh, the *song*. Do you mean this song?' He took a sheet of parchment out from inside his doublet. 'I'll just see if Tom is all right and then we'll go and learn it shall we?'

As the sun came out across her face, he saw what her brother had meant. Avis Carey truly was stunning looking, in her day.

FOURTEEN

The bit with the donkey was not going well. Old Adam was even-tempered enough when he was just turning the wheel to bring water up from the well beneath the castle. Decking with flowers had been tricky; what he hadn't eaten he had rubbed off on the wall. And then eaten. Standing still most of the time was his stock in trade, but he wasn't used to it when a rather second-rate castrato from St Thomas's Church was singing in his ear. The Island was rather embarrassed to be the de facto owner of the man, who had been brought down by the previous governor and rather left to his own devices when George Carey took up the position. His rather strange voice was at odds with the bucolic singing on a Sunday and he was missing the opera. So he was making the most of this opportunity – he had heard that there might be crowned heads in the audience and life as a singer in a great house was what he craved. His hoots could be heard at the bottom of the hill, merging with the braying of Old Adam.

A small child, chosen because of her angelic face, was proving to be almost as intractable as the donkey, just as smelly and far louder.

'All she has to do, Kit, *all* she has to do,' Sledd lamented, 'is to walk down the sodding central aisle between the seats strewing poxy petals while the orchestra plays. Her maundering mother has left her here for the whole rehearsal time and all the kinchin mort does is howl. She howls if it's quiet. She howls if it's loud . . . God help me, Kit, I will swing for that child.'

'It will be all right on the night, Tom. And if she's howling when the audience arrives, I will strew the poxy petals for you – that's rather a good line, by the way. And think what a coup *that* would be.' Marlowe smiled and put an arm round Sledd's shoulders, giving him an encouraging shake. 'It will be all right. I promise.'

Sledd dropped his voice to a mutter. 'And George Carey. He's got the stage presence of . . . of a . . . hedgehog.' He looked at Marlowe, who was trying to keep a straight face.

'A hedgehog, Tom?'

'Well, he has.' They both dissolved in laughter, which made the child howl.

'Let's get on,' Marlowe said. 'I doubt the audience will be very discerning, but we have reputations to keep up.'

'Kit?'

'Yes?' Marlowe turned back to where Sledd stood, still looking at the mansion.

'About Avis Carey.'

'What about her?'

'Her song. I haven't heard it.

'Need you?'

'I suppose not. But the orchestra are worried. They don't know it.'

'Of course they don't. I have only just written it. And anyway, Mistress Avis will be performing alone.'

Sledd blew out his cheeks in relief. 'Oh, it's a *poem*!'

'No, a song, with a tune and everything. I wasn't a chorister all those years for nothing, Tom. Trust me on this. There won't be a dry eye in the house.'

The playwright looked at the stage manager.

'And I do mean in a good way. Yes, in a very good way.'

It was a balmy evening as Tom Sledd lit the torches around the gallery. The groundlings were in position, to each side of the stage so as not to impede the view from the seats, and there were collective 'oohs' and 'aahs' as each flame burst into life. There were more 'oohs' and 'aahs' among other mutterings as the coaches arrived, the horses blowing hard up the long hill and the coachmen snaking their whips out. The velvet night was closing in and the Carey mansion was awash with candlelight, spilling out over the groundlings and the stage.

The Dillingtons came first, all beams and smiles, then the Oglanders and the Meux. The captains of each side of the Medina kept suitably far away from each other and there

was a kerfuffle as the mayor of Newport arrived. The
man was paralytic with drink already and George Carey sent
him quietly away into the knot garden flanked by a couple of
his stoutest guards. He was not to leave there until the night
air had sobered him up. Edmund Burley's carriage was the
last to arrive, as it had come the furthest, and then the leading
townsfolk arrived on foot, led by that upright citizen John
Vaughan. He bowed briefly to George Carey who barely gave
him the time of the evening.

A small handful of the great and good of Hampshire had
risked the water and had hired coaches on this side of the
Solent. They all knew that George Carey had the ear of
the Queen *and* the Masque had been written by the great
Christopher Marlowe, he of the mighty line, the Muse's darling.
The Earl of Southampton had had to send his apologies – there
was a war on – and now Cecily Meux would *never* find out
what it was he had whispered to Bet Carey that time during
a dance at the court of Queen Elizabeth. Bet Carey looked
even more dazzling than ever, the pearls in her hair shining
in the torchlight and her eyes bright.

'Lady Carey.' A gentleman in blue velvet doffed his cap
and bowed low. 'May I say what a pleasure it is to meet you
again.'

Across the stage, half hidden by the flats, Tom Sledd turned
to Kit Marlowe. 'Hey,' he said. 'Isn't that . . .?'

'Nicholas Faunt.' Marlowe nodded. 'Yes, it is.'

'What's he doing here?' the stage manager wondered aloud.

'That's what I'd like to know,' the playwright said. 'Coming
for a nibble, Tom?'

'Nah,' Sledd said. 'I've got to check things out here. That
bloody donkey's been giving me the evils all day. Now it's
dark I don't trust him further than I can throw him.'

It was hot in George Carey's great hall. The governor was
wearing a magnificent new doublet, laced with gold and
faceted buttons and peacock plumes nodded in his hat. The
wine was flowing freely and everybody was tucking into
the sweetmeats and morsels of pastry encasing expensive
and rare fruits and spices as if they had never eaten before.
The cook, peering round a door, shook his head as larks'

tongues were gobbled down as if they were dumplings, raisins soaked in the finest Malmsey were being guzzled as if they were hedgerow fruit.

'Master Faunt.' The governor took the projectioner by the arm. 'May I introduce the author of tonight's little extravaganza – Master Christopher Marlowe.'

'Master Marlowe.' Faunt bowed stiffly. 'I have heard so much about you.'

'Really?' Marlowe returned the salute with a deeper flourish. 'I'm afraid I've never heard of you.'

There was an awkward silence filled by a sudden guffaw from George Carey. 'Master Faunt is here on behalf of Sir Francis Walsingham,' he said, 'who was to have come in the place of the Queen. But, sadly, you know how it is . . . affairs of state.'

'Indeed.' Marlowe smiled and the little knot broke up to mingle, as good guests and hosts should at times like these.

'Thank you for the ringing vote of confidence,' Faunt said out of the corner of his mouth when he and Marlowe at last found themselves in a quiet alcove. 'Never heard of me, indeed.'

'Sorry, Nicholas.' Marlowe smiled and raised his glass to Ann Oglander as she glided past. 'I was not exactly expecting you tonight.'

'Oh, surely.' Faunt sipped his wine. 'A Masque by the great Kit Marlowe. I would not have missed it for the world.'

'Liar.' Marlowe bowed to Cecily Meux, who curtsied so deeply he could see just a hint of rouge on the nipples only half-hidden under the gauze of her gown. 'Why are you really here?'

'First, to tell George Carey that the Armada is, as of our latest Intelligence, making its way windward to the Lizard. It can only be a matter of time now. I would estimate we have two days, perhaps only one.'

'And second?' Marlowe's glance alighted on Bet Carey, who paused, still on her husband's arm, and smiled at him. Faunt noticed it but said nothing.

'Second,' he said, 'your cryptic message. In the Holinshed book.'

'Ah.' Marlowe was all ears. 'Phelippes cracked them?'

'Phelippes didn't see them,' Faunt said. 'Sir Francis understood at once.'

'Well, out with it, man,' Marlowe hissed. 'You can't keep me dangling. The safety of the Island may depend on it.'

'Indeed it may,' Faunt agreed. 'But it must remain, I fear, a closed book.'

Marlowe looked at the man, wondering how he could get his dagger point under Faunt's chin without anyone noticing.

'Let's just say . . .' Faunt may have read the man's mind because he spoke quickly. 'They were black propaganda directed against the Queen. Written by a traitor, would be my guess.'

'So we're no further forward,' Marlowe said. He was suddenly aware of little Ester, in her crisp new apron, standing at his elbow with a tray of gingerbread. She was looking up at him, open-mouthed. 'Thank you, no,' the poet said.

'Tut, tut, Master Marlowe,' Faunt chided. 'And you so fond of gingerbread.' And he helped himself to a piece before Avis Carey swept through the room like a sou'wester and whisked the girl away with her. 'You've been here, for God's sake,' Faunt hissed when the coast was clear. 'How much time do you need? Because, believe me, time is running out.'

Matilda Dillington curtsied to Marlowe as she rustled past in her carefully darned finery, covering her face with her fan and making eyes at him.

'Do you know *all* the Island ladies?' Faunt asked, rather irritated at last by this cattle market.

'Only some,' Marlowe said. 'Did you notice anything about them?'

'Well, apart from the last one, all rather young and lovely.'

'And alone.'

'Eh?'

'Only Bet Carey is with her husband. The others are unescorted.'

'So?'

'So.' Marlowe turned his back to the crowd so that Faunt

could see over his shoulder and his words did not carry too far. 'See that knot of gentlemen in the corner, by the fireplace?'

'Yes.' Nicholas Faunt was a master of seeing while appearing to be stone-blind.

'That's Henry Meux, Robert Dillington, Henry Oglander. The two on each side of the group are Richard Turney and James Norris. The one with the pie in his face is Edmund Burley.'

'What of them?'

'They are the principal gentlemen of the Wight,' Marlowe said, 'and the low-life in their midst is John Vaughan.'

'The pirate Vaughan,' Faunt said.

'Don't tell me you know him.' Marlowe was amazed.

'I know *of* him. So, ironically, does Philip of Spain.'

Marlowe's eyes widened.

'He was mentioned in the letters we intercepted between Philip and the Spanish ambassador, when we still had a Spanish ambassador, that is.'

'There's something amiss here, Nicholas; I don't like it.'

'You gave me the impression that George Carey had no friends.'

'I did,' Marlowe said, 'but there's having no friends and having no friends. Are you armed?'

Faunt raised an eyebrow. 'Is Medina Sidonia Captain-General of the Ocean Sea?' He glanced down to his boot where a dagger-hilt nestled, hidden from the world.

'You might need that later.'

He caught sight of Tom Sledd, hurrying across the floor, bowing and doffing as he passed more nobs than he'd scraped up shovelsful of pig shit. He bowed low to George Carey who smiled and clapped his hands. 'Ladies and Gentlemen,' he called. He waited until the hubbub had died down. 'Ladies and gentlemen, it is time. Pray take your seats for . . .' And he paused like the old Queen of the May he was. 'The Carisbrooke Masque!' There was a thunderous applause and everyone trooped out to yet more applause and more 'oohs' and 'aahs' from the groundlings.

*　　*　　*

The audience were settling into their seats, with much less shuffling, cat calling and vegetable hurling than Tom Sledd had ever seen in his life. They were holding playbills that George Carey had had printed down in the town. If his own name was bigger than anyone else's, it was possibly a typographical error. He would speak to the printer in the morning. Other delights on the programme included a Lovers' Idyll with music and a song, with no performer's name against it. Ariel's Song. What could that be? With a few more shuffles, the audience turned their heads to the great lit house with the stage set up before its doors and waited.

Tom had decided against the donkey entering from the hall of the mansion as all the other performers would do; Avis Carey was in a very buoyant mood but he didn't feel that it could possibly survive a pile of donkey shit in the middle of her polished floor. Beside all other considerations, it would present a hazard to her beloved Georgie and that would never do. The animal would be brought in from Stage Right. The other performers were ranged in order of appearance, carefully separated from each other so that there would be no confusing additions. During rehearsals, the Comic Gravediggers had had an upsetting habit of entering with the lovers and Benjamin's temper was uncertain enough without that additional problem. He had not taken well to the wig and had been found, still in his dress, beating Hell out of the bootboy, who he had heard laughing during his love scene with Tom, accompanied by the braying of Old Adam and the antiphonal braying of Master Bedgberry the castrato.

Tom Sledd was pleased with his own appearance and had decided to let Avis Carey have her head when it came to arranging his costume. He had never worn such splendid clothes and the only question on the mind of the audience would be why someone as handsome and well dressed as him would be in love with a girl in a dress made from an old sheet, with hair like straw and feet that looked like skillets. But, as he surreptitiously stroked his velvet breeches, he hardly cared. As another bonus, the horrible petal-strewer seemed to be quiet, so all was well in his little world of backstage.

He moved to the front of the small assembly and held up

his arms for quiet and, by the magic of theatre, everyone
obeyed and turned trusting faces towards him. He spoke quietly
but clearly. 'The audience is in, lady and gentlemen. I must
ask for quiet now and just be guided by . . .' He leaned over
to the boot boy who was his runner for the evening. 'Jeffrye
here who will tell you when to come forward through the
doors. I wish you all the very best of luck, thank you for all
your hard work; you have . . .' He threw his arms out in mute
affection. 'Thank you.'

Avis gave him an indulgent look and mouthed the words
of her song to herself, under her breath. Benjamin scratched
under his wig and hitched up his apple-enhanced breasts. There
was a tap at the door and the Masque was on.

Sledd broke every rule in his own book and dodged to
one side where he had left a curtain partly open so he could
watch the progress of the show. He had a sudden thought
and his stage manager's bowels turned to water. Where was
that dratted child? He hadn't made sure she was tucked away
in her place at the back of the audience. She could be
anywhere. But where? His eyes swivelled madly and then
his attention was caught by an 'Aaah' from the gathered people
sitting outside in the torchlit dark. He looked and breathed
again.

The child was walking like an angel through the audience,
strewing petals as though to the manner born. Holding the
basket for her, matching his stride to hers, was Kit Marlowe.
Before they had set off, he had let her throw some petals over
his head and one or two had caught in his curls and some lay
artlessly on his shoulders. Only he and Tom Sledd knew how
many tries it had taken to make sure they lay so artlessly. The
stage manager offered up a prayer to Saint Vitus – no one
could hear inside his head and a little Papist superstition now
and then wouldn't harm.

At the lip of the stage, Marlowe hoisted the child up on his
shoulder and extended his other arm to embrace the audience.
The child, miraculously picking up on the mood, extended her
arms too and then, to Tom's amazement, blew them all a kiss.
He closed his eyes – this saint business really worked. The
orchestra came in, on the note, all together and Sledd uncrossed

his fingers. Who would have thought that things could go so well?

But there was still Sir George to come.

If pauses could be pregnant, this one almost gave birth. At last, Sir George Carey emerged from his own front door and stood centre stage, one hand on his hip, the other across his breast. Marlowe, watching from the wings, saw everybody cheering and clapping. Everybody, that is, except the gentlemen of the Wight. They had ranged themselves to one side of the gallery, their respective ladies on the other. There was no applause here, just silent, grim-faced men with something on their mind.

When all was quiet and the groundlings had stopped shuffling and coughing, the Captain of the Wight held forth, spouting Marlowe's mighty line: '"And here, the Isle doth dance and shine, So far beyond this wit of mine, Encased . . ."'

But he was hardly past the second line before a shout went up and all eyes turned to the gallery. All the gentlemen of the Wight were on their feet and Henry Meux shouted: 'We have raised a Bill against you, Carey,' he bellowed. 'We demand that piracy be abolished.'

No sooner had he finished but Robert Dillington was adding to his words. 'That robbery and such like, tending to the utter discredit of the County and the displeasure of Almighty God, be abolished.'

'That the prize recently taken from the fleet of Spain be turned over to Her Majesty, according to the laws and customs of the sea.' That was Henry Oglander, glowering at the man across the flickering flames.

John Vaughan forced his way into the centre and leaped up on to the stage. 'We, the men of the Wight,' he said levelly to an astonished governor, 'demand that you lay down your staff and chain of office, that you surrender your goods and chattels and vacate these premises forthwith.'

'Traitor!' Carey spat at him.

'The pot,' Vaughan shrieked, 'calling the kettle black.'

'Guards!' Carey roared and suddenly the Masque was over. Old Adam brayed hysterically, lashing out with his hind hooves

as pikemen and billmen barged their way into the auditorium.
Torches were overturned and sparks flew. Men loyal to Carey
clashed weapons with men who were not. On the stage, the
governor brought his knee up sharply into John Vaughan's groin
and batted him aside. Women and children were screaming.

'Not the flats!' Tom Sledd yelled. 'Not the flats!' His stage
manager's soul could not bear to see good scenery go to waste.

But a battle was breaking out in front of George Carey's
mansion and this was not in the programme. The groundlings
had immediately taken sides and were joining in with a will.
This was certainly a whole lot more entertaining than watching
a lot of nobs making idiots of themselves in funny clothes,
although of course that would have been amusing enough.

'Look! Look! There!' It was a guard still on the ramparts
who halted the mayhem. 'The beacon! The beacon!'

They swarmed over Sledd's stage and Sledd's seating, dragging half of it down with them. Half of them made for the
gatehouse, the rest for the ramparts and the keep. And there
it was, out to the west, not one fire but two and a third beyond
that, pinpricks of light along the backbone of the Island. Men
who had been at each other's throats a moment ago stood,
sweating and panting in disbelief.

The Great Armada had come.

The castle seemed as quiet as death when all the shouting had
stopped, when the last carriage had rattled away bearing wives
and children back to their homes in the fastnesses of the Wight.
They had gone to bolt their doors, to bring in their cattle, to
do all the things a woman must do when the men are away,
fighting the don. The castle guards had stayed and were shoving
enormous planks through even bigger staples in the doors to
the gatehouse. The guests from the mainland would be guests
a while longer. Bet had persuaded her friends to stay too;
Cecily and Ann and, because she hadn't had the heart to make
an exception, Matilda. Their husbands' behaviour should not
be laid at the women's door. Not now, at least. The castle was
always ready for a siege. And now it was here.

Bet Carey sat slumped on a bench at the back of the raked
seats still standing in the courtyard. Her men had gone;

literally, every one. She wasn't good with women, but she feared she may have to get used to it, if only for a while. The torches were beginning to gutter now and soon would go out. Would the Spaniards attack in the dark? Would they wait for light? Would they take the castle by main force or would they tap politely on the door? They had guns, she had heard, that could punch holes in the curtain walls as if they were paper. She smiled to herself in the teeth of the end of her world as she remembered Bernardino de Mendoza, the ambassador at Elizabeth's court, before he was thrown out, lucky to keep his head. She had quite liked the man and he would always call 'Hola!' as he walked by or entered a room. Would the Spanish cry 'Hola!' at her door? She felt a little trickle of fear run up her back, turning her arms to gooseflesh and making her shiver. Then, from the dark of the stage came a voice, singing so sweetly in a minor key, not loudly but using the acoustic of the wall of the courtyard to give it power.

'Full fathom five thy father lies; Of his bones are coral made; Those are pearls that were his eyes: Nothing of him that doth fade, But doth suffer a sea-change Into something rich and strange. Sea-nymphs hourly ring his knell . . .'

The song faded into antiphony with its own echo and Bet shifted slightly on her seat, aware that she had been holding her breath.

Then the singer, with a stifled sob, sang just two more lines: 'Ding-dong. Hark! Now I hear them – Ding-dong, bell.' Ariel's song died away and there was silence. Then, a door closed softly and Bet knew that Avis, when she saw her again, would be her old, efficient self. They would never be friends, but at least she felt that now they were sisters under the skin.

George Carey had ordered the Carisbrooke beacon to be lit, roaring into flame in its iron brazier. Then he had ordered the Essex Militia out of their canvas and into their armour. Men had tumbled down the hill from the castle in the short summer night, buckling on swords, swinging bandoliers over their shoulders, checking their calivers for fuses and powder; there had been the shouts of the sergeants and the thud of iron-shod boots, a frantic leave-taking as the ladies clung briefly to their men. Then George Carey was riding to the sea.

'What's he going to do?' Martin Carey asked Marlowe, scurrying along to keep up with the man's stride.

'He's your kinsman,' the poet said, 'so by rights I should be asking you. But my guess is he's going to take on the Armada. The question is, will he be single-handed?'

All the way across the ford and into the still-sleeping streets of Newport, Carey was not single-handed. At least three hundred men marched behind his banner, swirling over his head in the stiff breeze of the darkness. Lights sparked to life behind lattice windows, doors were flung wide and bleary-eyed townsfolk stumbled on to the cobbles. 'It's the Armada,' various militiamen shouted to them. 'The dons are here. Arm yourselves!'

No one had rehearsed this moment. For all he had brought the Militia and the feudal levies up to a reasonable fighting quality, George Carey had made no provision for civilians. And nobody was listening as they grumbled among themselves as the soldiers tramped past their front doors. 'The castle. We've got to get to the castle. It's our only hope.' . . . 'Well, I'm going to die here if I have to.' . . . 'Nobody's getting me to get off my backside, least of all some bloody dago. We're staying put.'

The more realistic said nothing. They quietly dug into their hidey holes for the old Latin Bibles, long banned, and hid rosaries in their jerkins. 'George Carey? He couldn't knock the skin off a blancmange, he couldn't.'

They reached the quay before the Captain of the Wight decided to have it out with his dubious command. With the black hulk of the *Bowe* behind him, George Carey ordered his men to halt. There was an odd silence now, stranger still after nearly an hour of noise and thunder and the rattle of an army on the road. He looked at the faces in front of him, the men who would have to stand against Philip of Spain.

'Gentlemen,' he shouted so that everyone heard him. 'Here we are. The time has come. But after the events at the castle, I fear we are not as united as we should be. I will take my sailors here and hunt the seas for the dons. We may not make much of a dent in their formation, but we'll see the enemy face to face and make them rue the day they ever left Lisbon.' He drew his sword, brandishing it high. 'Those who are with me,' he said, 'stand by me now.'

At first, no one moved. Then Kit Marlowe stepped forward, smiling at the governor. 'I still have your sword here, Sir George,' he said. 'I'd like to return it to you, after it's been baptized in some Spanish blood, that is.'

'Good man!' Carey beamed and slapped him on the shoulder. Nicholas Faunt followed. No mere field agent was going to upstage him; besides, he was there as the representative of the Queen – how could he stay behind? Tom Sledd was next, still picking bits of painted plaster off his sleeves.

'Tom,' Marlowe murmured. 'Are you sure about this?'

'Me? Miss a punch-up? Come on, Kit. It'll be the best fun I've had in . . . ooh . . . hours.'

One by one, the others followed – Henry Meux, Robert Dillington, Henry Oglander, Turney, Norris, Burley. Carey's beam grew broader with every arrival, until his eyes were bright with tears. In five minutes, there were only two men still standing on the quayside.

'Martin,' George Carey said, frowning. 'You're with me.'

The man scuttled over to him. 'I'd be no use on board a ship, George,' he said. 'I'll get back to the castle, organize a defence.'

'Do as you're told, sir!' the governor snapped at him. He looked across at the last man standing. 'Well, well, Master Vaughan,' he said. 'No stomach for a fight?'

'On the contrary.' Vaughan brazened it out. 'I will be right behind you, Sir George. On the *Bowe*.'

'Very well.' Carey reluctantly gave the man the benefit of the doubt. He turned to his officers. 'Burley. Get yourself west. It may be Yarmouth is under fire already. God speed.'

'Sir George.' The big man saluted and went off to find his horse.

'Norris. Turney. To your posts, please. Turn your guns to seaward and the first Spaniard you see, I want him blown out of the water. Understand?'

'Sir!' Both men saluted and barely acknowledged each other as they parted to ride up the opposite banks of the Medina.

'I'll take a hundred men of the Militia,' Carey shouted. 'Sergeant Wilson, there's a Captaincy for you if you choose the best you've got.'

'Sir.'

FIFTEEN

For the next three hours, every man under Carey's command found himself hauling on ropes, heavy and wet, that cut hands and would not give. Slowly, inch by inch, the *Commander*, newly painted in the Queen's colours of green and white, slid out of her makeshift berth. Men from the town had come along to lend a hand, even the miserable vicar of St Thomas's, although he was so shocked by the language he heard from the sweating, grunting soldiery that he soon retreated and chanted prayers for everybody's safe return instead.

At last, the sails were unfurled with a roar of canvas and the wind took them, billowing wide. There was a clatter of boots as the company assembled on deck, the Militia in the centre with their pikes piercing the sky. The gunners hauled their demi-culverins into position below the planking and the gunports flew upwards. The *Commander* swung away from her moorings and Carey's banner streamed from the stern, snapping in the wind.

Avis Carey was leaning on the wall of the keep, wrapped in a blanket and staring out to sea. Dawn was beginning to lighten the sky to the east but she shielded it from her eyes with her hand. She could just see Georgie's stern lights, but couldn't tell what was going on; the light jigged and jounced around and she feared that the ship may capsize at any minute. She knotted her fist in the blanket and held it under her chin, muttering the rosary she had learned as a child. It calmed her a little, but even so her eyes kept unfocusing with fear and her foot tapped ceaselessly.

Bet had watched her for some time from the courtyard below. In the growing light, she could see the mess that the stage and the seating were in; planks of wood, splinters and sagging swags of flowers were all over the cobbles. Hats were scattered here and there as well as playbills with George Carey's name seeming to shout from the page. She picked one up and smoothed it out, tucking it into her bodice. One day, when the world was back to normal, they would want one of these, to remind them of the Masque and happier days. She dashed a tear from her cheek. She wasn't quite sure who it was for. Looking up again at her sister-in-law outlined against the grey sky, she lifted her skirts and began the long climb up the worn steps to try to persuade her down. It was a long drop from the keep and Bet was not at all certain that Avis would not be tempted to seek oblivion that way, should anything happen to George. Better to get her down to ground level, if she could.

Finally, panting a little, she reached the woman's side. She looked out to where the mouth of the Medina yawned into the Solent.

'Avis,' she said quietly. 'Come down with me. Come and eat something. You will need your strength for the day to come, I think. We all will.'

Avis Carey turned dull eyes on her sister-in-law. She dragged her focus to bear on her and seemed surprised to see her there. 'Bet?' she murmured in a voice rusty with disuse and the dryness of her throat. She licked her lips and when she spoke again her voice was stronger and more harsh. 'Still here? I thought you might have gone off with the men.'

Bet looked at her, her own eyes wide. 'What do you mean, Avis? Why would I go off with the men?'

Avis raised a sardonic eyebrow and looked out to sea again. She turned her head frantically left and right. In the moment she had looked away, Georgie's ship had disappeared behind the trees. But no, there it was, beyond the trees, turning west at the mouth of the river. She leaned on the parapet and peered closer, greedily taking in the last view of the *Commander* before she got too far away for Avis's short sight. She gave a sob that went right to Bet's heart.

'Avis.' She put a hand on the woman's arm. 'I know what we can do. We can go down to the quay and ask the men left there what is going on. Better that than staying here, always wondering. What do you think?'

Avis froze for a moment and then gave herself a shake. She turned away from the distant view and looked at Bet almost as if seeing her for the first time. 'You'd do that?' she asked.

'Of course. I do love your brother, you know, Avis. And you.' Bet could hardly believe the words coming out of her mouth and yet, amazingly, she knew them to be true.

The big woman stood there irresolute for two more heartbeats, then threw off her blanket and made for the stairs. From the first stopping place, she looked back at the mistress of Carisbrooke and shouted, 'What are you waiting for, Bet? The tide won't be right forever, you know!' And with a whirl of skirts, she was gone.

John Vaughan sat on the bridge of the *Bowe*, a lantern at his elbow. The dawn was rising, but he was totting up rows of figures and he needed the light. Some of his men had been a little mutinous, wanting to go and fight the dons. He had chosen them for their bellicose nature in the first place, he thought to himself, so now he had to ride that particular storm. He also had quite a lot of information on most of them – information that could have them twirling from a rope before they could say knife – so, muttering, they had continued their normal morning tasks on board while he assessed the damage that having the mouth of the river blocked by the *Commander* had done to his business. Finally, he drew two straight lines under the figure he had arrived at and, blowing out the lantern, pushed himself back from the table, a half-smile on his face. He was still all right. He could rebuild Mead Hole in a twinkling and soon be back in business. With the dons or with the governor, it didn't really matter which.

He hadn't heard her approach, but suddenly Bet Carey was standing opposite him, a hand on either side of his reckoning table, forearms taut, breasts almost bursting out of her bodice. Her chest was heaving and for a moment he wondered if he was asleep and dreaming. Like most men on the Island who had not actually sampled her charms, he had often spent time there in his sleep. 'Master Vaughan,' she snapped. 'Why is your ship still in harbour?'

He looked up at her and put on his most winning

expression, which dripped off his chin when he looked further and saw Avis Carey standing behind her. He knew he was beaten, but tried an excuse nonetheless. 'I fear the *Bowe* is not seaworthy at the moment, my ladies,' he said. 'She has barnacles on her bottom and I would not risk her out to sea.'

A sailor popped his head out of a nearby hatch. 'No, sir,' he said, sketching a salute to the women. 'She just bin scrubbed below for foulin'. We're fit to set sail any time you like.'

Vaughan turned on him but Avis was quicker.

'Excellent, my good man,' she said. 'Call your crew, Master Vaughan, and have them do whatever is necessary to get this ship out of this river. We must follow the *Commander*. She may need our help.'

The sailor was ready with his opinion again. 'Beggin' your pardon, Mistress,' he said. 'We can't overhaul the *Commander*. The *Bowe*, she ain't built for that kind of running. But we could wait in the Solent, watch for'n, if she should need our help.'

Avis opened her mouth, but this time Vaughan was the quicker. 'He's right, Mistress Avis,' he said. 'We can heave to, to help your brother's ship if she comes to harm, but we could never catch her in a month of Sundays.'

Avis was reaching over the table, ready to haul the man to his feet, but Bet, expert at reading men in any weather, knew he was speaking the truth. 'Let's settle for that, shall we, Avis?' she said. Then, turning to Vaughan, 'Where do we sit? Is there some kind of viewing platform? I doubt I can keep Avis below decks, you know.'

Vaughan looked at her with a worried frown. Lined up on the quay he could see other women there, the wives of his fellow conspirators who, not hours ago, had done their level best to topple George Carey. 'You can't come with us, ladies,' he said. 'The sailors won't have women on board ship. It's bad luck.'

Avis and Bet folded their arms in unison. They planted their feet on the deck and looked at Vaughan under their brows. It was clear he would have more luck moving Carisbrooke Castle than these two.

'But, on the other hand,' he said, standing up and gesturing for his crew to start hauling the ship into sailing rig, 'luck is just a state of mind. Lean on the rails, ladies, for the best view. Master Page!'

The captain sprang to attention on the lower deck.

'Haul sail and make for Mead Hole.'

'That's bad luck, you know,' Tom Sledd said as he caught sight of Benjamin, still in his farthingale. 'A woman on board ship.'

'Stow you!' the lad snarled at him and pulled off his wig, kicking himself free of the skirt. Judging by the wolf-whistles that followed, he began to wish he had kept it on.

It had been still dark as the *Commander* slid past Richard Turney's fort at Cowes and the little garrison there saluted as the stern lanterns flickered past them and swept on into the open sea. There was that bloody wind again, Tom Sledd moaned to himself as they butted free of the river. Why was the damn thing always blowing in his face, whichever way he stood and whatever direction he was coming from? The little ship churned and rolled as the cables creaked and groaned. The low headland of the island was dark to their larboard, the curve of Gurnard Bay and Thorness. Soon they were slicing the sea beyond Newtown and running with the tide along Hamstead Ledge. The dawn was lighting the sky behind them as the ship buffeted below Edmund Burley's guns at Yarmouth. No firing yet. The dons had not got this far east and that was a good sign. Kit Marlowe stepped down from the quarterdeck where all the officers and gentlemen had gathered. The main deck was solid with militiamen, leaning on their pikes and watching as Colwell Bay snaked to larboard.

'That's Hurst Castle,' Marlowe heard Sergeant Wilson say. 'Narrowest point to the mainland, that is. Reckon we could hold the Armada here all by ourselves!'

There was a ripple of laughter. Marlowe wondered if it was like this on board the Spanish ships, anxious men making small talk, cracking feeble jokes, moaning about the weather. Or were they all kneeling in fervent prayer, kissing their rosaries while their black-robed priests sang *Te Deum, pro nobis*?

'Shit!' the helmsman at George Carey's elbow hissed. Carey

had seen it too, the sea mist like a wall that so often cloaked the Island and made it invisible. It was seeping into their nostrils already, smelling of salt, but it hadn't quite reached them yet. Totland should be to larboard and the coloured cliffs of Alum beyond that. But there was nothing, just grey above the rolling sea, whispering and restless. The fog moved stealthily towards them, like an animal stalking its prey, glowing with a fantastic magick that could be hiding anything in its coils. There was a stir from the men on deck and everyone gritted their teeth, ready for whatever may come.

'Steady, rudder,' Carey murmured. The last thing they needed was the weather to be against them when they could almost hear the roar of Medina Sidonia's guns. The wind had dropped and the sails were not so full now, but the momentum of the sea kept them surging forward, into the unknown.

'Dear God, no!' No one knew who said it, who saw it first. The single voice came, not from the crow's nest where the sailor there was drenched in mist and shivering with cold. It came from the main deck, from a foot soldier who had never been this far out to sea in his life, a lad from Essex, from dry land.

For a long electric moment, there was silence on board the *Commander*. The mist was clearing as though a man was drinking smoke and blowing the rings away. And beyond the mist came the Armada, a vast crescent of timber, canvas and iron, more ships than any man on the *Commander* had ever seen in his life before. As sea mists will, the one that had shrouded the ship moments before had gone now and the sun shone bright on the sails and brass and gold of the Spanish galleons. The sky behind them was as black as pitch, rolling clouds coming in from the west, thunderhead anvils building and collapsing, then building again, each time bigger and blacker than before. In the depths of the cloud, beyond the ships, lightning flickered but there was no thunder that the men on the *Commander* could hear. Their ears were filled with the snapping of the canvas as the wind got up again and the roar of their own blood.

George Carey let his eye roam over the wall of ships that filled his horizon. He knew their banners; so did Nicholas

Faunt and Kit Marlowe. The blood-red bars of Aragon, the rampant lions of Castile, the chains of Andalusia: all the panoply of the greatest power in the world was bearing down on the Wight, churning forward like an unstoppable juggernaut for the narrows. And in his heart of hearts, George Carey knew that he had nothing in the Wight to stop that. They would bat aside Burley's cannon at Yarmouth, blow Turney and Norris off their perches at the Medina estuary. Nothing could stop them. Nothing.

'Hard a starboard!' Carey was suddenly galvanized into action. 'Bring her round, Master helmsman.' The man wrenched the wheel, hauling the ship round, and the *Commander* swayed and swung, militiamen slipping and colliding with each other against the deck rail.

'Are we in range, Master gunner?' he called down to his artilleryman.

The man looked at him as if he was mad. At best he could bring ten guns to bear against that great and terrible fleet. Ninety pounds of iron smashing into any one of those galleons would hardly leave a scratch.

'Barely, sir,' the man shouted. There was a vicious wind rising from the north-west and it brought a sudden squall of rain. It stung the faces of the men clinging to the *Commander*'s rail and lashed the billowing sails. The Armada was changing course, whether to combat the wind or by design was impossible to tell. The leading ships were dipping to starboard, veering south, away from the Solent and the wind was behind them.

'Fire!' Carey commanded. He could see the whole Armada slipping away from him if he did not hurry and although the pinnace could easily outdistance the big galleons, he had no wish to sail in too close. The militiamen scattered as the guns along the *Commander*'s hull roared and bucked, their carriages sliding back. Below decks, the gunners toiled and sweated, stripped to the waist for action, hauling on ropes to check the recoil.

Carey scanned the sea, heaving in the squall as it was. Explosions of water burst ahead of the crescent's left horn, but the shots had fallen short. 'Reload!' he bellowed and the

Master gunner on the middeck yelled the same to his lads under the timbers. It was then that Tom Sledd saw his life pass before him again. There was a muffled roar and a burst of flame and smoke from the nearest Spanish man-of-war as she fired a broadside at the *Commander*. Her guns were bigger, her aim was better, who knew the reason? Not Tom Sledd, stage manager of the Rose, certainly. He saw the deck rail disappear in a shower of splinters and the roar and crash as the foc'sle disappeared and holes gaped in the canvas over his head. Men standing alongside him a moment ago were no longer there. Others were lying on the shattered deck, slick with blood. They were moaning and crying. War had come to the Wight.

'Hard a starboard!' Carey shouted, helping his helmsman to control the wheel. There was no time to reload and fire again because the wind was roaring through the shredded canvas now, threatening to tear the sails down. The only chance was to reach the shelter of the Solent and even then they would not be out of danger. Carey clung to the stern rail as the *Commander* veered and swung. Marlowe was on one side of him, Faunt the other. Henry Meux was shaking his fist uselessly as the Armada was blown south. Robert Dillington was white and rigid, frozen to his spot on the deck.

Nicholas Faunt made his way across the heeling wheel deck and hung on to a rail. 'As a landlubber, Sir George,' he said, sounding for all the world as though he were making small talk at a party, 'I have to ask what we do now.'

The Captain of the Wight looked at him. 'We pray, sir,' he said, as his banner was ripped from its housing by a sudden, sharp gust, 'and we do it hard.'

The thunder, which had just been a rumour so far, opened its throat and roared defiance at all of the ships ploughing through the increasingly angry sea. Christopher Marlowe had never considered himself a particularly good man; on the contrary, he had done many things he sincerely regretted. And yet, search his soul though he might, he could think of nothing that would make him deserving of the dismal, choking death by water that he seemed to be in danger of experiencing within the next few minutes. A better sailor than Tom Sledd, he nevertheless was not happy when he had to look up at a breaking wave from his place hanging on to a hatch cover for grim death. The sea should be below a man on a deck. It was the world turned upside down.

All around him, men were crying, to their God and for their mothers. Marlowe shook his wet hair from his eyes and saw Tom Sledd, just an arm's length from him, hanging on by one pale hand to a piece of spar which had broken loose in the rigging and which had become jammed across the deck. His eyes were closed and it was only his fist clenched on a staple hammered into the wood that told Marlowe he was still alive. The poet called the boy's name and his eyes fluttered open. With the next heel of the deck, as the ship climbed the sheer face of a wave and hung, teetering on the crest as it seemed to decide whether to flop back and turn turtle or race down the other side to plunge with its own momentum to the bottom of the sea, Sledd let go of the spar and slid into Marlowe's side, where he clung, with his head buried, as he prayed for it all to be over.

'What are you doing, Master Vaughan?' Avis Carey asked the man. She knew a ship heeling into land as well as anybody.

'I'm putting you ashore, madam,' he said. 'You and your ladies.'

'Master Vaughan . . .' Bet was standing elbow to elbow with her sister-in-law. 'May I remind you that you are within an inch or two of my husband's gallows?'

'Do what you like to me on land, Mistress,' he said, 'but on this ship *I* make the decisions, not George Carey. You see that storm?' He was pointing to the black clouds rolling in from the west. 'The *Bowe* won't stand against that. And who knows what's behind it. The galleons of Spain, I shouldn't wonder. This is Mead Hole. You'll be safe here. Page, when we anchor, send a man up to Osborne's manor. We'll need as many wagons as he's got, horses, donkeys, anything. And water. And blankets. Got it?'

'Got it, sir.' Thomas Page was still a little bewildered at the side of his master he was seeing now. The man was dangerously close to being a patriot.

* * *

By the time the *Commander* was swept on past the estuary of the Medina, she was listing badly, water gushing in through the gunports on her starboard hull. The top-gallant yards had long gone, one of them blown off by the Spanish broadside, and the foremast was splintered and leaning at a dangerous angle where its canvas and rigging trailed in the rolling whitecaps. The wind was dropping and the sudden squall that had blown the ship twenty miles before it showed signs of finally abating.

Tom Sledd, sitting up but still hanging on for grim death, was the colour of the *Commander*'s paint. Blinking, he looked towards the land and recognized it finally for where it was. 'That's it, Kit,' he said, pointing to the shallow bay the ship was tacking into. 'That's Mead Hole. But someone seems to have burned it down.'

There was a tearing sound and the mizzen splintered completely, the weight of it hauling the *Commander* over on to her starboard hull. Her guns on that side disappeared below the water line and the larboard artillery broke free of its housings, all ten guns sliding down the sloping deck, ripping ropes free of the grappling rings and crashing into the submerged hull. Men were catapulted into the sea, splashing among the crashing timbers. Everyone was shouting above the wind and the rush of water. Men carried along with the undertow waved desperately, then vanished in the surf.

Marlowe found himself clinging to a spar with one hand while keeping a militiaman afloat with the other. The man was panicking, kicking out with his feet and threatening to take Marlowe with him. They bobbed below the surface and Marlowe heard the most terrible sound of his life – the roar of the sea with him under it. He held his breath, feeling Carey's sword tangling momentarily in floating ropes. Then he was free of it, spar and militiaman gone from his grasp. His lungs felt as if they would burst when he surfaced next. The *Commander* was almost submerged and moving away from him, but another ship was coming to her rescue, hauling sail and pulling alongside. He saw the anchors splash down and the chains slide behind them. It was the *Bowe*, battered but still upright and men were swarming all over the dripping hull and keel of the stricken *Commander*, trying to right her.

Carey's ship had run aground on the long ledge of the beach off Mead Hole, its bowsprit buried deep in the sand and its masts collapsed over it and spread with wet, shredded canvas. There was debris everywhere, timbers, ropes and rigging surging at the tide's ebb. Out to sea, the squall, like a black demon over the land, was roaring to the east to vent itself along the Hampshire coast. Of the Armada there was no sign. Perhaps even now they had driven their anchors into the ledge below Chale and Brighstone and Freshwater. Then the beacons would blow out and this part of Gloriana's England at least would become the newest colony of Spain.

Marlowe dragged himself ashore, barely able to feel his feet. His Venetians clung to his legs and his boots were full of water. His doublet and shirt were slashed in a less elegant way than ever his tailor would suggest and his hair was plastered to his forehead. Men were lying sprawled on the sand of Mead Hole, dead or dying or too exhausted to move. Benjamin would never move again. He was lying in Tom Sledd's arms, the rouge gone from his cheek and his shirt in tatters. Tom had buried actors before. He could do it again.

Marlowe patted the boy's shoulder and stumbled off to the group further up the beach. Robert Dillington was sitting on the sand, shaking, while his Matilda fussed around him, loading blankets over his shoulders. Henry Oglander was standing locked in the arms of his Ann, both of them crying. Henry Meux had looked long and hard at Bet Carey, then he had let Cecily wrap her cloak around him and help him up the sand.

George Carey was kneeling below a stand of silver birch and Sergeant Wilson was with him. And yet the sergeant was not with him. His back had been broken by the falling timbers when the broadside had hit them and he had not withstood the surge of the tide. Carey called two militiamen over to him. 'Find a blanket for your Captain, boys,' he said to them. 'I won't have him buried here in the sand.' He looked back to the wreck of his ship with tear-filled eyes. 'Oh, my pretty lads,' he said to Marlowe. 'Drowned like rats.'

Marlowe looked around and saw Bet making her way to her husband. George got up and the pair held hands briefly before she wrapped him in her arms.

'Master Marlowe! Master Marlowe!' It was Avis Carey, thundering down the sand towards him. She saw her George and smiled triumphantly. Like her, the man was unsinkable. 'The boy?' She squeezed Marlowe's hand and he realized he was too weak to respond. 'Tom?'

'Over there,' Marlowe said. 'He's all right.'

'Martin?' Marlowe heard George Carey calling. 'Where's my kinsman?'

Everybody was looking up and down the beach, across to the *Bowe* that was still taking men off the drowning *Commander*.

'He's gone,' Tom Sledd said. 'I saw him go down for the third time.' He looked out at the grey, rolling breakers. 'We'll find him,' he said, 'when the sea gives up its dead.'

SIXTEEN

George Carey and his drenched, exhausted party clattered under the barbican as night fell. Not twenty-four hours earlier, the courtyard had been alive with torches and music and the excited hum of a crowd intent on a Masque by the legend that was Kit Marlowe.

Kit did not feel much like a legend tonight. Servants fussed around them, cooks and gardeners and stable lads. The guards still patrolled the battlements and the beacon still crackled and spat as the faggots burned in the brazier. Ester was running around crying, forgetting her lowly position entirely and hugging everybody except Master Marlowe. Avis was too tired to clout her round the head; she would do that in the morning.

What was left of the Essex Militia were making their way across the Island, but many of them had slept in the shelter of Arnold Osborne's house beyond the silver birches that ringed Mead Hole. Still others lay on the beach where the dead still rolled in with the tide. John Vaughan had picked up as many of the living and the dead as he could and had made his way back down the Medina to lick his ship's wounds and to see if he could patch his life together again.

Tom Sledd and Avis Carey sat among the ruins of the stage and thought about what might have been. Tom had had worse performances, and a lot longer than the Masque of Carisbrooke Castle. Avis hummed her song quietly under her breath and Tom knew that she could hear the applause, see the roses flying through the air, feel soft hands patting her on the back. Little did she know how much sweeter the imagined accolades always were than the real ones, which he had come to learn were usually few and grudging when it came to your nearest and dearest.

She had swept into the castle like a smaller version of the storm at sea, demanding hot water, blankets, clean clothes and food and, in a remarkably short time, the survivors of the wreck were warm, dry and fed. The dead were laid in rows in the great hall, with a guard on the door and candles at their heads and feet. Sir George Carey would not let them be forgotten in a hurry. But now, Avis looked deflated and tired. And, thought Tom, surprised, younger and somehow vulnerable.

She broke into his thoughts. 'Tom,' she said, 'do you pray, ever?'

He smiled. 'I prayed a lot today,' he said. 'I sent a little prayer to St Vitus last night, for the success of the Masque. So I suppose you could say that I have had very mixed results.'

She smiled and moved closer around the edge of the stage. 'I have a lot of regrets, Tom,' she said. 'My life isn't what I thought it would be by now.'

Tom Sledd patted her hand. 'None of us can look into the future and get it right, Mistress Carey,' he said.

'Can you call me Avis, please? I . . . No man except Georgie calls me Avis, and I would like you to. Just tonight, of course, and when no one else is here.'

'Of course,' he said. Always thinking of the proprieties, Mistress Carey. 'So, Avis, that's what I believe. I have seen some things . . . things I can't forget. I've lost a lot of people in my life.' A tear sprang to his eye and he wiped it away. 'But you just have to keep on, moving on. Perhaps that's what you need, Avis. To move.'

'Where would I go?'

'London. You are a cousin of the Queen, after all.'

'I've never thought of that,' she said, with a smile. 'Everyone always says Georgie is but . . . no one thinks that I am too.'

'You are though. Come to London. I could show you the sights. Half price tickets at the Rose. How about it?'

She chuckled and patted his hand. 'I miss confession, Tom, do you know that? I know you shouldn't say it, but when I was a little girl, I loved the feeling that I could go to the church and tell God everything and he would forgive me. I miss that.'

Sledd felt his shoulders stiffen. Somehow, he could feel a storm brewing, one every bit as dangerous as any he had gone through today. He chose his words with care before he spoke again. 'God is still listening, Avis, surely. If He was there then, He is there now.'

She leaned forward, gazing into his eyes. 'Can I tell you my sins?' she said. 'Please, Tom. I just can't tell them straight to God. I would feel . . . well, I need to tell a person.'

He met her eyes and saw the need there. 'You should be telling this to Sir George,' he said. 'Family.'

'If I had had a son, Tom, I would have liked him to be like you. But, somehow, I never had the time. I had to look after Georgie . . . Please, Tom. Let me confess to you. But look away. I don't want to see your face.'

'Let's sit like we sit when we learn our lines,' he said. 'Back to back.'

They shuffled round on the wreck of the stage and Sledd braced himself to take her weight, but she felt as light as air. He knew she was holding herself stiffly, still Lady Avis, even in this pain.

'Go on,' he said.

Her voice came softly, and he could feel its vibration in his back. 'Ever since he was a boy, I have looked after my brother,' she said. 'I nearly shot him once, you know, by accident, and after that I have been watching out for him. I feel as though he is on borrowed time; God called him that day but he didn't go. I try to make his path easy, when I can. I don't want him to be hurt. So, when I found out about Bet and all those men, I had to do something.'

Tom Sledd felt as if he was still in the icy sea, with the water closing over his head. He couldn't open his eyes, nor speak. His hands were heavy by his sides. He felt as though he couldn't move if his life depended on it.

'I let the first ones live. She wasn't serious about them and usually it was just the one time. Then she started going back, to the same man over and over again. I couldn't have that.' Her voice rose and she controlled it with a cough and began again. 'They were easy to dispose of, Tom. All I had to do was leave a note and they would come. Panting for it, as a rule. One of them saw it was me before I could get a grip on his neck and he even offered himself to me.' She laughed, with no mirth in it. 'He thought I was jealous, you see. Thought he could buy his life with a quick . . .' She sobbed. 'By taking me against a wall. Him, I allowed to suffer. For the others, it was very quick.' She waited but Tom couldn't think of what to say. 'Tom?'

'I'm sorry, Avis. What do you want me to say?'

'Tell me God forgives me, Tom. Tell me Georgie would forgive me.' She sat up slowly, giving the stage manager time to take his own weight and he slewed round to face her. There were no tears now and her face looked smooth, wiped clean. Confession had been remarkably good for her soul.

Tom Sledd had faced death only a few short hours before. He had felt water close over his head. He had felt the heart of a man stop beating when it was pressed against his own. He thought that he had probably been through enough for God to perhaps feel he should be given some slack. He held her hand and squeezed it, then raised it to his lips. He bowed his head. 'God forgives you, Avis,' he said.

'And Georgie?' Her eyes were alight with hope.

'If he knew,' Sledd said. 'But shall we lay this burden on the Lord? Not on Georgie.'

She looked at him. 'You are very wise, for such a young man,' she said, then looked up at the keep. Noises that had been getting louder and louder for the last little while had finally broken through. 'Whatever are they doing up there?' she said. Then she looked again and leapt to her feet. 'Georgie! He was supposed to be resting! I told Bet to make sure he was resting!'

Sledd pulled her back down. 'He's safe with Master Marlowe and Master Faunt, look,' he said. 'They are probably just helping him go through Master Martin's things.'

'Poor Martin,' she said.

'I never heard your song, Avis,' Sledd said, conscious that he needed to keep this frail mind busy. 'Sing it to me.'

Very softly, she started to sing.

Carey and Marlowe walked on the battlements to the south. There were no lights twinkling across that broad sweep of blackness, no sign of a Spanish camp getting ever closer.

Outside the castle gate, a huge crowd were settling down to sleep, having been held out by the garrison at halberd-point. Tomorrow, the Captain of the Wight promised them, once he had news of what was happening, they could come in and prepare for a siege. There would be plenty of time; the dons would not be here tonight.

'I can't shake myself free of it, Christopher,' Carey was saying. 'That bloody crescent. Those awful ships. I had no idea. Look.' He paused on the uneven steps to the keep. 'I confess I'm not too steady at the moment. I must go to Martin's rooms, you know, to . . . see to things. Will you hold a candle for me?'

'I'd be delighted, Sir George,' Marlowe said, 'but I don't think that will be necessary.' He pointed across the ramparts to the rooms on the far side above the well. There was a candle there already. In fact there were three or four.

'Who's had the damned impertinence?' Carey said, finding his Governor's voice again. 'Nobody goes in there, except . . .'

'Except Master Martin.' Marlowe finished the sentence for him. It was something playwrights felt entitled to do. He held Carey's arm. 'Let me go first, Sir George,' he said.

'What?' the governor frowned. 'Why?'

But Marlowe did not wait to explain. He kicked open the door and stood there, the dagger still at his back, George Carey's second-best rapier somewhere at the bottom of the Solent.

'Where will you run to now, bookkeeper?' he said softly.

Martin Carey had spun round at the noise behind him. He was wearing boots and a cloak and was busy stuffing papers into a satchel. 'Master Marlowe,' he said. 'You survived. Thanks be to God.'

'Why don't you complete the business?' Marlowe asked him. 'Why not cross yourself as you did over Hunnybun's body? Why not say a *pro nobis* for those less lucky than I?'

'Martin!' George Carey was at Marlowe's elbow. 'You're alive! Heaven be praised! Christopher, this is wonderful.'

'No, Sir George,' the projectioner said. 'I'm afraid it's not. There is a cuckoo in your nest.' He leaned his exhausted back against the door frame. 'He stands before you.'

Carey frowned. 'What are you talking about, Marlowe?' he said. 'Martin, what's he talking about?'

'Will you tell him, Comptroller, or will I?' Marlowe asked.

For a moment, Martin Carey dithered, looking from his uncle to the playwright and back again. Then he stood up straight. 'Let me,' he said with a look of contempt for them both on his face. 'It won't make any difference soon anyway. You saw that crescent, both of you,' he said, eyes bright and teeth bared. 'It's only a matter of time now. All right, the *Comendador* mistimed the whole thing. Medina Sidonia sent that boy to do a man's work. But the Captain-General of the Ocean Sea will be in the Wight by now. The rest, as they will say in the centuries ahead, will be history. I've been the poor relation for long enough. This time, I intend to be on the winning side.'

'The feeble Holinshed passages,' Marlowe said. 'Your attempt to put your uncle here on the rack. I must confess it nearly worked. What will we find in your satchel there, Master Martin – the accounts of Carisbrooke Castle or letters from the King of Spain that will get you hanged?'

'Oh, make no mistake, gentlemen,' he said. 'It is you who will feel the rope, but not before the Inquisition gets its inquisitive little hands on you. They have ways of hurting you that make Richard Topcliffe's little toys look like babies' soothers. Now, get out of my way.'

Marlowe barred the door and folded his arms. 'What about the murders?' he asked. 'Using black propaganda against George here, helping no doubt to stir up the great and good of the Wight against him, blackening the Queen, inviting José de Medrano and his minions, all that I understand. But why kill Hunnybun, Compton and the rest? They couldn't all have discovered your little plan, surely? A corn chandler, a draper, an inn keeper, a farmer and a lawyer?'

Martin Carey blinked. 'I don't know what you're talking about,' he said. 'Now, let me go. I have places to be. Friends to meet.' He suddenly threw his satchel at Marlowe. Normally, the projectioner would have ducked or caught it and his dagger would have been in the man's ribs. But tonight, his reflexes were slow and his body tortured. He lost his balance and

Martin was out on the wall-walk. He turned to his left, but Nicholas Faunt was walking towards him with a deadly step and Nicholas Faunt had a knife in his hand. Martin ducked to his right and George Carey faced him.

'In the name of God, Martin,' he growled. 'It's over.' Suddenly, he was being driven back to the wall by a sword blade, the tip pricking his throat.

Martin Carey stood back, arm extended as he had been taught, and held his uncle many times removed as a spider holds a fly. He increased the pressure an extra inch and George Carey was bending backwards, out over the blackness that waited below the wall. 'I should have done this years ago,' Martin said. 'All that clever stuff with letters and innuendo. Steel was the answer all along.'

'Martin!' The shriek made them all freeze. Avis Carey was striding along the ramparts, closing in on George and Martin from the right. 'What do you think you're doing?'

'Stay out of this, Avis, you mad old bitch. This has nothing to do with you.'

'No, Martin,' she said softly. 'No, I can't let you hurt my Georgie. Not after everything.' Marlowe saw Martin's arm flex and George Carey jerk back a little more. The Captain of the Wight was a fingertip's width away from death and neither he nor Faunt would reach him in time. Only Avis could do that and she launched herself at him, taking the rapier point full in the chest as she used her weight to twist the traitor away from her brother. Before anyone could grab them, they both hurtled over the edge of a low wall and into the gaping mouth of the well below. Their screams died away in a hideous echo as they fell foot by foot, bouncing and scraping on the stones as they went. Then there was silence.

'One hundred and sixty feet,' George Carey whispered in horror, half his family gone before his eyes. He looked up at Marlowe and Faunt, black and still against the night sky. They closed to the Captain of the Wight and between them helped him down the uneven steps. Bet was waiting there, uncomprehending. 'I heard a scream,' she said, staring at her husband's white face. She looked at Marlowe, who shook his head.

'Look after your husband, my lady,' he said. 'It has been a long, long day.'

Bet put an arm around George Carey's waist and he leaned on her. They could hear him whispering to her as she led him away. 'Avis, Bet. She just . . . Avis.' She leaned round, raising a hand to his face and the watching projectioners knew she was wiping away a tear.

Tom Sledd poked his head around a flat leaning against a wall of the courtyard. 'Kit?' he said. 'What's going on? Where's Avis?'

'Mistress Carey is dead, Tom,' Marlowe said gently. 'She . . . can I tell you the details later? I must have a drink and for choice a lie down.'

'Dead?' Sledd could hardly believe it. Down in the court-yard, Avis had finished her song and then had suddenly leapt to her feet, looking up to the keep above her head. She had turned to Tom, telling him curtly to stay where he was. 'She just ran off,' he told them. 'Said it was family business.'

'It was indeed,' Marlowe said. 'She saved her brother's life.'

'Ah.' Tom Sledd folded his arms and fell into step behind the others as they made for the front door of the mansion. 'She decided to lay it on the Lord after all.'

George Carey stood on the top step of his entrance way looking every bit the master of the Island. At his side stood the beautiful and notorious Elizabeth Carey, dressed in black but with real diamonds on a net over her hair. Her nipples peeped just a little over the edge of her bodice and as she offered her hand to the departing men, they could see that there was just the slightest touch of rouge. She nodded to Tom Sledd, lingered over retrieving her hand from Nicholas Faunt and pressed Marlowe's to her bosom, so that for the rest of the day it smelled of civet.

Sir George Carey came down the steps and he walked with them over to where their horses waited. 'Don't mind Bet,' he said to Faunt.

Faunt blustered. 'I have no idea what . . .'

Carey caught him a buffet around the shoulder. 'Don't think I didn't know what you and she were up to the . . . No, let me get this right. It *wasn't* the last time we were at court, was it? No, I think it was the time before that.'

Sledd and Marlowe exchanged sardonic glances, as Faunt tried to look innocent. 'Sir George, I assure you . . .'

'Oh, Master Faunt,' said George Carey. 'Don't insult my wife by claiming not to remember. She's a very memorable woman, I can vouch for that.'

Sledd found his voice. The secret he shared with Avis Carey and her God was weighing on his mind. 'Excuse me, Sir George,' he said, uncertainly. 'Do you know about . . . about . . .?'

Carey looked at him with the whole gulf of station between them, but they had stared death in the face together and he thought he could afford to be generous. Besides, Avis had been fond of the lad. 'Yes, yes, Sledd,' he said. 'I would have had to be blind and deaf not to, wouldn't you say? And of course you mustn't forget –' and he pulled the three closer together and dropped his voice a notch – 'Ann Oglander's last three are the living spit of me.' He turned his head so that they saw him in profile. 'Got the nose.'

'Oglander?' Marlowe asked.

'Hmm,' Sir George conceded. 'An urgent matter at Nunwell. Yes, Master Marlowe.'

The grooms came round from the horses' heads and gave the three a knee up into the saddle.

'Keep safe,' Bet Carey called. 'Come back and see us soon.'

The three rode together out of Portsmouth with its guns trained on the sea, away from the Island whose spell had held them, and on along the road to the north-east. Two days later, south of the river where the spire of St Mary Overie stood tall over the stews of Southwark, came the parting of the ways.

'Well, Kit.' Faunt sat his roan in the shadow of the church. 'Until the next time.' He extended his hand.

Marlowe smiled. 'One day,' he promised, 'I'll tell you about Harry Hasler.'

Faunt's eyes narrowed. 'One day I'll listen to you,' he said and he made for the Bridge.

'What *do* you do for that man, Kit?' Tom Sledd asked.

The playwright looked at him. 'It's better you don't know,' he said. 'Wait a minute.' He stood in the stirrups and looked to his left. 'Unless I'm much mistaken, that's the roof of the Rose over there. Shall we?'

It was a tired Nicholas Faunt who clattered under the archway into Her Majesty's Palace of Whitehall. A guard in the Queen's livery held his horse while he forced his aching legs to carry him up the stairs to the first floor and then along the passageway. The Spymaster sat with his spectacles on his nose and a glass of Bastard on the table beside him.

'Ah, Faunt.' He reached over and poured a second glass. Back to the surname. That was good. 'You've heard the news?'

'There were rumours all the way up, sir,' he said. 'Good and bad. I half expected the Duke of Medina Sidonia to be sitting where you are tonight and a very different flag over the gateway.'

'God breathed, Faunt,' Walsingham smiled, 'and his enemies were scattered.'

'They were?'

'All the way along the south coast in the teeth of contrary winds. Oh, there were a few clashes – Drake, Frobisher, Hawkins, the Lord Admiral, of course – they did their bit. We shall say, when the reckoning comes, that our guns drove them off. They will say it was God's will. They're being washed up all around the coast. If it was really their intention to join up with the Duke of Parma, they can't do it now.'

'You won't be needing this, then?' Faunt said, pulling a piece of parchment from his doublet. 'It's a speech I asked Marlowe to write for the Queen; you know, to stir the troops.'

'Ah, well, no, actually.' Walsingham took it from him. 'Her Majesty is still at Tilbury with Leicester's army. *They* don't know what we do, yet.' The Spymaster's mind was racing. 'A good move, don't you think? We'll put her in armour, on a white horse naturally, and get her riding up and down, spouting this.' He read it quickly. 'Oh, yes, capital stuff. Excellent.'

'Er . . . that's my bit, there,' Faunt was keen to point out. 'That "body of a weak and feeble woman" bit.'

'Of course it is, Faunt,' Walsingham patronized. 'But it's

this bit that counts – "I have the heart and stomach of a king, and a King of England too." She'll love it. Pure Marlowe! Marvellous!'

Marlowe and Sledd paused at the bottom of Maiden Lane. The flares were lit all along the roadside and sellers of new milk, gingerbread and apples were all calling their wares. The musky smell of Master Sackerson came to them in waves.

'Well, Tom,' Marlowe said. 'Home.'

Tom Sledd hung back. 'I don't know, Kit,' he said. 'I left without saying goodbye. They probably don't want me. Johanna won't want me. She'll have found someone else, I expect. Henslowe, he won't want me . . .'

'Tom Sledd?' A head was suddenly thrust out of a window high in the eaves of the Rose. 'Tom Sledd? Is that you? Get yourself up here this minute. There's work to be done. Master Kyd is back from his travels and has some changes he thinks will improve his play.' Philip Henslowe's smile could have lit the street, without the flares. He forced an arm out and waved imperiously. 'Come on. Come on.'

Marlowe smiled down as the stage manager slid off his horse and ran up the hill and disappeared inside the theatre. The playwright dismounted too and walked the horses in the same direction, careful to keep on the other side of the road from the Bear Pit. The bear upset the horses; the horses upset the bear.

He hitched the horses to the rail outside the side entrance and pushed open the door. The smell hit him at once. The pig, of course; slightly rotting vegetables . . . he sniffed . . . make-up . . . very old costumes, not washed since the Rose was built and probably even long before that. Tobacco. Fresh smoke. He turned round and there, sitting on the front bench in the gallery, was Will Shaxsper.

'Will! How has it been here without me?' Marlowe asked.

'Have you been gone? I haven't noticed.' Shaxsper looked as dejected as always and just a touch balder.

Marlowe leaned on the rail and looked up at the man.

'Women trouble?' It was a fair guess.

'Writer's block.'

'Oh, you've decided to try the writing again, then? In that case . . .' Marlowe turned and pulled his satchel round so he could rummage in its contents. 'Perhaps these notes might help. Something I had some thoughts on while I was away in the south. An island. A terrible storm. *Very* strange people. Anyway, see what you think.'

Shaxsper leaned towards the light and flicked through the pages. 'Hmm,' he said, thinking aloud. 'Prospero. Caliban. Ariel . . .' He looked up. 'Oh, God, Kit! Not a *song*!'

Marlowe shrugged and grinned a rueful grin.

'Well.' Shaxsper had a sudden thought. 'How much do you want for this?'

Marlowe spread his arms. 'Nothing.'

'Nothing? Are you sure?'

'It's yours.' He turned to walk away. 'I call it "The Storm" by the way.' He made for the stairs where he could already hear Sledd and Henslowe in furious argument about the cost of lumber.

Shaxsper called to him and he turned back. 'Yes, Will?'

'You don't mind if I change the title, do you, Kit?'